DEATH
IN
DISGUISE

THE REV & RYE SERIES

Death at Fair Havens
Death in the Woods
Death in Disguise

DEATH IN DISGUISE

A REV & RYE MYSTERY

MARIA MANKIN &
MAREN C. TIRABASSI

Death in Disguise is a work of fiction. Names, places, and incidents either are products of the author's imagination or are used fictitiously. Any resemblance to actual persons, living or dead, or locales is entirely coincidental.

Published in the United States by Brain Mill Press.

Print ISBN 978-1-948559-86-7
EPUB ISBN 978-1-948559-87-4

Cover design by Ampersand Book Covers.

DEATH IN DISGUISE

1

WANDA THREW THE PILE OF MAIL ON THE TABLE, grabbing the only piece that wasn't a bill or junk mail to read as an "endless meeting day" treat. It was a postcard from Luke Fairchild, dear friend, local funeral director, and occasional heartthrob. "Short, plump, energetic, twice-divorced clergywoman" was a certified subgenre of lonely hearts, according to the Manual on Ministry. And for everyone who never asked, marking "clergy" on an online dating site drew uniquely unexpected and undesirable contacts.

But Luke was...well, the photo postcard of him in swim trunks on a white sand beach brightened this February day. He had been at his second home in Jamaica for a few weeks, and, as usual, he'd remembered how much she loved to receive "real" mail.

The card was not filled with his usual jokes about the weather or lack of tropical corpses, though. Wanda sat down to read it and then read it again.

Dear Wanda,

I wanted you to be the first to hear. On January 6, my beloved and I eloped. Epiphany has always been my own version of a new year, and we decided after all our years of friendship, and the many months of long-distance love, we were ready to take the next step. My only regret is that you were not here to perform the wedding. I know you would have made us weep at the beauty of this sacrament. I look forward to introducing you to Irie when we come back from our honeymoon in late February.

Your dear friend,
Luke

Luke Fairchild, dear friend, funeral director...now spouse? She was reading it for a third time when the sound of cardboard hitting the floor drew her attention.

"Drop it!" she said. Wink did. He glanced up at Wanda, his muzzle light green. He'd heard that tone of voice. Unfortunately, a nearly empty quart of Brigham's mint chip ice cream was such an exceptional prize, Wanda's Jack Russell picked it up again and ran for the stairs.

"Aunt Wanda, your sneak thief is heading under my bed!" Lance shouted from the top of the stairs.

"Did you catch him?" Wanda was not far behind the dog. At fifty-three and eleven months, the Stone Ridge

Trinity Church pastor was in the best shape she'd been in for years, and she was hardly puffing at all after the sprint up the steps. Of course, at fifty-*two* and eleven months, she had not yet had her life threatened by three killers and a drug dealer. Physical fitness had never seemed so logical. It didn't hurt that all the exercise had put full-fat ice cream firmly back into her freezer rotation.

Lance, Wanda's seventeen-year-old nephew, had Wink firmly in hand, but the dripping quart was still firmly clamped in the dog's jaws.

"Drop it!" Wanda demanded again, trying to wrestle the damp cardboard from her terrier's grasp.

"Watch this." Lance set Wink down, but before the Jack Russell could abscond with her ice cream again, Lance whipped out a Slim Jim. The beef jerky stick was infinitely more appealing. Wanda snatched the masticated carton and considered that adolescent and canine probably understood each other's 24/7 appetites. Wink took the Slim Jim down to the kitchen to gnaw, and Lance slumped into the disreputable swivel chair in his bedroom.

Lancelot Bates had been living with his aunt for four months, ever since his mother—Wanda's sister, Mickey—had dropped him off and headed to Italy on a romantic adventure that quickly soured. Mickey was currently living in the UK with Wanda's second ex-husband, Brian, and Brian's husband. After being scammed by Enzo, her much younger Italian paramour, Mickey had told Wanda that she needed "time." Time for what, Wanda wasn't sure, but it seemed to involve a continued break from parenting responsibilities.

At first, Wanda had been furious with her sister for dropping Lance on her with no warning, but living with him had been the best thing that had happened to her in years. Well, that and solving two murders in less than a year with her friend Prudence Rye. Coming home to a sweet, goofy teenager and his equally nerdy friends filled a hole in Wanda's life she hadn't realized was there. She loved the vibration of stampeding feet overhead as she worked on a sermon and the sight of her nephew and the dog curled up on the couch watching Netflix or playing video games. Even the sneakers and sweatshirts that were absolutely everywhere made her grin. If Dungeons & Dragons got too loud, she turned off her hearing aids.

Wanda had recently given up not only online dating but drinking as well. Some people apparently could meet and date through online platforms without cocktails, wine, or beer. She couldn't. AA raised her feminist hackles, but the friends she'd made at the Monday women's meeting were a source of amazing support. She still loved chocolate, sparkly stilettos, and troublesome terriers, but none of those got her into (much) trouble.

She thought of the postcard on the table and felt only a twinge of regret at what might have been. Luke was the friend who had pushed her to give up alcohol when everyone else had remained tactfully silent. More than she needed a partner, she needed real friends. Maybe Luke's wife, Irie, would become a new one.

"How's your campaign going to get a comfort dog into the sheriff's office?" Lance picked up an article that had fluttered to the floor during her tug-of-war with the terrier.

"I'm still trying to understand the differences between therapy dogs, emotional support dogs, Hero pups, search-for-the-lost hounds, and I'm-going-to-chase-you-down-and-tackle-you dogs before I make my pitch," she replied.

Lance followed Wanda back downstairs to her office. Wink had finished his Slim Jim and was curled up in his bed by her desk. Lance scratched behind the pup's ears, and Wink sighed loudly. "If you volunteer Wink, you could get an all-in-one!"

Wanda picked up Wink's favorite chew toy, a rubber pumpkin she'd acquired for a dollar the week after Thanksgiving. She gave it to the dog before sinking down into her desk chair to straighten all the piles that had been disturbed. She wasn't the best organizer, but this was chaos. To be fair, her office at the church was the opposite of this room, but that was due to Lisa Vaughan, the Trinity UCC administrator. Lisa's skills kept Wanda employed. If Wanda's conference minister wandered in here, an exorcism would follow.

"Wink's unreliable, at best," she said with a smile. "We're proposing a 'comfort dog,' who could immediately intuit the most fragile person in the situation, whether that person was family to someone detained, a victim of a recent crime, or a police officer who'd witnessed a traumatic event."

"Let me guess—Sheriff Ryan Phennen is not in favor of this plan, since he is not in favor with you?"

Wanda and Ryan had dated on and off for several years. They were a terrible match, but every so often they seemed to find themselves back in each other's orbit. When Wanda gave up drinking, she'd also given up on throwing herself back into a situation neither party actually wanted anymore.

Wanda knew Ryan was not upset about that, but about the fact that buying a support dog would take a chunk of the budget away from the before-school sports program he was trying to get off the ground. He'd gone to a conference and learned about Wake-Up Basketball, and ever since he had been trying to organize something similar at the middle and high schools in the district. His funding progress had been slow. The dog Wanda was proposing would be attention-catching, and therefore money-siphoning.

"You are wise beyond your years," Wanda said. "Why don't you direct a little of that wisdom at your homework?"

Lance groaned, but he scooped Wink up and headed back to his room, dog and pumpkin toy cradled in his arms like a baby doll.

"Hey," Lance called down.

"Hey yourself!"

"Did you finish that book about the vet and the dog?"

"*Until Tuesday: A Wounded Warrior and the Golden Retriever Who Saved Him*? Yes. It was wonderful! It was a difficult read in light of Luis Carlos Montalván's death."

"I can't believe you finished it in time for your meeting tonight," Lance said. "Isn't book club in half an hour?"

Wanda looked at her watch, then double-checked the clock on the stove. "Twenty-three minutes, in fact!" She hurried past him and bolted up the stairs to her room, Wink hot on her heels.

"Don't forget that Leslie and Nicole are coming over for pizza!"

The three were fast friends: Wanda's nephew, with his blue glasses and auburn man-bun, who could paint, draw, and write but had barely mastered multiplication; Bellona Pond's fragile blond newshound daughter, who whispered deftly insightful critiques of how adults were destroying the world; and Nicole Laferriere, whose voice could lift the roof off a three-story building, if not yet an opera house. Last year, Wanda could not have imagined those girls at her house several times a week, but now she was used to seeing their shoes and backpacks by her front door when she came home.

She called out "Don't forget to take Wink for a walk!" from the depths of her closet. Lance wouldn't forget, and even if he did, Wink would remind him. She emerged a minute later with one boot on and a cardigan that needed to be rebuttoned. She was trying to put her hair up and brush her teeth simultaneously. None of it was working.

Lance let out that exaggerated sigh teens reserve for the inexplicable behaviors of adults and abandoned any attempt at homework to fix himself a snack-before-the-pizza-before-the-bedtime-snack. Just in case the girls were late.

2

THEY WOULD NEVER CALL THEMSELVES THE THURSDAY Mystery Club, though their book club did meet on Thursdays, and the members did spend most of their time discussing murder. Honestly, they were just not as smart (or as old) as Osman's fictional crime-solving Brits, but when Wanda and Rye had joined in December they quickly discovered that this group, like Osman's, was more interested in how the book of the month connected to a cold case than they were in literary clues.

Rye decided that suited her just fine, and Wanda was on a mission to make friends outside of both church and bars. This fit the bill. Harvey's Bakery even stayed open late for the meeting. If the content didn't keep Wanda's attention, Rye knew their superb coffee and pastries were compelling.

In addition to Rye and Wanda, who were the group's newest members, there was Greg Engstrom, a librarian and mystery enthusiast who organized and ran the club. Greg also happened to be engaged to Wanda's best friend, church musician Tony Tomeo, who tagged along for the company (and good food).

Greg was the most knowledgeable person Wanda had ever met. Wanda had spent a lot of time with him since he and Tony had started dating, and he seemed to be an endless repository of little-known facts, detailed myths, and insightful research. He was, as Tony pointed out, also funny and handsome. A middle-aged man with a slight build, dark-rimmed glasses, and curly blond hair, Wanda would call him sweet rather than good-looking, but when she saw how Tony gazed at him, she kept her opinion to herself.

They were also joined by Elena Mendoza. Elena's husband, Gerard, was the principal at Stoneridge High and Rye's boss. In addition to his work for Wanda's church, Tony led the school chorus, taught a little music theory, and accompanied anything that needed a piano, so Gerard was his boss, too. Rye had enjoyed getting to know Elena on her own terms and not in Gerard's considerable shadow. She was a dazzling craftswoman. She sewed her own clothing, refurbished furniture, and knew how to quilt, knit, and crochet. Elena was also a masterful chef, and she often brought a savory dish to share. She had four daughters at home and was used to cooking for a crowd.

Camila Santos was another high school connection at the book club. She taught biology. She and Rye had become close friends soon after Rye moved back to town, and, many weekends, Rye and Camila met up with Camila's twin sister, Ana, who taught Spanish and French, though their birth language was Portuguese. They'd go for a run or have dinner and a movie at home. Teaching at the high school meant all three preferred to keep their local outings to a minimum, lest they run into students or, worse, parents of students, during their limited time off.

Recently, Ana had been spending more time with her boyfriend, and Rye and Camila had gone on a few adventures that the quiet Ana probably wouldn't enjoy. Beating the record for riding the bucking Bronco at a bar one state over had been a favorite for Rye, although she'd also enjoyed the dueling piano show Camila had invited her to a few weeks ago.

The final member of their little band was Officer Jaz Malone. Rye had met Jaz in a professional capacity several times in the last year, and Wanda had taken self-defense classes with her, but neither knew her outside of work. Even at book club, because the topic of conversation often strayed toward murder, Jaz kept her professional hat on.

Over two months, Rye had only learned three personal details about the woman. One, Jaz was madly in love with her husband, who owned the best tea shop in town. Two, she was a huge gymnastics fan and went to every competition within driving distance. Three, she hated chocolate. Rye could forgive her this last fact because Jaz always saved her a salted chocolate chunk cookie when Rye was running late to the meeting.

As a rule, Rye had a great time at these meetings, but she was antsy tonight. She had been casually seeing Claudia Ramirez, the drama teacher at Stoneridge, since early November. Claudia had decided to take a leave of absence after the death of her friend Jonathan Thorne and had spent December and January visiting extended family in the Philippines. Since she'd been back, Rye had only seen her once outside of work. She and Claudia had a narrow window to spend time together each week, and between Claudia's local family, who she frequently stayed with on the weekends, and her new second job at the Lilac Cottage Playhouse, their schedules hadn't lined up.

Tonight, though, Claudia had promised to be available when Rye was done here, and they were going to have a real date. Rye had a change of clothes in her car. Her thick auburn curls had been styled for once. She hadn't eaten dinner, and her stomach was rumbling, even after helping herself to a madeleine and a mug of fragrant orange blossom tea.

Greg had shared with them that this week they would be listening to an episode of a local true crime podcast about the unsolved murder of a man named Lionel Burgess. It didn't seem to connect to the soldier and his dog in *Until Tuesday* in any way except that both stories ended tragically.

"Burgess was thought to have been killed in a break-in," Greg was saying as he scanned his page of notes, "although the evidence suggests the perpetrator was known to the victim. There was no sign of forced entry, and nothing of value was taken." He glanced up at Rye, who had been zoning out. "Rye, was this before your father's tenure as sheriff?"

She reached her hand out for his notebook. "Who did you say the victim was?" Rye studied the description of the podcast.

"Lionel Burgess," Elena Mendoza said. The elegantly dressed brown-skinned woman was usually as flamboyantly outgoing as her husband, but tonight she had been quiet.

Rye glanced over at Elena. The woman was discreetly wiping her eyes with the cuff of her sapphire silk blouse. She was about to ask if Elena had known the victim when Camila gave her a quick hug from behind.

She had come in late, and her hands were freezing. Rye handed her the dirty chai, extra hot, that she'd ordered for her. Camila wrapped her hands around the mug. "Are we already done pretending we're here to discuss the book?" she asked.

Wanda laughed. "Oh, yes! Greg and Tony pushed us through *Until Tuesday* in about fifteen minutes. It might be a record!"

"Good," Camila said. "I didn't read it anyway."

Rye gave her a light punch on the arm, but Camila just smiled. "I tried, but I'm so behind on grading, I've given up fun for the new year."

"We probably should get back to the questions I found online about the author's death," Elena replied, "and how inmates have continued training dogs to companion returning soldiers. I shared *Tuesday Tucks Me In* with children in the after-school program I teach on Wednesdays." Rye watched her closely, but all signs of sorrow had been erased from Elena's expression. She was as briskly organized as always.

Wanda handed Jaz the plate of cookies. "I'm more interested in this case Greg found. It was before my time here, but I've heard Ryan talk about it. I think it was one of those cases that defined the department. How Hardy handled his involvement is still lauded by those of us coming up."

"What do you mean?" Rye started scanning the details in Greg's notes again. A date caught her attention. "I don't believe it."

"What?" Wanda asked. Rye handed her the sheet without a word, but even after reading it over twice, Wanda wasn't sure what had caused Rye's face to go gray.

"Lionel Burgess was murdered the day my mother disappeared," Rye said.

Camila put down her tea and leaned forward. "Do you think the cases might be connected?"

Rye knew Camila was a fan of telenovelas. Her imagination tended to run wild, but this time she might be right. "I don't know."

"Should we listen to the episode?" Greg asked. He looked worried. "I won't play it if it will upset you, Rye."

She shook her head. "No. Go ahead." Rye closed her eyes. "Let's hear it."

"So? WHAT DID YOU THINK?" CAMILA ASKED AS SHE, Rye, and Wanda walked to the parking lot.

Rye was still processing the story she had heard. The podcast's host was well-prepared. Lionel Burgess had worked at the DMV, where he was well-liked according to his colleagues. His neighbors said he kept to himself. One man interviewed, though, whom the group had immediately dubbed "Mr. Bigot Braxton," complained about what he'd considered to be a "parade of men and women coming to the house at all hours of the night."

Police had discovered no sign of forced entry or a struggle. Burgess's parents and siblings had told the police that, to their knowledge, nothing of value had been taken from the house except for a set of suitcases gifted to him the previous Christmas, which Lionel's mother had engraved with LMB—Lionel Marius Burgess.

The host also noted that in the photos she had seen of the crime scene, there was a rack of suits and stacks of milk crates that appeared to be filled with sanitary products, formula, and diapers. Police had not been able to trace any connection between Burgess and the halfway houses in the county, and they'd concluded he might have been involved in a human trafficking ring brought down later that same year.

"I hate podcasts," Wanda replied. "I feel like I'm so easily swayed by the story when I can't examine any of the evidence myself."

"I know," Camila said. "At first, I felt like she was painting a picture of a regular guy who was being persecuted by his neighbor for being Black and gay. I felt for him."

"But then she started talking about his potential connection to human trafficking," Wanda said. "I was not prepared for the interviews that supported that possibility."

"What do you think, Rye?" Camila asked.

"I don't know," she replied. "The evidence for his involvement is circumstantial at best."

"Do you think..." Camila paused and shook her head. "Never mind."

"What?" Rye asked.

"What if your mother was taken?" Camila asked. "She might have struggled. Burgess was killed with a bookend, right? Maybe she grabbed it and hit him as she was trying to escape. If Burgess had a partner, he or she could have grabbed your mother and made her disappear."

"She doesn't exactly fit the profile of the other people released from human trafficking in this area," Wanda pointed out. "It sounds like the women were brought in from countries in South America and Eastern Europe. They were undocumented and largely didn't speak English. Your mother was a U.S. citizen, employed, and married to a man in law enforcement. Taking her would attract too much attention."

"Unless she killed Lionel Burgess and someone panicked," Rye replied.

"We don't even know if there was another person," Wanda said. "We don't even know your mother was there!"

A woman screamed, and, as one, the three women turned toward the sound. Rye took off first, with Camila and Wanda close on her heels. She rounded the corner, skidding on the ice, and almost smacked into Elena Mendoza. Her face was pale, and her black hair had come out of its chignon. She looked shaken.

"Elena! What happened?" Rye asked.

"I was walking to my car, and someone grabbed my purse," she said, pointing down the street.

Rye and Camila ran in the direction Elena had indicated, but by the time they reached the corner, the only people in sight were a few couples headed into Zucca for dinner. Rye thought she recognized Claudia among them, her plum wool coat distinctive, but Camila was pulling at her hand, ready to head back to Elena. Rye gave one last glance over her shoulder at the women heading inside, then returned to her friends.

Jaz had called it in by the time they came back to their meeting, and Camila crawled into the back of Jaz's car with Elena to keep warm. Rye dug her hands in her pockets, wishing she'd brought gloves and a hat tonight.

"See anyone?" Wanda didn't look any warmer.

Rye opened her mouth to mention Claudia, then realized Wanda was talking about the mugger. "No. They must have taken off through one of the neighborhoods." She glanced into the backseat at Camila. "Did Elena notice anything about her attacker?"

"I think those questions fall under my jurisdiction." A deep voice spoke from behind Rye, probably taking the words right out of Jaz's mouth.

Rye turned to see Sheriff Ryan Phennen standing behind her. He looked like he'd come from a date rather than the station. In his early forties, he was fit, and when he was off duty he dressed to impress. Tonight, under his charcoal peacoat, he had on a royal blue cashmere sweater and dark jeans. Ryan's younger brother, Sergeant Tyler Phennen, and his girlfriend, Camila's sister, Ana, appeared behind Ryan a moment later. Tyler was not in uniform either. In fact, he looked like he had shed his uniform for the most comfortable clothes in his closet. Rye hid a smile to see how well-matched he and Ana were in their joggers and hoodies.

Camila climbed out of the car and gave her sister a hug. Ryan slid into the seat she'd vacated beside Elena.

"Would you give Ana a ride?" Tyler asked Camila as he pulled on his parka. "I'll stay and take Ryan home when we're done here."

"I suppose so," Camila agreed with a grin, throwing an arm around her sister's narrow shoulders. Though the women were identical, they managed to look very different. Ana wore her dark hair in a pixie cut and favored soft fabrics in creams and blues. Camila kept her hair long and wild, and she almost always had on black or gray jeans with fitted tees or tanks. Camila also had a leather moto jacket she wore three seasons, claiming she never got too cold. Rye envied the effortless punk energy Camila gave off. She had personally been freezing since moving back from Texas and currently had on a puffy jacket, wool sweater, and silk long underwear under her jeans.

"I'm going to head out, too," she told Wanda. "Tomorrow I'll talk to Gerard. If Elena saw anything, I'm sure she'll tell her husband about it tonight."

"I need to get home and check that a certain three teenagers have left my house intact," Wanda agreed. "Are you sure you're okay? That was a lot tonight."

"I will be. I need to think about it."

Wanda gave her a hug. "Okay. Let's talk soon?"

"Definitely," Rye replied. She pulled out her phone and texted Claudia to solidify their very tentative plans for late supper. Claudia wrote back immediately.

> *Sorry! Something came up. I'll see you at school tomorrow.*

Rye spent the drive home contemplating that final period at the end of Claudia's text. Contrary to what Wanda and Hardy believed, punctuation in texting was paramount. Claudia never wrote a single character without intention. Rye hit play on *evermore* and turned up Taylor Swift. At the next red light, she texted her father that she'd be home in time to watch NCIS with him after all.

3

WANDA TOSSED AND TURNED AND WOKE UP GRUMPY. For the first time, she wished that she had joined a book club that rotated between thriller, cozy, and police procedural, with a side of discussion about how P. D. James, Sue Grafton, and Ngaio Marsh presented their particular English-speaking countries. She could have handled a conversation about why there were not more SSRIs prescribed for fans of Scandinavian noir or why people enjoyed recipes in their reads. They shouldn't be dredging up local cases—Wanda had enough murder in her life without exhuming graves. Book clubs were for escaping.

Grumpy was not the way to prepare for the Interfaith Council planning meeting for Mardi Gras, though. Some members of the Christian subgroup thought Mardi Gras was a perfect excuse to extend Lent backward and talk about sin, while others believed it was a time to show non-churchgoers that church folk knew how to party.

The group had pushed planning late because some members had been on sunny vacations encouraged by congregations who thought clergy should be refreshed between Advent and Lent. Wanda had never served such a church and didn't actually like the idea of a Caribbean cruise, but to be offered a break after Christmas would be wonderful. It surely would provide some lively preaching points for the imagination-impoverished year of Bible passages they were "encouraged" to preach. It was a three-year cycle, and this year's weekly dose of Mark and Joshua was filling Wanda with ministerial ennui. She took another sip of her coffee, willing it to overcome her attitude before she had to be open-minded. Helpful. Pleasant, even.

Wanda had ideas for the Mardi Gras service—that wasn't the problem. The challenge was selling them to a tricky audience. She put her hands at two and ten on the steering wheel, her prayer mandala, and asked God for patience, and the universe for the tongue of Peitho, personified spirit of persuasion, herald of Aphrodite. Covering all bases.

When she arrived at Saint Athanasius, which was hosting both this meeting and the service, her spirits were lifted just turning into the parking lot. The church shared the lot with Stoneridge High School, and she could see students down on the track and soccer fields on this bright morning. This was definitely the spot to have a Mardi Gras celebration. It would tie into a parade, led by the Stoneridge Jazz band and starting at the front door of the school.

It also didn't hurt that the best cooks in town went to Saint Athanasius Orthodox Church, including several Greek couples, a woman from Moldova, one from Romania, and one from Ethiopia. Recently, a young man from Russia doing a university exchange had joined. Apparently, his blinis were amazing.

The members of the clergy group had descended on a tray of pastries provided by those same gifted chefs. First was the Reverend Colleen Sullivan from the Unitarian Universalist church. Colleen had eight inches on Wanda's five-foot-two, and with her clergy shirt and collar she wore black jeans and pink bejeweled Converse high-tops. She possessed an interesting assortment of the brand, and she only dressed up (or down) to black flats for the most solemn occasions.

Rolf Anderson, a slightly stooped man in his fifties, head shaven but with a bushy, strawberry blond beard and eyebrows to match, had been at the Lutheran church for a year. He had good ideas but preferred to wait for someone else to present them. He returned Wanda's smile as she came in, and Wanda restrained herself from handing him a napkin to take care of the crumbs in his beard and on his tie.

Lana Grenier, who had just returned from maternity leave, was nursing her son while devouring a plate of food. She was at First United Methodist and had once told Wanda she would rather perform an infant baptism on horseback while sporting a sequined red tube top then ever again hold a denominational national office. Someday, Lana might be able to listen to jokes about splitting churches, but that time had not come yet. Wanda sat next to her, knowing this would put her in proximity to baby snuggles and in a position to refill Lana's coffee cup with decaf as often as necessary.

Father Bogdan (easy to remember, he always said, since he was Bogdan Bogdanovic, like the basketball player), the genial head of Saint Athanasius, was happily playing host and attempting, futilely, to get the meeting started before folks went into a sugar coma. They had all settled down with full plates balanced on their laps when a commotion at the door signaled the late arrival of Josh Gagne, the twenty-nine-year-old pastor at Rising Star Baptist, and Bruce Upton, pastor at Jordan Baptist since before his colleague was born. They came in talking loudly with their own coffees and breakfast sandwiches from the new food truck, Dad Yolks, that was parked by Bruce's church.

Father Bogdan invited Rolf to pray. Wanda knew it was to make sure Rolf said something, anything, during the meeting. He then invited Bruce to take notes, which everyone knew was to keep Bruce's comments to a minimum.

After a brief welcome, Bogdan continued, "I am glad to volunteer Saint Athanasius for the Interfaith Mardi Gras Supper. This year, our Great Lent begins six days after the Ash Wednesday that kicks off most Western churches. We will not be fasting yet and can happily provide a spread of savory dishes and desserts." He smiled warmly. "My wife, Agatha, also suggested we might close our time together by inviting everyone outside to see the parade go by."

"That sounds like a wonderful suggestion," Wanda replied, pleased that someone else was thinking along the same lines as she was. She didn't know Agatha well. Agatha was younger than her husband and seemed reluctant to join in with meetings like this, even though Wanda knew she would be coordinating the food and volunteers.

Josh glanced around. He was handsome in a way that reminded Wanda of her childhood Ken doll—blonde and plastic—although the look on his face was rarely as pleasant. She'd overheard one of her parishioners describe him as "smoldering" at last year's Easter sunrise service, but for her taste he was just too pouty to be attractive. "I hope we'll have a prayer service and time to grieve our sins," Josh said sternly. Wanda covered her snicker with an almost convincing cough.

To everyone's surprise, Bruce spoke up. "Ash Wednesday is soon enough to talk about sin. And most of our churches"—at this, he aimed a pointed look at Colleen, who offered a drive-through "ashing" in the church parking lot rather than a service—"will be having such an opportunity."

It seemed Wanda would not have to use any of her prerehearsed speeches about the difference between Mardi Gras and Ash Wednesday, because the normally silent Rolf raised his hand. Bogdan acknowledged him. "I don't know as much as I should about Orthodox tradition, but I would love to hear more about Forgiveness Sunday and Clean Monday. Those practices seem like themes we could learn from and incorporate into this service."

Several others in the group were not familiar with Forgiveness Sunday, when parishioners turned to one another to ask forgiveness instead of asking only God, and only in silence. Clean Monday encouraged congregants to start Lent with a clean conscience, with forgiveness, and with renewed Christian love. The custom of scrubbing the house during that first week of Lent reflected that idea of beginning the season with a fresh start.

Wanda spoke up. "I think this will stick with my congregation—that we let God clean away the corners of our lives, and then we do the same by straightening up things around us in our heads, our homes, and our hearts. It's a commonsense Lent. We all know about cleaning—the work and satisfaction. We don't beat our breasts and say, 'I am a terrible sinner.' We say, 'I've smudged this, I've put dirty fingerprints all over my life. I have made a mess of things I was given. God help me.'"

Josh snorted. "Some folks need to beat their breasts."

"Certainly they do, if that helps them make a new beginning," Wanda said. "But people have plenty of opportunities to hear it put that way."

Colleen stood and threw her plate away. She had been uncharacteristically quiet. She was an extrovert's extrovert, already standing out with her fire-red hair, height, and high-tops, and she wore a button that typically stopped people cold. It was big, maybe three inches in diameter, and read, *This is what a rape victim looks like.*

Colleen's local ministry was the same as most clergy—worship services, pastoral care, urging and supporting justice work, and an outreach program focused on food insecurity that fed hundreds of people a month. But nationally she was an advocate for worship spaces as real sanctuaries where people could break the silence about sexual violence. Naming church as a safe place for people to talk about date rape and incest, trust abuse and lifelong PTSD, was her crusade. If she thought Clean Monday belittled the damage that lasted a lifetime, her colleagues would pass on it.

Colleen met Wanda's eyes as she sat back down. "I think that one of the reasons we talk together and eat together is to understand across faith lines, to learn one another's beliefs, practices, and metaphors. I always like to learn."

"I have another idea," said Wanda.

"Of course you do," murmured Lana, passing Wanda a sleepy, full-bellied baby.

Wanda's smile almost touched her ears, but she was not distracted. "I was thinking we might ask someone in the cleaning profession to speak. What about Martina Suarez?"

Martina was the custodian at Saint Athanasius, but she had also come to work at Trinity when the church's custodial staff, a father-and-son team, had been on leave following a family emergency. In fact, Martina cleaned most of the houses of worship in town on an occasional basis, although she also maintained a few private clients. "We talked when Martina was at Trinity in October. I know she's a faithful Roman Catholic, and there hasn't been much Interfaith participation from Saint Mary's since Father Paul has been filling in as hospital chaplain. I think Martina would enjoy the opportunity to connect."

Father Paul Kelly was a good friend of Wanda's. Although he was out of town this week visiting his mother, he had given her the okay to offer up this suggestion. It was the one idea Wanda had not expected to meet resistance, but a chill was in the air. Lana and Josh looked away, and Bruce stared down at his notes. Wanda used her favorite technique of letting the silence stretch.

"I'll speak to Martina about it," Father Bogdan said after a long moment. No one else in the room met her eyes, but he smiled warmly. "I've heard rumors she's a wonderful singer."

"Those aren't the only rumors," Wanda heard Bruce murmur to Josh. No one objected outright.

When the meeting ended, Lana took her son back and tucked him into his car seat, shushing him back to sleep as she walked out with Wanda. Wanda wanted to ask about her hesitation and if she had any idea why almost everyone seemed against asking Martina to speak at the service—and hopefully perform, too. It was common knowledge that she had studied to be an opera singer and generously sang for the annual events of many nonprofits.

She knew Lana would be honest with her, but Wanda didn't get a chance to ask. Josh squeezed between them and knocked Wanda's bag out of her hand in his hurry. Lana took off to the parking lot while Josh hastily scooped her belongings off the pavement with a huff, as though this were her fault. Wanda reminded herself that she could only be impatient until Lent began, when she would have to give it up for six weeks.

"You know, you should never underestimate sin," Josh said. "Mardi Gras is a big opportunity for it." He wore a strong aftershave that some people might find appealing. It gave Wanda a headache.

She stepped back, slinging her bag onto her shoulder. "Well, if that's the case, I vote that at the Mardi Gras supper we focus on practicing gluttony."

"Not everything is a joke, you know." His jaw, which really was the definition of chiseled, looked like it might have gotten that way from constant teeth grinding and the complete lack of a sense of humor.

Wanda usually loved working with young clergy— they had energy, passion, and great ideas. Josh just made her feel old, and like she'd better restrain herself from calling out a self-righteous troublemaker. "Josh, someday you may realize that if you can't laugh at all, you'll end up miserable and alone."

He ignored her. "Martina Suarez is not an appropriate guest speaker. I've recommended to Bogdan that we consider Gary Sheed. He's an upstanding member of my congregation with impeccable character, and he's a tall building window washer. I'm sure he would speak to the cleansing of sin with more proficiency than Ms. Suarez."

He gave a sniff, and Wanda, who had reached full sugar crash levels of irritation, pulled a crumpled tissue out of her pocket and pushed it into his hand before walking away. She could hear him sputtering in dismay as she got into her car. As she pulled out of the parking lot, she turned her hearing aids to a restful off position. It was time for a well-deserved break.

IT WAS FRIDAY, SO WANDA FINISHED HER SERMON IN the church office and decided to leave it there in order not to waste the entire weekend messing with it. Lisa, the jewel of administrators, was finishing up as well. Pre-K pickup was in a few minutes.

"Wanda, Tony was here earlier, but he and Greg are out tasting wedding cakes. Again." Lisa held up a clear plastic container filled with leftovers from yesterday's tasting to share with her four-year-old daughter, Lily. "They do seem to be taking that part of wedding planning seriously."

"Did he need me for anything?" Wanda hadn't seen Tony except at book club this week, and it felt like ages since they'd gotten a chance to catch up with the wedding plans.

"No. He did want to thank you, though," Lisa said with a sly grin.

"For what?"

"You didn't volunteer him for the Mardi Gras service. He's helping the Jazz Band that evening, but he knew you might trick him into double duty with promises of…loukoumades?"

"Fried honey donuts. I'll save him some."

"He's also happy that the Ash Wednesday service is not all Taizé and has some upbeat music," Lisa said. "I'm sure I don't think of Ash Wednesday as upbeat." She openly admitted that she came to church for Lily's sake rather than her own, but she had enough opinions on services that Wanda wondered if somewhere in Lisa's family tree there was a minister or two.

"I'm trying something new this year. I want to have the confession and assurance of grace in the beginning of the service and then challenge people to decide how they can use their freshly granted forgiveness to change the world. Ashes are a sign of our transitory lives, and it's a waste of time to wallow in our own personal mistakes rather than making a difference."

Lisa looked thoughtful, though Wanda guessed she might already be planning the weekly Friday night dinner that she and Lily brought to Fair Havens Assisted Living to share with Grandma Dottie.

"Where do you get those lucky-o-donuts?" Lisa asked as she buttoned up her coat.

"On Mardi Gras at Saint Athanasius. There will be kites for the kids to fly, and we'll have the best seats to see the parade." Wanda grinned at her admin. "And as a thank you for not asking for help with the bulletin, could I ask you a teeny, tiny favor?"

"Maybe," Lisa replied, wisely noncommittal.

"Have you ever planned a pancake flipping race?"

"A what?"

"Firefighters versus kids."

Lisa raised one eyebrow. "No idea what you want me to do, but you know firefighters are my weakness, so yes. I'll do it."

As far as Wanda was concerned, firefighters were everybody's weakness, whether they wanted to admit it or not. She just smiled and said thank you.

4

RYE WAS GLAD THAT SHE HAD FINISHED UP HER WORK in time to make the Stoneridge High School MLK Jr. concert. It had been a tradition for the past decade, although this year they had needed to postpone it two weeks due to a snowstorm over the holiday weekend.

Ever since Tony had taken over directing the chorus and turned them into a group worth hearing by people other than their parents, concert tickets sold out early. For this show, Tony had chosen BIPOC chorus members for all the spotlight roles. He had discussed the decision with Principal Mendoza, who brought it up to the staff. Tony had confided to Wanda and Rye over coffee one morning that he hoped he'd covered all his bases in making the choice, and that he'd eventually decided to have an open conversation about it with his students.

The chorus, a reflection of both the school and its community, was 70 percent white, and of those who made up the remaining 30 percent, most had Latin American and Asian heritage. Stoneridge currently had six Black families, and only one of those students was in chorus. Nicole Laferriere was undoubtedly the star of the group and had been since freshman year. No one complained about showcasing her prodigious talents, nor those of the other well-deserving singers who had earned solos.

Rye knew it was an ongoing joke that this generation of students was "too" woke, but she was in love with their passion and acceptance. She also suspected that the people who complained the loudest were the same ones who had been too afraid to take a stand when they were young and on fire with possibility.

She felt a tap on her shoulder and looked up to see Ana, who made a gesture for Rye to follow her. The two walked quickly up the aisle along the wall. When they left the cozy warmth of the auditorium, Rye didn't have to ask why Ana had come to get her.

Outside, there were protesters. Rye walked briskly to the front door and opened it. A group of about twenty people were standing on the sidewalk holding up signs and chanting, "Make America Great and Free, Great in the World and Free for Me!"

Tyler Phennen was already taking charge of the situation. Ana must have called him in before she went to find Rye. It was a good thing, too, because Rye would not be handling these people as calmly as Tyler was.

"What's going on?" Rye asked.

She recognized a few of the people in the crowd—parents whose students weren't even in chorus, a few members of a local self-named "True-Church," and, sadly, a retired teacher Rye had known in her own days as a student.

The True-Church members were not a surprise. Rye had been fielding nasty emails from them for months. Nothing that happened in the school was too insignificant to escape their notice and general condemnation. The parents, too, were frequent visitors in her office. Rye and Gerard had many conversations about how to handle their animosity, but Hardy's voice was the one Rye channeled when their names appeared on her calendar. He had told her that as sheriff he often worked with and offered substantial assistance to people whose views were vocally abhorrent to him. "It's my job to protect and serve," Hardy would tell Rye. "I don't have to like them, but I do have to respect their humanity."

It was a lesson Rye had taken many years to learn, and she still wasn't all that good at it. Her overwhelming desire at this moment was to start punching, in fact, but she was at work. And a role model. She needed to handle this accordingly.

"Hey, Tyler," she said, crossing over to where he was observing the crowd.

"Rye." Tyler looked down at her and smiled. "Sorry about this."

"Is there anything we can do?"

He shook his head. "You know there isn't. Not unless they become violent or public property is destroyed. They have a right to be here."

Rye ground her teeth together. "I don't want the kids to see this."

"Me neither, but I'm not sure what we can do about it."

Ana sidled up behind them. "I have an idea."

RYE LEFT TYLER TO KEEP AN EYE ON THE PROTESTERS. He promised to update her if there was any change. She snuck back in and passed Claudia a note as Tony was introducing the final song.

"It has been my honor to work with this amazing chorus to prepare a concert to bring people together in the spirit of Martin Luther King Junior's work." Tony paused, and the audience responded with a round of applause. "Before we end our program tonight, I'd like to offer you all an opportunity to hear a special duet between former opera singer Martina Suarez and soloist Nicole Laferriere. They have been working on this piece for the All-City Choir but have agreed to honor us by singing it here tonight." Tony beckoned Martina, in a beautiful blue dress, to join Nicole at the mic in front of the stage.

The next thing anyone heard was Martina's bright soprano, and then Nicole's wide-ranging alto, beginning Odetta's version of "Oh Freedom."

There wasn't a dry eye. By the end, the audience was on its feet, and the room was filled with an electricity that Rye hadn't experienced outside of protest marches. She stood poised by the exit, watching as Claudia rose to address the crowd. As the head of the drama department, Claudia had a knack for commanding the attention of full auditoriums, and the crowd quieted quickly.

"Before you leave tonight, I want to ask all of you a favor. I've been informed that in front of the school there are…protesters." She seemed to struggle to keep her voice neutral. Several voices in the audience booed this news. Claudia held up a hand. "We cannot legally ask them to leave, but we can steal power from their hatred. If you all leave by the cafeteria doors"—at this, she pointed toward Rye, who waved a hand to indicate they should follow her—"they won't have the privilege of upsetting us. We can all walk out to our cars through the back parking lot, and they will have spent a night in the cold for nothing. We will not acknowledge them. We will not approach them. On this night, after being uplifted by our talented music department, we will give them nothing. They cannot steal our joy."

A loud whoop followed this, and the audience got up and headed toward Rye, who held the door until the last of them had filed out. She greeted many by name and received enough high fives to make her glad she wasn't sitting in the back of a squad car for having punched out an ignorant bully. As she headed back in to grab her jacket, she was stopped by Wanda.

"I think one of your students needs a little extra help," Wanda told her, nodding her head in the direction of a girl sitting in the third row, her head down on the back of the seat in front of her.

"Thanks," Rye replied, giving Wanda's hand a squeeze and Lance a low five as the two headed out with Tony.

Rye slid in beside the girl, who didn't bother to lift her head up. She wore a jean jacket that had clearly had something sewn on and then ripped off of the sleeve.

"Hey, Corrine," Rye said softly.

"My mom's out there protesting, isn't she?"

"Yeah, she is." Rye studied her. When Rye had seen Corrine earlier in the week competing with the debate team, her jacket had sported Black Lives Matter and Protect Trans Lives patches. Her cornflower hair had been in two braids then. Now, her head was shaved, the nicks still visible.

"She took my car away. I have to go out there to get a ride home."

Rye squeezed her hands tightly into fists and let out a slow breath. "I can give you a lift, if you'd like? Or if you'd feel more comfortable, I bet Lance is still in the parking lot. His aunt would be happy to take you home."

Corrine shook her head. "That would just make things worse." She sat up and pulled a package of wet wipes out of her backpack. Rye watched as she used a compact mirror to make sure she got all evidence of makeup wiped away before she stood up. "Do you think everyone else is gone yet? I just don't want the whole school to know…"

Rye pulled out her phone and texted Ana, then showed Corrine the thumbs-up that Ana sent back. "I think you're in the clear. Can I walk out with you, at least?"

Corrine shook her head. "I don't think that would be a good idea." She slipped on her backpack and gave Rye a wan smile. "But thanks for asking."

Rye watched Corrine until the door of the auditorium swung closed behind her. She sagged back in her seat.

She wasn't surprised when she heard the first few notes of the piano play. Rye laid her head back and listened as Claudia played "God's Eye is on the Sparrow," the grief building in her chest until she finally began to cry.

Some days, there was so little she could do.

When she was finished, Claudia stood and put on her jacket before walking over to offer Rye her hand. "I'm keeping an eye on her, too," Claudia said. "I know that doesn't feel like enough, but…"

Rye tried to smile and failed. "It helps." She let Claudia pull her to her feet and followed her out the front door to be sure all the protesters had left. Although they never engaged in any displays of affection at school, tonight Rye held Claudia's hand tight.

She was surprised to see a light on in the office. Rye dug out her keys and let herself in, with Claudia following. Gerard Mendoza was sitting at his desk, his wife pacing back and forth in front of him.

Rye knocked gently on the doorframe. "Still here?"

Gerard gestured to Elena, who was in the middle of delivering an angry tirade about ineffectual police procedure on school campuses. "We're letting off a little steam before we go home to put the girls to bed."

"It's unacceptable that they couldn't remove those people!" his wife responded, clearly nowhere near burned out yet. Claudia offered Elena a fist bump in solidarity, and the older woman gladly took the opportunity. Rye watched Claudia surreptitiously rub her knuckles as Gerard tried to defuse the situation.

"You would have had to convince the police that we had evidence they would create a life-threatening disturbance, and not only that, but prove that they had intent to cause destruction of property or violence."

"It does start to sound like *Minority Report* when you put it that way," Rye agreed reluctantly.

"How can we be sure they won't turn up at the Mardi Gras parade next Tuesday?" Claudia asked.

"I'll speak to Sheriff Phennen about our options," Gerard replied.

Elena threw up her hands and began to pace again. "Ryan Phennen is powerless when it comes to this sort of thing. You know who's going to show up for us? Parents." She came to a stop in front of Rye. "Because I'm going to make them. No matter what happens, these children will not have to face off against a bunch of narrow-minded bigots alone."

"I'll be there. You may end up having to bail me out afterward, but hopefully the school board will understand, given the circumstances."

Gerard gave Rye a look that said under no circumstances should she test that hypothesis. Rye bared her teeth in an approximation of a smile. He turned to look at his wife and was met with an identical "don't test me" look.

He sighed, clearly beaten. "At least do me a favor and share a cell so I only get one call for bail."

5

THE NEXT DAY WAS A WELCOME PAUSE FROM DRAMA OF any kind. Wanda was glad to get the bulletin planned for Sunday and visit a couple of shut-ins. The hours melted away. The landline began to ring as Wanda finished making her 'cocktail-hour' cup of tea. The music of Parquet Courts drifted down from Lance's room. If he was wearing headphones and there was that much spillover, they would be seeing an audiologist soon, but at least she knew by the sound of it he was working on a paper for his English class.

Even if he hadn't come straight home from school and drama club and ensconced himself in his room, Wanda knew from experience that he didn't really register the sound of the house phone ringing. The landline was a holdover from church days past that she couldn't quite let go of. Besides, it was the number Mickey always used.

Sure enough, Birmingham, England, was on the line.

Michelle—or Mickey, as she had always been called—was Wanda's very own reminder that the parable of the prodigal "son" could replay itself ad nauseum through history and still have a fresh sting with each new generation of siblings. Wanda always struggled to preach on the story with impartiality, given that her sister was still out in the world spending not only their meager inheritance but also Wanda's patience in equal measure.

It was only when Lance had come to live with Wanda that she had started giving Mickey a little grace. That was mainly because she didn't want her sister to come back to the United States and take Lance home to California. She would miss him too much. Wanda figured any sibling progress was a good thing though.

Mickey and Lance's father had never married. Wanda had never even met Sean, though she knew he lived in Florida with what Mickey called "his new family." Given that he and Mickey had been together for less than a year nearly two decades ago, Wanda wasn't sure why that designation had stuck, but when Wanda had asked Lance if he wanted to visit his dad for Christmas, he'd looked at her like she'd sprouted two heads and told her he didn't have a dad—just a father he wasn't interested in getting to know.

Nor did Lance seem particularly eager to reunite with his mother. Mickey's abrupt departure still rankled, though he seemed to love Stone Ridge the town, as well as Stoneridge the school. Lance had gotten a lesson in New England politics when he'd learned the story behind the name discrepancy—that one distracted engraver had made a mistake on the granite sign intended for the high school, then had the temerity to die before the problem could be remedied. The engraver's children had no interest in the business and sold it before the school could file a complaint, and the new owner refused to fix the error unless he was paid in full to do so. The district had refused, and Stone Ridge's high school had henceforth been known as Stoneridge.

Wanda and Lance had dinner together almost every night. When Leslie and Nicole were over, she was happy to feed them, too. At least twice a week, Rye came over to eat, often with Hardy in tow, and he always cooked lavish meals for them to share. Wanda acknowledged that she was not being very pastoral, but she hoped her sister was happy enough in England to stay there for a good long while.

Lance did talk to his mother once a week. These calls typically consisted of Mickey talking and Lance occasionally saying, "Yes, I'm still here." Only when Mickey told him something interesting about England was he engaged. He obviously wanted to go visit the country, if not his mother.

Wanda sighed and picked up the phone. "Hi, Mickey. How's it going?" The music upstairs rose in decibels. Wanda took the phone into the kitchen and carefully shut the door. "Sorry about that. Lance is finishing an essay."

Mickey didn't seem to think it was odd that her son chose to listen to ear-splitting indie rock while he worked, and Wanda recalled that Mickey used to do the same when they were teens. The band changed. The genetics did not.

"He's mad at me! Can you believe that, Winnie? How could he be mad at me? I haven't even seen him in months!"

"What did you do?" Wanda asked suspiciously.

Mickey continued as though Wanda hadn't spoken. "What's weird is that he should be happy for me. He's always telling me I sell myself short with the men I date. They're all self-involved and immature."

"He was right about Enzo. You moved to Italy with him, and it was less than a month before he was scamming you."

"Enzo is old news, Winnie." Mickey sounded more cheerful than Wanda had heard her in a while. There could be only one reason for that. "I met someone."

"Oh?" Wanda had a more cutting response at the ready, but she gritted her teeth.

Mickey laughed. "Well, he's an old duffer."

"You're dating an incompetent golf player?" Wanda asked. She was stalling. Wanda had never heard her sister use the word "old" when describing a boyfriend, at least not in a few decades, and she had no idea what this meant.

"No. I mean yes, he's not very good, but he only plays for the sociability of it, and never with Scots. They're so serious about golf, did you know that? Floridians have nothing on the Scots."

Having no interest in golf or Florida, Wanda let this comment pass with a neutral, "Oh?"

"He's fifty-seven, Winnie. Older than you!" Mickey replied. "And he doesn't dye his hair or dress very well. I've been helping with that a bit. He's quite fit, you know, but he dresses like an elderly librarian."

Wanda knew that her sister actively looked for young, attractive men who spent at least as much time getting ready as she did. Mickey had Botox, then switched to Xeomin. She spent hours at the gym and longer on her makeup afterward. Even as a teenager, Mickey had been insecure about her looks, although she had always been the stylish, "beautiful" sister. The fact that Mickey was admitting to dating a man who didn't bother with any of this was far more shocking to Wanda than that she'd bounced back so quickly from her last love affair.

"And his name?" Best to have that information in case Mickey got into trouble again.

"Robert Chambers. I really like him. Robert's so relaxed and unpretentious. Do you want to know something?"

Wanda sighed. When they were kids, Mickey would always say "do you want to know something," and whatever it was she had to say ended up getting Wanda in trouble.

"Do I have a choice?"

"Sometimes he rolls his eyes at me just like you do."

Wanda thought that sounded promising. "What's the catch?"

"No catch. We go to the park and craft fairs. We shopped at a farmer's market—can you even imagine me there, much less cooking the produce we find? He's teaching me how to cook. And he told me I should read some C. S. Lewis—not Narnia, though—and—"

"Go to church?" Wanda supplied.

"How did you know?"

"Educated guess. Only that part is a little suspicious."

"He doesn't care if I go. But that's where he is on Sunday morning and Wednesday night, because, get this—"

"He sings in the choir?"

"How do you know these things?"

Wanda ignored Mickey's question. "Here's another guess. You told Lance all this, and he hung up on you."

Mickey paused. "How did you know that?"

Wanda thought about her nephew. He couldn't seem to help taking care of people—his friends, his aunt, his mother. He had been protecting Mickey from her bad choices his whole life. He would probably be talking to his therapist about it for years.

"It's the idea of you finding a stable partner, or at least one you think is a good person. How can Lance trust that it's not the best-played scam of all and it won't blow up and hurt you? And if it doesn't, what does that mean for him, Mickey? Will you live in England? Will he have to move again?"

There was a very long pause. "I have to go." And then she hung up.

Wanda set the phone down very gently on its cradle before she picked up the pillow on the chair by the phone and screamed into it. When she was done, she went to get some water boiling for pasta. It was Lance's night to cook, but making dinner was probably the last thing on her nephew's mind.

LANCE SCOWLED THROUGH PENNE AND MEATBALLS. He would have cooked something better, but Wanda didn't think his mood had anything to do with the menu. Still, with an adolescent boy, she deemed it wise to wait until he was full before fixing him with "the Look." She waited for him to speak first.

"Well, at least the salad didn't come out of a bag," Lance grumbled.

"Hey, some slack is requested. It was your night to cook."

He stared at her for a moment before recognition dawned. "I'm sorry, Aunt Wanda. I totally forgot. I was going to air fry egg rolls and make rice with peppered eggplant."

"That will be delicious tomorrow," Wanda replied. "Are you going to share the cause of your culinary amnesia?"

"You know, or you wouldn't ask."

"I just talked to Mickey, and her big news was a boyfriend. Not a trophy catch this time. Not a guy trying to impress her. No mention of his quads, or expensive dinners, or the make of his car."

Lance shrugged. "Yeah, Robert sounds great."

"You don't trust him."

"Do you?"

Wanda could tell he was truly asking. He trusted her opinion. "I know nothing about him beyond what Mickey has told me. So, no. Not really." She paused. "But I want to, if that makes sense?"

Lance pushed a cucumber slice into a puddle of dressing. "Sort of."

"Would I rather Mickey spent time learning to love and trust herself rather than jump into another relationship?" Wanda asked. "Yes. But if there's one thing AA meetings have drilled into my head, I can't fix someone who isn't looking to change."

"So I should be happy that this guy seems like he won't screw her over?" Lance asked. "Or should I just hunker down and wait for the next implosion?"

"I think that's a question for Sam," Wanda replied. Sam was the therapist that both Lance and Wanda had found, independent of each other, after the murder investigation in the fall. "I could give you advice, but we don't know what's going to happen with Robert, so anything I say could be contradicted tomorrow."

"If it works out, do you think she'll stay there?"

"I think it's way too soon to know." Wanda looked at her nephew, who was tracing his long fingers lightly across the lines of the tablecloth. "Who knows where she would live, where you'd choose to live—"

"You mean I could stay here? If I wanted to?" Lance seemed genuinely surprised.

"Of course! You can stay here as long as you want. I love having you here, Lance."

He stood up abruptly and gave his aunt a quick hug before he started clearing the plates. Wanda intuited that he had reached his capacity for sharing feelings and left him to it.

She wanted to meet Robert, at least over Zoom. Maybe she and Lance could be on a call together sometime soon. Wanda wanted to believe this relationship might be a fresh start for Mickey, and that Brian and his husband were a good influence on her sister.

But if Robert was just another problem to be solved, she wanted to know that too. And soon.

6

Someone was at the door. Both aunt and nephew were relieved by the distraction. Lance dropped the dishes into the sink of soapy water. "I'll get it."

It turned out to be Hardy, and he was carrying a King cake. Wanda recognized the intricately braided confection with white icing and purple, gold, and green sprinkles. Making a King cake was a lot of work, and a lot of sugar.

"I need taste testers," Hardy announced. "This is my contribution to the Mardi Gras Supper. I've never made a King cake before, so I've been tweaking the recipe. This is the best one I've made."

"How many others were there?" Wanda asked, amused.

He tilted his head, considering. "Three. And a half." Hardy helped himself to a knife and grabbed three plates for them. It still surprised Wanda that he knew where everything was in her kitchen, but he'd been here often enough in the last few months that it made sense.

"It can be made and eaten from El Día de los Reyes Magos through Epiphany. The last chance is Mardi Gras," Hardy continued.

Lance was already helping himself to a huge slice. "Is this the cake with the baby in it?"

"Yes," Wanda replied. "So please try to chew your food, at least enough to identify whether or not there's a hunk of plastic in it."

Lance just shoved another big bite in his mouth.

"In the King Cake, even the sprinkles have meaning. Mardi Gras colors are gold for power, purple for justice, and green for faith," Hardy told them as he cut moderately large slices for Wanda and himself. She accepted the plate with a smile. Hardy's cooking was legendary, and she knew he rarely, if ever, shared a recipe he wasn't positive was perfect.

Wanda and Lance had started self-defense classes with Hardy before Christmas, but Wanda and Hardy had been grabbing coffee and dinner, with and without Rye, since the incident at Fair Havens. He was good company. It had helped Wanda's recovery from trauma to have Hardy around. As a rule, he didn't drink much either, and once she shared her sobriety, he went cold turkey with her. That helped.

"I got it. I got the baby!" Lance sputtered and spat out the little figure. Wanda considered herself lucky they weren't giving him the Heimlich. "So what does it mean? Do I have good luck this year?"

"It means you have to bring the cake next year," Hardy said, grinning.

"You also get to be king for the night," Wanda said, "and some people do believe it can bring prosperity to the one who finds it."

"Does that mean I can punt on the dishes tonight?" Lance asked. "Being king and all?"

Wanda snorted, but Hardy nodded. "Sure. You go finish your homework, and I'll do the dishes."

Lance sighed. "Being king isn't all it's cracked up to be."

"You could be doing the dishes and your homework," Hardy pointed out.

Lance made a quick escape upstairs.

"He likes you," Wanda said as she brought their dishes over to the sink, where Hardy had already rolled up his shirt sleeves and started to scrub.

"I like him, too."

"We both got a call from Mickey."

Hardy glanced up. "What did your sister have to say?"

"She has a new beau."

He snorted. "I hope he's an improvement over the last one." Hardy's background in law enforcement had helped Mickey discover how Enzo was scamming her.

"Me, too," Wanda replied. "He's older."

"He'd better be a lot older than me," Hardy said, "if he's old enough for you to mention it!"

Hardy didn't look his age, which Wanda guessed was between fifty-five and sixty. He occasionally needed his cane to get around when his leg bothered him, but she'd noticed him using it less and less. His hair was threaded with gray, and he was in excellent shape—a fact she'd learned firsthand when he'd started teaching them self-defense. Hardy was seemingly tireless, joining in on the workouts every time.

Wanda knew many of the women he dated were much younger than she was, and he seemed to be able to keep up with them just fine, although they never lasted long. On some level, she thought, he still mourned the disappearance of his wife. Someday, Wanda might feel brave enough to ask him about it, although she probably should have attempted that before she quit drinking.

"Enzo was what, twenty-eight?" she asked. "The new guy is closer to sixty."

Hardy growled at the mention of Mickey's ex-boyfriend, a very effective con artist. "What else do you know about him?"

"His name is Robert Chambers. I assume he lives in Birmingham, although Mickey didn't say. He goes to church. Plays golf. Apparently makes my sister happy."

"Lance doesn't trust him," Hardy concluded.

"He doesn't trust his mother's judgment, with good reason," Wanda replied. "And I think he's feeling displaced. If this does work out, he won't have to watch out for his mother all the time." As she said this aloud, she knew who Lance should be talking to—not that she would say so to Hardy.

Hardy put the last dish in the drying rack and wiped his hands, carefully folding the towel and placing it on the edge of the sink. "I agree with Lance. I think he's right to be concerned."

"I know, but I also want to give Mickey the chance to prove us wrong. It goes against her history, but my gut tells me this might be different. I'm going to call Brian and see if he knows anything about Robert."

"Your ex-husband?" There was an edge to Hardy's voice.

"One of them," Wanda replied, arching an eyebrow at him.

Hardy didn't say anything as he boxed up the rest of the cake. He seemed less relaxed than when he'd arrived, but Wanda knew he was already thinking about checking out this new guy. He clearly had his suspicions. He would probably feel better if he had more information.

Wanda grabbed his coat and walked Hardy to the door. "Thanks again for the cake and the dishwashing."

He looked down at her without speaking. They were close. Wanda felt a little rush at the intensity of his gaze, but she just opened the door and let the cold February night cool her cheeks.

"I'll see you soon," was all he said.

Wanda waited until he had gotten into his car and then closed the door, leaning against it and banishing any wicked thoughts his look had inspired.

"Tea," she thought. Yes, a nice cup of chamomile tea would be just the thing, and a call to Rye to ask a favor.

7

TUESDAY HAD BEEN A LONG DAY, AS WAS YESTERDAY, and today was starting out the same way. Rye glanced at the clock. Of course, it was only ten. She sighed and looked at her inbox. Three more emails had popped in from parents while she was answering the last one. There was a knock at the door, and she called "come in" with relief. She didn't have a student down for an appointment, but that was how her workday often went. Students were sent to the office, and she had to figure out what they needed next. That sounded like a dream compared to responding to these messages.

Claudia poked her head in. "Do you have a minute?"

"Sure." Rye waved her in.

Claudia closed the door and sat down in the chair across from Rye. When they had started dating, they'd decided on a strict disconnect between their personal lives and their professional ones. Rye knew it wasn't doing much for the relationship—flipping the switch on and off was easier in theory than in practice.

"How's your day going?" Rye asked, aware the silence between them was stretching out too long, a sign that Claudia had something she needed to get off her chest.

"Nicole just told me that she's being scouted by a pastor at another church."

Rye was startled. This wasn't what she had been expecting. Neither Rye nor Claudia went to church, although Rye knew Claudia heard a lot of gossip from Tony about choir students who attended Wanda's church, where Tony played the organ on Sundays. "What? When?"

"After the concert. She said a guy named Pastor Josh came up and started telling her about the praise band they have, and how they sing a lot more modern music at his church. Apparently, they also have a thriving youth group that goes on a lot of fun trips."

Rye bristled. "Wanda's youth group goes on trips!"

"To soup kitchens and caroling at Fair Havens," Claudia pointed out. "Apparently, the Baptists go to concerts and have weekend retreats. Which do you think is going to appeal to a teenager?"

"Fair enough."

"Anyway, I just wanted to let you know so you can tell Wanda. I know she and Tony love having Nicole in the choir, but they should brace themselves."

"Thanks." She studied Claudia's face. "Something else is bothering you," Rye said. It wasn't a question.

"What are you planning to do about the protesters at the concert?"

In less than forty-eight hours, Rye had sent an email to all families, taken meetings with Mendoza, the school board, and SOAR (Students Organizing Against Racism)—a group of Stoneridge kids working with students from a nearby community college to establish a high school branch of the activist group—and she was in the process of writing up material for the assembly they would be having at the end of the school day tomorrow. The police might not be able to limit protest gatherings on public school grounds, but the school was not going to brush the incident under the rug.

"We have the assembly tomorrow," Rye replied. She didn't bother to list the other things she'd been doing. They'd had a fight about it the preceding night when Rye had stayed late to finish the notes on the SOAR meeting for the school board.

"As though that will change anything," Claudia said. "How many times have we received threats about this sort of thing just this year?"

Claudia's family had immigrated to San Antonio from Makati City soon after Claudia was born, and she'd lived in Texas until she was twelve, then moved to the Chicago suburbs, where Claudia had a tough time finding a community. She'd been on the receiving end of abuse from the white students who made up most of her school and dealt with aggression from boys who thought she should be grateful for their attention.

The protest outside the concert had rattled her, stirring up unhealed hurts. On top of that, Rye knew Claudia was still deeply shaken by her friend Jonathan's murder in November, as well as her ex-girlfriend's death the year before. Claudia was noticeably more fragile.

It was originally something they had in common— the death of a girlfriend. Even a few years after the fact, Rye had to stay vigilant and watch for the signs that indicated her medication wasn't working as it should, or that she needed to reconnect with her therapist. But recently Rye had begun to realize that there was a significant difference between a year's healing for

Claudia, which had been interrupted by more trauma, and her own state of mind after years of processing her feelings of regret, grief, and self-recrimination.

"Claudia, you know I've been working on this nonstop. I'm not sure what you want me to say right now," Rye said. She rubbed her temples. Their first few dates had been so sweet that Rye had started imagining a future for them, but Claudia had barely texted while she was in the Philippines, and since she'd come back, she'd seemed distracted. Rye had gotten used to feeling like she was always saying the wrong thing or using the wrong tone.

Claudia bristled. "I came in here to ask if you had a plan—a real, concrete way to effect change at Stoneridge. You have nothing, and you act like it's my fault for asking!"

Rye stood up and walked around the desk, pulling the second chair close to Claudia's. "That wasn't what I meant. I'm sorry if it came off that way." She held her hand out, not touching Claudia's, but available. "I wish I could say for sure that what we're doing is working, but I've gotten more threats this week than in the rest of my career combined."

"Why didn't you tell me?" Claudia asked.

Rye's thumb stroked the back of Claudia's hand. Her own fingers were rough compared to the smooth skin beneath them. She thought of how she had seen Claudia put hand lotion on so slowly, first one hand, then another, smoothing it over and over. "I didn't want you to worry."

Claudia stared at her. "What?"

"I didn't want to add one more thing to the long list you've been dealing with."

Claudia pulled her hand back. "I'm not a child, Rye. You don't get to decide what I know and what I don't."

"I didn't mean it like that—"

"You don't get it. I don't just need to be a part of the conversations. I need to be leading them."

"You're right. I'm sorry."

"What are you going to do about it?" Claudia asked. "'Sorry' won't cut it here, Rye."

Rye stood up and went around her desk to print a few pages that were up on her screen. She handed them to Claudia. "This is a synopsis of everything I've been working on since the concert. It's what I distributed to the school board. I'll email it to you as well, so you can click through the links. If you want, you can look it over and tell me if I'm missing anything."

"I want to lead the assembly," Claudia replied. "I've done this before, and I know what needs to happen."

Rye was relieved. "That sounds great." She studied Claudia, her head already bent over the notes, dark hair swinging forward over her shoulders.

"I'm still mad at you," Claudia said without looking up. "This isn't a get-out-of-jail-free card for well-intentioned white girls."

"I know."

A sharp knock on the door broke the tension in the room. Rye had never been so grateful to admit a student coming back from suspension. Claudia left without another word, closing the door softly behind her.

Rye had not gotten a chance to ask whether Claudia had been at Zucca's last Thursday night when she'd chased after Elena's mugger. Maybe that was for the best. She wasn't sure she wanted to know whether Claudia had been out with someone else. She turned her attention to the student in front of her.

"Devon Hansen, welcome back."

THE INTERFAITH MARDI GRAS REFLECTION WAS HELD in the sanctuary and had included explanations of the Greek Orthodox traditions of Forgiveness Sunday and Clean Week. Martina Suarez was introduced as bivocational, a cleaner and musician, and she gave a simple story of how satisfying it was to visit churches, schools, and people's homes to make things bright and fresh and to lift their spirits. She finished by singing a cover of Raye Zaragoza's "Rebel Soul," which startled those who thought of her as an opera singer.

Rye was mesmerized by the performance, although she glanced across the stage once and saw that Pastor Josh needed to fix his face. He looked as disapproving at having the woman perform as the regular high school custodian did when a student threw up junk food and beer in the middle of a hallway, burped, and said, "Sorry, bruh."

After the service, there was a rush downstairs for dinner. The social hall was lined with tables sagging with beef, chicken, and fish prepared and shared. No pork and no shellfish. Dishes like spanakopita and moussaka were marked 'dairy.' Members of the Reformed synagogue were pleased by the courtesy, though many of their plates were not strictly kosher. The cooks were delighted to please, having wondered whether anyone from the synagogue would attend. (Wanda had remarked not quite under her breath that they certainly wouldn't attend if they were not invited.) Pancakes were a traditional choice for the night, and they were popular with the kids, but the busiest tables were those filled with homemade Greek goodies.

Rye looked around and waved when she saw Camila and Ana lined up to snag fresh pancakes being flipped by volunteer firefighters. Wanda and Elena Mendoza had cornered Greg and Tony at one of the prime tables near the desserts. Rye's own plate was getting full. She'd have to make a second trip for sweets, but she grabbed a gooey baklava and popped it into her mouth as she slid into a chair beside Claudia. She was in the middle of an animated conversation with Lance, Leslie, and Nicole about the spring play for the statewide competition.

"I don't want to do another depressing show!" Nicole insisted, a fork halfway to her mouth.

"But they always win," Leslie reminded her. Leslie's blond hair had been dyed bright purple since Rye had seen her at the concert.

"Do we care?"

"Yes!" Leslie said, at the same time Nicole said, "Of course not!"

"That's easy for you to say, Nikki! You'll be rolling in scholarships. I don't think most colleges are going to be handing me money for the time I've spent playing D and D," Leslie argued. "And if we can get to go to state finals, it's an overnight trip! Right, Ms. Ramirez?"

"They're holding the competition in Amherst this year, so we would get to spend the night."

"Who chaperones that?" Rye asked Claudia.

"Why? Are you volunteering?" Leslie asked with a smirk.

Lance laughed. "I doubt they'd let teachers who are dating chaperone a bunch of teenagers on an overnight trip."

Leslie's mother was walking by with a plate of her own. Bellona paused at the table to look over her glasses at Rye and Claudia. "You can count on that, ladies."

"I'm sick of moping around," Nicole said. "Lent is starting up, so all the hymns I sing in church are dirges." Nicole tossed her goddess braids over her shoulder out of the way and took a huge bite of pancake, dripping with syrup. "Why can't we find a one-act play that's good enough to win without the gloomy melodrama?" She looked up. "Lance, why don't you write something for us?"

Lance blushed, the heat igniting at the tips of his ears until his pale, freckled skin was suffused with it. He shook his head. "I don't think so."

"That's not a bad idea," Leslie said. "All the ideas you've come up with when we do LARP have been great."

"What about the story you wrote for English last week? I bet we could turn that into something." Nicole turned to Claudia. "If we did, could we use it for the show? I mean, after you read and approved it?"

"I don't see why not," Claudia said. "I can't promise anything, but if it's appropriate for school, I would be happy to consider it. Of course, I don't think Lance is convinced yet."

The girls turned on their friend. He didn't stand a chance. Rye nodded to the far end of the table, where a few seats had opened up. The three kids scooted down, and Rye and Claudia were joined by the twins.

"Rye," Camila started without preamble. "Did you talk to your dad about the podcast?"

"What podcast?" Claudia asked.

"It's about a man who was murdered here in town on the same day Rye's mother disappeared," Camila said. Ana shot her sister a glance, but Camila didn't notice. "Rye thinks there might be a connection between them."

Claudia glanced at Rye. "I didn't know you were looking into stuff with your mom."

"It came up at book club last Thursday," Rye replied. "I was going to tell you about it, but you were busy that night, and I just forgot."

Claudia studied her plate. "I see."

"It would be good to have answers, right?" Camila added. "And if anyone would have more information, it would be your father."

"Sometimes it's better to leave well enough alone," Claudia replied. "What if she learns something she wishes she hadn't?"

"Let's talk about something else," Ana said. Rye smiled at her gratefully, but Camila and Claudia looked mutinous.

The four of them sat in tense silence, listening to Leslie and Nicole sweet-talking Lance into playwriting.

When Claudia finished eating, she stood up and held out a hand to Rye. "Are you coming?"

Rye looked down at her plate, still half full. "We have a little while before the parade. I'm going to finish eating, and then I'll come find you, okay?"

"Whatever you want," Claudia replied. She grabbed her coat and her plate and walked off without another word.

Camila stood up, too, leaving her food behind and heading out of the hall.

"What just happened?" Ana asked as she watched her sister follow Claudia out the back door.

"I don't know," Rye said with a sigh. "But I do know I won't be getting a goodnight call from Claudia tonight. Again."

"Do you want to talk about it?"

"What's there to talk about?" Rye pushed her food around on her plate. "I'm a terrible girlfriend. I never know the right thing to say or do, and I'm also pathologically afraid of being alone, which makes me incredibly needy."

"Rye—"

"It's okay. I've had eight years of therapy, Ana. I know I'm a mess."

"Maybe you need a new therapist."

Rye looked up. "What do you mean?"

"If your self-esteem is really that low, I don't think your current one is doing the trick."

"Shannon has been with me through everything," Rye said. "Aside from my dad, she's probably the longest relationship I've maintained."

"But you pay her," Ana said, "so I'm not sure that counts." She examined a piece of baklava before stuffing the whole piece in her mouth. She chewed and swallowed it slowly before continuing. "I know you've depended on her, and that's great. I'm glad you have someone you trust. But either she's not doing her job or you aren't being honest with her, Rye, because you're a catch. You're smart and loyal and passionate. I've even seen you be funny, on occasion." Ana winked at her, and Rye smiled back.

"So why am I so terrible at relationships, then?"

"I don't know, Rye. Why are you so terrible at relationships?"

"You're supposed to tell me I'm not," Rye pointed out.

"I've never lied to you before, and I'm not about to start now." Ana dipped her napkin into her sister's water cup and carefully cleaned the honey off her fingers. "I supported this thing with Claudia from the start, but you and I both know something isn't right."

"And something wasn't right with Andy, who, on paper, is also perfect."

"I love Andy. Sweetest guy in the world—"

"After Tyler," Rye interjected.

"That goes without saying," Ana continued. "But if I were your therapist, I would say you have trouble differentiating between romantic and platonic love. Do you like spending time with Andy?"

"Yes, of course."

"Do you want to make out with him?"

Rye wrinkled her nose. "No."

"Do you want to smell his stinky morning breath every day? Or let him be the grouchy one even after you've had a really bad day?"

"Definitely not," Rye replied. "I couldn't even stand the fact that he didn't separate his light and dark laundry."

Ana laughed. "What about Claudia? How does she sort her laundry?"

"She has a service. They pick it up and return everything clean and pressed."

"And?" Ana arched an eyebrow, waiting.

"It's a waste of money!" Rye exclaimed. "There's a washer and dryer in her unit!"

"And when she's having a bad day?" Ana asked gently.

"She changes into another outfit. I know. I know. Her clothes and her money are not my business. I mean, I don't know whether you hang your delicates, or if Wanda has a pile of identical black skirts on her closet floor."

They both laughed.

"And when Claudia's having a bad day?" Ana prodded again.

Rye sighed and glanced over at Lance, who had clearly been convinced to save the day. She watched as he started scribbling notes on a napkin, Leslie leaning over his shoulder to offer constructive feedback.

"We usually end up in a fight because I say the wrong thing," Rye replied finally. "I hate it. I hate being the reason she's upset, but I also don't know how to fix it."

"Does she at least still make your heart race when she comes in the door?"

Rye looked down at the table and blinked away tears. "Maybe I'm just meant to be alone, Ana. I mean, I look at you and Tyler, and I can't imagine having something so comfortable." She glanced up. "Not like boring-comfortable, but…safe."

"I think you'd better talk to your dad," Ana said after a moment. "And your therapist." She reached across the table and patted Rye's arm. "Because no one you're with is ever going to replace a mother."

9

"WANDA, ARE YOU COMING TO THE PARADE?" LANA asked as they made their way down the stairs after straightening up the sanctuary.

"Yes! I just want to thank the kitchen staff. Save me a spot!"

The noise when Wanda opened the door to the kitchen was as sudden and loud as the one nightclub Wanda had visited years ago in Miami. She winced, reaching up to adjust the volume on her hearing aids. She looked around at a chaos of dishes, racks of trays with food, a counter full of desserts still being placed on platters, and about twenty people who were talking, laughing, and clattering seemingly every pot or pan they laid hands on.

She stayed pressed against the door as she adjusted and overheard the conversation of two women standing over a sink full of soapy water.

"What do you mean somebody knows?"

"Somebody knows, and it's going to ruin Violet's future. She's young. She didn't think…"

"It'll blow over."

"Do you think so?"

"Can you afford to pay?"

"No. You know I can't."

The door of the hall swung open, whacking Wanda in the back. She stumbled in and immediately lost sight of the conversationalists.

"More baklava," someone called out behind her.

Wanda snapped back to attention. She grabbed a pot lid and took out a strap with a snap and a small mallet that Tony had given her this afternoon. Tony had told Wanda she could put the strap through the handle of any pot lid, suspend it, then hit it with the soft mallet and get a reverberation that would cut through conversation. She had already used it to introduce Bruce for the grace, to encourage a round of applause for the firefighters, and, ten minutes ago, for the fifteen-minute warning for the parade. Every time she set down one lid, it disappeared, presumably to be washed. Fortunately, there was no shortage of lids.

It worked.

"Hi, I'm Wanda Duff from Trinity Church."

A voice from the back replied, "We know—runner up for most kourabiethes eaten!"

"Tell me how many more till I win!" Wanda laughed along with them. "On behalf of the Interfaith Clergy group, I want to thank you all for the amazing meal, for cooking and serving, as well as for making the contributions from the other faith communities look wonderful."

Same voice. Was it Agatha? "Hardy Rye can bring the King cake any time. It seems like it was half gone before it made it onto one of the tables!"

Wanda noticed Martina wearing an apron over her presenter clothes and standing by the giant refrigerator.

She gave her a warm smile. Martina didn't seem to notice. "I don't want to keep you from the parade—"

The volume in the room rose again immediately. Wanda beat a hasty retreat before she gave herself a headache or got pulled into drying dishes. She ran into Rye in the dimly lit hallway.

Rye gave her a hug, and Wanda realized her friend had been hiding out. Although the kitchen and social hall were buzzing, this spot by the stairs was dark and quiet.

"Are you all right?" Wanda asked.

"I just needed a break."

Wanda leaned against the wall, enjoying the silence. It was her world. She loved when someone else valued it, too. After a minute, Rye held out a picture she had been holding in her hand. In the middle of the photograph stood a woman who had to be Melanie Rye. The resemblance to her daughter—at both the age of the little girl in the picture and the woman standing next to Wanda—was startling. It looked like they had been photographed at a town event. Next to Melanie, with his arm around her shoulder, was a young black man with a megawatt smile. Wanda turned the picture over. *Mel and Lionel with Pru, Founders Day Parade.*

Rye took the picture back and looked down at it. "I was in second grade the day she left. No one met me at the bus stop. I walked home, and when I got there, my dad was sitting on the couch. He said my mom had called him, but when he'd come home to check on her, she was gone. She hadn't taken her little suitcase. She always took the same one. It was dark green with brass latches."

"Do you think something happened to her?" Wanda asked gently.

Rye didn't answer. She just looked at the photo, her hand smoothing a path over her mother's face.

"Do you think your mother might have had something to do with Lionel Burgess's death?"

"It's a pretty big coincidence. Her friend is murdered the same day she leaves town? He would have let her into the house if she'd come over, and if something had happened between them, she would have left in a hurry."

"Maybe he died protecting her," Wanda replied.

"She wouldn't let that happen," said Rye.

Wanda felt helpless, knowing that it was not memory speaking, but the heart-saving mantra of two decades. The trail of this case wasn't just cold—it was glacial. There was no way Hardy hadn't turned over every leaf looking for his wife. "Have you shown that to your dad?"

"He was probably the one who took the picture."

"Maybe. But if you have questions, who else are you going to ask?"

Rye looked tired. She tucked the picture into her jacket pocket. "I'm not sure I'm ready."

Wanda could understand that. "Let's go to the parade. Getting pelted with bugle beads is going to be a completely new experience." She winked at Rye, then shook her hair. "And, just so you know, this is silver glitter, not dandruff, as your father suggested!"

Rye cracked a smile. She pulled Wanda's coat off a hanger and handed it to her before finding her own. Wanda knew that Rye had undoubtedly spent her life constructing a story around her mother's disappearance, and if this picture cracked open an entirely new narrative, it would mean a lot of things—not least of which that book club was not just a bit of fun to be had on Thursday evenings with a cup of coffee or tea.

She watched as Rye reconstructed the emotional mask she wore as vice principal. Wanda followed the confident, cheerful administrator back into the social hall, swiped more dessert, and headed for the show.

10

THE STONERIDGE JAZZ BAND WAS AMAZING. WANDA and Rye pushed their way to the front of the crowd to join Ana and Tyler watching students march from the high school toward downtown. The church provided the perfect vantage point for them to cheer the kids on and collect a few strands of the Mardi Gras beads the middle school chorus was throwing from their flatbed disguised on each side by truck-sized masquerade masks.

The weather was mild, and even though it was long dark, the night felt closer to spring than the dreary winter they'd been having. The slush had even melted, which felt like a miracle, if only a temporary one.

Some folks followed the band downtown, and others went to their cars. Ana decided to find Camila. Rye and Wanda headed back toward the church, Wanda scanning the crowd looking for Lance.

"The three musketeers are following the band for a few blocks," Rye said. "Then Leslie is going to drive them to her house. Lance told me you could pick him up there 'at your convenience.'"

"Those were his exact words, huh?" Wanda said, using her fingers to detangle a strand of beads from the hairs at the nape of her neck. "Maybe I should let him spend the night so he can find out just how 'convenient' it is."

Rye laughed. "You think letting him sleep over at his best friend's house on a school night would be teaching him a lesson? His very cute best friend?"

"Okay, when you put it that way, I will definitely not be doing that. Wait…are they dating? He hasn't said anything about that."

"And I'm sure you would be the first person he would confide in about it," Rye said. "And no, I don't think they are. No evidence of it at school, at least."

Wanda squeezed Rye's arm. "They do know you're watching."

"I don't exactly spend my whole day following them around. Other students bring all the salacious gossip right to my doorstep, so no snooping is even required." Rye pulled on the front door. It was locked. "Let's go around to the back and see if that door's still open. I want to collect Dad's King cake platter."

They walked down the path, smiling at the last few people who were heading to their cars. "You'd tell me if anything was going on between them though, right?" Wanda asked.

"You'd be my first call."

"I just don't want to think I'm losing my touch. I can usually spot a youth group romance from a mile away, so if I'm missing one under my nose…"

"You haven't missed anything. The three of them are good friends. None of them seem remotely interested in dating, at least each other. Nicole is trying her best to collect as many music scholarships as she can. I know she wants to apply to Juilliard and Berklee. And, although she's never said it in so many words, I'm pretty sure Leslie isn't interested in dating at all."

"So it sounds like you're saying I can leave Lance there overnight," Wanda replied.

"I said I think Leslie isn't, not Lance. And certainly not Nicole," Rye said. "Besides, teenagers like to experiment, even if it ends up going nowhere."

"Or, worse, ends up ruining the friendship."

"Exactly," Rye confirmed. "Better not to risk it on a whim. Have you read that book I told you about, *Ace* by Angela Chen? Definitely wouldn't leave your ward overnight until you've had 'the talk' with him."

"I'm sure Mickey has talked to him about all of that," Wanda replied, although, now that she thought about it, she wasn't certain at all.

Rye grinned. "Oh, dear sweet Wanda. I never thought you, of all people, would be so timid! Human sexuality, gender spectrum, consent—this cannot be covered in one conversation."

"I know!"

"So you've had at least one with him?"

"It's on my to-do list." Or it would be now.

Rye chuckled. "I can't wait to hear about how that goes!" She pulled open the door and stepped into the hall. They went through the kitchen door, and it was just as dark and quiet as the entrance had been. "Wow. I wouldn't have expected them to finish packing up the leftovers so soon."

"They haven't. The kitchen crew is still outside talking. Someone must have turned out the lights to save electricity." Wanda pointed at the tables. Even in the dark, the shrouded platters were visible.

"Wanda," she said softly, pointing to a spot on the floor. "Hit the lights."

Wanda fumbled for the switches. Both women blinked at the bright light, but as their vision cleared, Wanda's eyes followed the path of the stain. She and Rye started toward it at the same moment.

"Look," Rye said. She stopped a few feet away from the drinks table. In front of it, a body in a blue dress lay face down, blood seeping through the fabric. At her side, not far from her hand, was a knife, smooth-edged and deadly.

Rye glanced up at her friend. Wanda crossed herself.

"Do you recognize her?" Rye asked.

"Of course. If you saw her face, you would, too. That's Martina Suarez, the woman who spoke and sang in the service tonight...and at the concert." She squatted down next to the body, already pulling out her phone. She made the sign of the cross again, compulsively. "She was Roman Catholic. She needs some kind of rites."

Rye glanced around. "We need to call the police, now."

"We will," Wanda said. She was kneeling near Martina, holding her phone in front of her like a prayer book. "Loving and merciful God, we entrust our sister to your mercy. You loved her greatly in this life; now that she is freed from all its cares, give her happiness and peace forever. Amen."

"Amen," Rye murmured, then offered Wanda a shaky hand to pull her up.

"She seemed like such a nice person," Wanda said softly.

"Seemed like it?" Rye asked.

"Somebody obviously didn't think so," Wanda said, glancing at her friend. "Or we wouldn't be about to place a call to my ex."

11

"I SHOULD HAVE KNOWN," RYAN PHENNEN SAID, BARELY
ten minutes later. He'd been in the parade in the back of
a truck wearing an oversized sheriff's hat, which he'd left
at the door. He looked from Wanda to Rye. "I should
have known it would be you two." Rye adopted a look of
wounded innocence, but Ryan ignored it. "It seems like
every time I turn around, you're stumbling over another
dead body. Honestly, it's implausible."

"We're social butterflies," Wanda said. "We just get
out more than you do."

"It's my job to find them," Ryan muttered. He flipped
open his notebook. "Let's just get this over with. I'll
need you to go down to the station to sign your official
statement, but for now, tell me what happened."

Rye nodded for Wanda to take the lead. "Martina
was in the service tonight. Father Bogdan explained
an Orthodox custom...never mind." Wanda shook her
head. "She had a speaking part and a song. I remember
waving to her when we came down for dinner. She was
in the kitchen."

"And when was that?" Ryan asked.

"Five o'clock?" Anticipating his next question, Wanda continued, "She seemed busy, so I didn't stop to speak to her. I wanted to compliment her on the lovely presentation, but she was in the middle of helping the aunties carry out food."

"Whose aunties?" Ryan looked up.

"There's a formidable community of home chefs at this church, and they all work together to put on events. People started calling them the aunties, although at this point not all of them are women. I think the name just stuck," Wanda replied. "Anyway, a lot of people were being fed, and the marching band was coming by at six thirty, so it was all hands on deck. I went in to thank the cooks at about a quarter after six, and they were rushing to finish the cleanup. Martina was there. I met Rye in the hall, and we went outside."

"I came in to grab my dad's jacket maybe five minutes later. The front door was still unlocked at that point. There were people in the kitchen and social hall."

"Was the victim here?" Ryan asked.

Rye closed her eyes. Her father had taught her memory tricks when she was a kid. She'd used them in a talent show one year, and they frequently came in handy. But she had been distracted by the photograph of her mother. After a minute, she opened her eyes. "Yes. She was talking to Elena Mendoza."

Ryan looked up. "Are you sure?"

"Yes. Elena was wearing a gorgeous scarlet jumpsuit, and I asked her about it. She told me she made it last year for a wedding."

"And?" Ryan was still staring at her.

"How many people do you think were wearing a one-of-a-kind red jumpsuit tonight? Rye was unable to keep the sarcasm out of her voice. "And Martina's wearing crushed velvet with sequin detailing all over the bodice. Neither of them would have been mistaken as anyone else here." Rye gestured to her own clothes—a navy suit with a mint green blouse she'd worn to school— and then to Wanda, who had on a long black skirt and maroon sweater.

"We're talking about the person who may have been the last one to see Martina Suarez alive," Ryan replied. "It's important that you get it right."

"Most of us looked like we were going to Sunday School, Ryan. The two of them were dressed for the opera. I know who I saw."

Wanda picked up the story. "The front door must have been locked between the time Rye got Hardy's coat and the end of the parade. We had to go down to the parking lot and through the door leading into the kitchen. The lights were off, but the food hadn't been taken away yet." She glanced up at the clock. "That was around seven. We called you as soon as we found her."

"Apparently, a few members of the PTA took leftover food downtown for the kids to eat when they finished up the parade. They volunteered to come back and take the rest of the food to the shelter. Agatha Bogdanovic is organizing it," Ryan replied without looking up from his pad.

"What a great idea!" Wanda exclaimed. "The kids must have loved that! And there's still this much here for the shelter? I wish I'd thought of that!"

"This food's part of a crime scene now," Ryan pointed out.

"Are you kidding? She wasn't poisoned! The knife is right there!"

"Have you done a tox screen?" he asked her. "I can't say definitively that she wasn't poisoned before she was stabbed. The food stays."

Rye jumped in to interrupt before Wanda lost her temper. "When we came into the social hall, I saw something on the floor. I asked Wanda to turn on the lights so we could get a better look." She glanced back at the cordoned-off bloodstains. "Then we saw Martina's body."

"No one else was in the room? You didn't hear or see anyone at the entrance into the hallway or in the kitchen?" Ryan asked.

The women glanced at each other and shook their heads. "If I'd heard someone, I would have gotten us out of there immediately," Rye said. Wanda looked like she might protest, but then she followed Rye's gaze to the body at their feet, now covered with a sheet. "If someone was willing to stab this woman, I doubt they would hesitate to take out any witnesses, especially if they thought we couldn't protect ourselves."

"I can defend myself!" Wanda protested.

"And my father taught me just about every move in the book for disarming an attacker. But do you remember his cardinal rule?"

"Don't put yourself in the position of needing to use the skills," Wanda replied.

"That's a lesson you could stand to learn," Ryan muttered. "Look, a stabbing is a personal and violent crime. It's not like poison or pills. It requires a different way of thinking—a different kind of person—the type who is willing to get close to their victim, to cause them intense pain, and to be a breath away when death comes. This could have been an abusive family member or an explosive argument. Maybe an attempted robbery."

Wanda interrupted him. "I'm sure there's no money kept in the church. Nothing of any real value to steal, though nobody knows that except other clergy. We did a course on building safety, and that was key. And the custodian would have her keys!"

"The building was open on this level. No one needed to take her keys," Ryan replied.

Rye lit up as she realized what Wanda was thinking. "Custodians have keys to the building, but also to every room inside!"

Ryan bent down and carefully pulled the sheet back. The three of them studied the woman carefully. Ryan put on a glove and gently rolled her to each side to check for pockets. Only a man would look for pockets on a cocktail dress. "Nothing."

"She didn't wear them on her neck, or attach them to a cart, did she?" Rye asked Wanda.

Wanda shook her head. "Usually she wore a belt, and the keys were clipped to one of those extendable lanyards on it. But she's dressed to perform. She told me before the service that her sister bought her this dress as a birthday gift years ago. She had a huge apron on to protect it when she was helping the aunties. Maybe her keys are in there?"

Ryan glanced around. "Do you know whether Ms. Suarez cleaned other buildings?"

"Yes, all over town," Wanda confirmed. "She filled in for all the regular sextons when they were on vacation, and I think she cleaned some homes as well. She kept her rates down. Business was booming." Wanda's phone buzzed. She glanced down at it. "Lance needs a ride. Can I go?"

"Come down to the station first thing tomorrow morning," Ryan said. "If you think of anything else tonight, call me."

"Call you or call the station?" Rye asked.

"Wanda can call me. You can call the front desk."

Rye winked at Ryan. His face flushed beet red.

"Of course," she replied. She stood up and gave Wanda a hug and quick kiss on the cheek. "If you and Lance want company, just let me know. Hardy and I will be on call."

Wanda could feel Ryan tense next to her, so she settled on giving Rye a "don't make trouble" look before grabbing her coat and heading out to the parking lot.

12

HARDY RYE STOOD ON THE PORCH LEANING AGAINST the railing as Rye pulled in. He waved at her to come inside.

"Hey, Dad," she said, giving him a kiss on the cheek and stepping into a bear hug.

"Hey, yourself." He waited for her to say something more, then turned and followed her into the house.

"Want some pie?" Hardy asked as he stumped into the kitchen. Rye followed him. "It's grasshopper."

"Chocolate and mint? You know it." Rye dropped into a seat at the kitchen table and immediately forgot how stuffed she'd been an hour ago. "Although I know a bribe when I taste one. You just want to hear about the dead body."

Hardy tapped his police scanner. "I already heard."

"Wanda and I found her."

"Ryan called. Are you okay?"

Rye picked up her fork and took a bite. Her father was an excellent cook, and he'd been trying new dessert recipes lately. This was her favorite. "I guess."

"I know you've had more than your fair share of murder this year, but this had to feel different. This is the first body you've seen. That's bound to shake a person up."

Rye thought about the photos of bodies she'd had to look at when her ex-girlfriend had been driving drunk. June had been responsible for the death of a single mother and her three children. Every day that June was incarcerated, she was in danger from other inmates. When Rye had gotten the call about her death, which had been ruled a suicide, it was clear to her that June had been abused to the point where Rye could barely recognize her.

Rye had also worked with grieving families whose teenage children had died by suicide or in drunk driving accidents while she was in Austin. Since she'd come back here, her worst experience had been finding Leslie Pond unconscious in the bathroom after taking too many pills. That trauma was tempered by witnessing how much better the girl had been doing in the last six months. Therapy—for both Rye and Leslie—had done a lot of good.

"It was awful," Rye replied. "Wanda said she was a nice person."

"But you don't think so?" her father asked.

"I didn't say that."

"She might have been in the wrong place at the wrong time. It does happen," Hardy pointed out.

"Of course it does. But in a church basement? On a Tuesday night? The only valuables in the building were religious icons not quickly pawnshop converted by the run-of-the-mill thief," Rye argued. "It doesn't seem like a random attack to me." She took another bite of pie. "Besides, if you were breaking into a church that was already open on a night when a lot of strangers were wandering around, would you go out of your way to commit a violent crime? Or would you try to blend in? Be polite and unremarkable?"

"Personally, I'd opt for the path of least resistance," Hardy said with a smile.

"Oh, and then there are the keys."

Hardy raised an eyebrow. Rye knew she had his attention now. "What keys?"

"Her keys—you know the big key chain custodians carry around? In her case, it could have had keys for any number of places, including homes that she cleaned. Her apron, where the keys were stored, is missing. My guess is that her attacker wanted the keys, and Ms. Suarez didn't want to give them up for whatever reason."

"That reason might be the key to the whole case," her father replied.

"No pun intended?"

"I never joke about dead bodies," Hardy said.

"Liar!" Rye retorted. "Anyway, Wanda and I are not going to investigate this. It's not our business at all. I'm letting it go."

Hardy waited. Rye hated those purpose-driven silences. She had a lot of practice rebuffing them, but tonight she was off-balance. She felt for the photo in her back pocket and pulled it out. "I found this."

Hardy slid the picture across the table and stared down at it. His fingers brushed across the photo the same way Rye had done all day. "Was this in one of the boxes in the storage room?"

"It was."

"Any reason you're carrying it around now?" Hardy pushed it back to her.

Rye picked up the picture and stared at her mother. Melanie looked so cheerful. "Did you take this?"

"No."

Rye looked up in surprise. "Do you know who did?"

"Your mom's friend from work. Elizabeth? No. Elena."

"Elena Mendoza?" Rye put down her fork.

Hardy shook his head. "I think her last name was Ortiz."

"Was she married?"

"I don't think so. I never met her in person. She and your mother and Lionel would sometimes go out for drinks, though. Why?"

"My book club is looking into Lionel Burgess's murder."

Hardy put his glass of water down on the table, steepling his fingers. It was a tell. He always did it when they were shaking. "Why?"

"I don't know. I'm not in charge of what cold cases we discuss."

Hardy stood up and walked to the sink, slamming his plate and fork down with unnecessary force. "Whose idea was it?"

"Probably Greg Engstrom, the librarian. He loves local mysteries." Rye stood up and walked over to her father. "Why? Do you know something you aren't telling me?"

"No." The frustration clear in his tone. "I don't. There's nothing to know. That case was ... it was mishandled."

"By you?" Rye asked quietly.

"Of course not." He looked at her, shocked. "I wasn't allowed anywhere near it, and I don't think I could have handled it if I were. We had a few other things going on here."

Rye leaned into him. After a minute, he turned and gave her a stiff hug. "So you don't think Mom had anything to do with it?" she asked.

Hardy glanced back at the table, where the photo was sitting, face down. It was so quick, Rye almost missed it. "No, sweetheart. I don't." He turned and headed upstairs without even a goodnight.

Rye looked after him. Hardy Rye never left dirty dishes in the sink.

13

Wanda showed up at the police station at eleven.

Jaz was at her desk typing up some reports. "He hoped you would have come in earlier."

"Give me a break! It's Ash Wednesday. We were trying out 'Ashes to Go' this morning."

"What's that?'" Jaz asked, her expression amused.

"Ash Wednesday gets its name because ashes were an ancient Jewish symbol for repentance or grief. Some churches burn the palm leaves from the previous year's Palm Sunday service to mark parishioners with the ashes. People come to the church early in the day so they can wear the ashes, letting other folks know they believe in human mortality and God's forgiveness," Wanda replied, preacher mode activated.

"I know what Ash Wednesday is," Jaz said with a laugh. "I was raised by a Roman Catholic and a Baptist. Long story short, we had a lot of church in my family."

Mortified, Wanda noticed belatedly that Jaz had a smudge of ash on her forehead. "Jaz, I'm sorry."

She waved a hand dismissively. "It's the 'to-go' part I didn't understand," she said. "Is it like grabbing Jesus with fries and a Coke?"

They both laughed at that. "It's not far off," Wanda said. "Many people who don't attend church regularly feel uncomfortable coming into the building to get ashes but would still like to have them. I spent an hour offering them to passers-by at the mall, then went to two different McDonald's. So, yes, Jesus and hash browns." Wanda shook her head. "I have to admit it's not my favorite thing. People feel a little strange when a person starts doing churchy things by the pretzel stand, you know? But the church council willed it, so off I went!"

Jaz lowered her voice. "I'll buy you a piece of cake if you go in and offer to put ashes on Ryan's forehead."

"I wouldn't do that," Tyler said from his desk across the aisle. Jaz and Tyler had become partners in January, and Wanda thought they made the best team. "Ana and I went to church this morning, and he tried to scrub my forehead when I got here."

Wanda and Jaz burst out laughing at the idea of the sheriff spit-cleaning his little brother. Wanda knew the Phennens were not religious, and she also knew that Ryan had zero sense of humor about it. She would never take Jaz up on her enticement—at least not as long as she was working as an ordained pastor—but she had to admit that finding little ways to annoy him did have its charms.

They had barely gotten themselves under control when Ryan emerged from his office with Father Bogdan. Jaz stood up to have Father Bogdan sign his statement, and Ryan gestured at Wanda to come inside.

Once they were both sitting, there was an awkward silence. Wanda didn't know what to say, since she really had shared everything she knew the night before. Ryan finally broke it. "You are not involved with this situation, do you understand? You are not going to ask people questions, snoop around Martina's places of employment, check out her background. Being stabbed in the back is murder. It's my jurisdiction, not yours."

Wanda took several deep breaths, taking small satisfaction in making him wait for her reply. "I invited Martina to the service. Her contribution was my idea, and it was definitely not the unanimous decision of the interfaith group. In fact, most of them didn't seem to like her. I feel responsible—not for her death, but for potentially putting her in a position to be killed." She put her hand up to forestall his retort. "That being said, I do hear you."

"Good. I'm glad we understand each other."

Wanda continued as though Ryan hadn't spoken. "I am going to look into this, of course. I won't do anything illegal."

Ryan looked like he wanted to lock her in a cell. Instead, he stared at a point between them on his desk. "Fine. Contact the other clergy and ask them about Martina. Subtly, if that's even possible for you. Let me know what you find out."

Wanda could only presume she was in a remake of *The Invasion of the Body Snatchers*. She stared at him. "You aren't going to fight me on this?"

"What's the point? You're going to do whatever you want, aren't you?"

She stood to go, knowing full well he was petty enough to change his mind if she pushed. It was then she heard a little yip. Wanda turned back to Ryan, whose face was turning red. "Do you have a dog here?"

"No," he said, but as if the pup had been summoned by her question, a beagle-headed, long-legged, tricolored mutt scrambled around the desk and began to sniff Wanda frantically, long tail flapping against Ryan's desk.

Now it made sense. This was clearly the reason Ryan had conceded so quickly.

"The department changed its mind about getting a comfort dog?" Wanda reached out a hand for the dog to sniff. She had been preparing a presentation on the necessity of having a dog in that position for the community, but Ryan had assured her several times it wouldn't be happening.

"We need a comfort dog like Alaska needs snow," he replied. The dog had already put his paws up on Wanda's stomach and was trying to climb into her lap, even though he was clearly not lap sized. "He was brought in last night. Stayed here with the night crew. I need someone to take him for tonight…for the next few nights."

Wanda looked up. "And you weren't going to ask me?"

"It's temporary." Ryan shrugged. "I didn't think Wink would tolerate a roommate."

"Why wasn't he brought to the SPCA?" Wanda allowed the dog to sniff her face, accepting the delicate tongue to her nose before gently pushing him down and giving him head scratches as he pressed hard against her leg.

"Jaz is still checking to see if there are family members who might want to take him in." Ryan rubbed the back of his neck. "He's also…vocal."

"Meaning?"

"He's a foxeagle—a beagle and foxhound blend—and he has the bark to prove it." On key, the dog lifted up his head and began baying.

"Hush now," Wanda said, putting her hand firmly around his snout. She stared straight into the dog's eyes and repeated herself. "Hush." Reluctantly, the dog flopped down on the floor and blew out a sigh. When he tipped over, Wanda gave him belly rubs. "Good boy." She glanced up at Ryan. "I see what you mean."

"Martina Suarez may have loved Mozart, but I don't think that was why she named him 'Figaro.'"

Wanda's heart skipped a beat. She looked down at Figaro, who she knew must be confused and missing his person right now. When she reached for the leash, Ryan reluctantly held it out. "I'm not sure Wink is going to like sharing the bed with this big guy, but I'll take him for as long as you need. God knows what he would do to that sterile abomination you call an apartment."

Ryan shuddered. Wanda knew he was pet tolerant but not an animal lover—especially if the animal in question were to come anywhere near the crisp white-and-chrome museum he called home. "Thanks, Wanda," he said gruffly. "I appreciate it."

She glanced up, surprised. "You're welcome."

Wanda emerged from the office with a firm grip on Figaro's leash.

Jaz gave the pooch a huge hug, and he wiggled like a puppy with every inch of his body, tail-tip to snout. "Is Figgy going to a new home? Huh, my sweetie? I'm going to come visit you and make sure the preacher-lady doesn't give you too many commandments."

"Better make it soon. Ryan assured me he'll get the shelter involved in finding a forever home if you don't find a family member to take him in."

Jaz's response to that was an arched eyebrow, indicating disbelief that Ryan would take even one more action, having gotten the dog out of his office. She gave Figaro special attention, scratching his long beagle ears. "Who's a big sweetheart?"

"Me. Also a big sucker," Wanda said as the dog tugged on his lead.

Jaz stood up. "Before you leave, would you say a prayer over my new rosary? I gave my old one away to a woman who lost her home in a fire. I figured she needed it more than I did." Jaz fingered the beads as she spoke. "I take it everywhere. Even keeps me awake in stakeouts, if you believe it."

"I do," Wanda said. She'd had too many experiences with prayer not to believe this prayer memory device didn't have power in its own way.

"Anyway, my priest and I got into a disagreement about my splitting time between his church and my mother's Baptist church, and I haven't completely forgiven him for some of the things he said." Jaz grinned suddenly. "Sort of ironic, don't you think?"

Wanda chuckled. "It is. And if you don't mind having a minister way left of center doing the blessing, I'd be happy to do it, though you might try Father Paul. He's a special brand of priest."

With prayer beads in her left hand and Figaro's lead gripped tightly in her right, Wanda said a prayer, inching her fingers around the circle with Psalm 91, since it would go into some tough situations, before handing it back. Jaz gave her a hug. "When you need some less-holy protection from evil, give us a call, honey."

The other interview room door opened. Tyler shook hands with Elena Mendoza. She looked exhausted.

"Elena, how are you?" Wanda allowed Figaro to tug them over.

She rubbed her face. "I'm not so good. Do you have time for a coffee?"

"Sure, if there's someplace Figaro is welcome. He's ... he was Martina's dog, and Sheriff Phennen can't locate any family, so he's with me for a couple days."

"You can use the break room," Jaz offered. "We've got coffee and tea in there."

Elena looked like staying at the station was the last thing she wanted to do. "It's nothing. We can get together some other time."

"How about four o'clock at Harvey's?" Wanda suggested. "I have to deliver ashes to Fair Havens, and by then school will be out and I can get Lance to take care of the dog. I'll be able to give you my full attention."

A look of relief crossed Elena's face. "That sounds great."

"See you later." Wanda waved, then looked down at Figaro. "How would you like to visit Fair Havens Assisted Living?"

14

OF COURSE, BY THE TIME SHE GOT HOME, WANDA WAS later than she'd hoped. The Fair Havens service was simple, and everyone came, though only a few received the ashes. Father Paul had been there to give ashes to the Roman Catholics at breakfast time, and others were overtouched and had avoided it.

It also may have been a bad idea to give the residents the bowl of ashes from last Palm Sunday's palms to anoint themselves. She hoped Andy and the cleaning crew would forgive her. Figaro had been a favorite and ate all the crumbs off the floor. She told Andy about Martina's death, and he gave her a hug and said that Martina often came to Fair Havens to sing for the residents.

"She sang opera here?" Wanda asked.

"Opera? No. Songs from musicals. Also, the Beatles were a hit, and the Beach Boys, too."

Wanda thanked him and waved at her little Fair Havens family before taking her new canine ambassador home. Figaro was willing to trot right into the parsonage, just as he had at Fair Havens. By-product of living with a cleaner, Wanda assumed.

"Lance!" she shouted, hoping the loud music indicated that he was not wearing headphones.

"Yes?"

"Come downstairs! I want you to meet your new best friend."

"No!" Lance called back.

"What?"

"No! If it's the vacuum cleaner, I'm going to do it later. If this is your way of asking for help with your phone again, you should Google it! I'm in the middle of working on this play I got suckered into writing." There was a pause. "I love you, though!"

Wanda was not used to hearing those words from him yet. She felt herself smile, even as she raised her voice over the racket. "Lance, please turn off the music for a minute."

The music stopped. She had never believed in miracles more.

"We have a canine guest. His name is Figaro. We're keeping him until—"

Lance bounded down the stairs, Wink at his heels. "Who's this sweetheart? Who's a good dog?" Wink and Figaro were sniffing each other already, even as Lance tried to pull the larger dog into his lap.

"Lance, don't get too attached. He's not ours. We're just keeping him for a few days—"

"Sure, sure." Lance's tone sounded suspiciously like Ryan's had when Wanda had assured him they wouldn't be keeping the dog. "What's your name?"

"This big boy is Figaro. Figaro, this is Wink." Wanda knelt down beside her terrier. She picked him up and let Wink lick her and sniff all the smells. She knew she was going to be late to meet Elena, but she wanted this introduction to go smoothly.

"Hi, Figgy. Oh, you are such a lovebug. I'm going to call you Figgy Puddin'," Lance crooned into the dog's snout. Figaro licked him across the face, and Lance laughed with delight.

Wink wiggled out of Wanda's arms and immediately climbed up into Lance's lap, asserting his possession over this human. Wanda was a little jealous, but she knew that Lance dropped a lot more food than she did and probably smelled more interesting, too.

"Oh, Wink, yes. You're such a good boy, too," Lance murmured, burying his head in the little dog's back as he scratched Figaro's ears. All of a sudden, he jumped up and ran back to his room. The dogs followed, sounding like a parade of elephants as they pounded after him.

Lance popped out just as quickly, and the three reversed direction, stampeding directly toward Wanda. She sidestepped as Lance led the dogs out to the yard, tennis ball in hand. "I'll be back in an hour," she called to him, and Lance waved to acknowledge her. His attention was on the dogs, though. Wanda tried to recall if she had ever seen him happier than he was at this moment.

As she walked back to the car, she stepped over Lance's boots, a hat that had fallen off the coat rack, and the basket of dog leashes that had been knocked over in the race to play. In less than four months, she had gone from having one staid terrier companion to having three rambunctious males to contend with. Wanda hung the hat back up and grabbed her purse. She didn't hate the change—not at all.

WANDA SAT IN THE COFFEE SHOP WITH A CUP OF ginger tea and a book—not one of Greg's picks, though she was sure he had recommended *All Boys Aren't Blue*, George M. Johnson's memoir manifesto. She was trying to finish it before the youth group met again. A few of the kids had been talking about the book, and Wanda had been trying to find time to read it so she at least could approach the loop, if not be in it.

She didn't mind the opportunity to sit and relax, but she was getting concerned. It was four-thirty, and Elena had not yet shown up or answered her phone.

Wanda finally went to the counter. The barista dragged her attention from her phone. "Can I get you something else?"

"I've been waiting for a friend. I don't suppose anyone's called?" Wanda knew it was a long shot—why would Elena call the restaurant rather than Wanda's cell phone? But she wasn't sure what else to do.

"Oh, yeah," the girl said. "Someone named Mendoza called about five minutes before you arrived." She looked longingly back down at her phone.

"Did she have a message for me?" Wanda prompted.

The barista lifted her head again. "It was a guy. He said she wasn't coming. Told me to look for a sharply dressed woman in a red jacket." The barista examined Wanda. She seemed like she had more to say about how "sharply dressed" she considered Wanda to be in her brown corduroy slacks with the cream sweater Wanda had gotten on clearance at Kohls, but she obviously thought better of it. "Your coat is black."

Wanda sighed. She wore her red jacket when it was wet or stormy, or when she was walking Wink, but for pastoral care or even a coffee date she tended to grab her long black wool coat instead.

"Okay. Thanks." Wanda went back to her table and texted Rye to get Gerard Mendoza's number. She wondered why Elena hadn't called herself. When she didn't get an immediate response, Wanda bussed her table, left a reluctant tip, and headed home.

Wanda's plan to find the number in her messy office and call Principal Mendoza was delayed by the chaos she encountered in her normally peaceful home. She hoped the two dogs were playing and not trying to inflict mortal injury on each other. Figaro chased Wink around the living room, kitchen, pastor's study, up the stairs and down again, and then they swapped places and Wink chased Figgy. Lance was laughing so hard that tears were running down his cheeks.

"Aunt Wanda, they're having so much fun! If they slow down, I throw the sock monkey, and they get all riled up again."

Wanda laughed. "I'm sure they do." She gave the dogs a pat as they stopped to sniff hello. "I need to make a call in my study. Do you mind keeping them out here for a few minutes? We can take them on a w-a-l-k after I'm done."

Lance nodded and threw the sock monkey up and over Wanda's head. The dogs went crashing after it, and she closed the door to her little study. It at least muffled the noise.

Wanda picked up her phone. It rang a few times before Gerard picked up. "Hello?"

"Gerard, hi. This is Wanda Duff. I was just calling to check on Elena. We were supposed to meet this afternoon, but she never showed up. I couldn't reach her."

There was silence on the other end, and then Gerard cleared his throat. "Elena's phone was taken when she was mugged. She's had a bad headache off and on since it happened and hasn't felt up to going to the store to replace it."

"I'm so sorry," Wanda replied. "I don't want to keep you, but this has been long enough that you should have her see a doctor about the headaches. I'm sure you're busy with the girls right now, but please let Elena know if she needs anything, she can reach out, day or night. Otherwise, I'll see her tomorrow at book club."

"I'm not sure whether she'll want to go. Talking about the cold case has been…difficult for her."

Wanda was curious about what he meant, but this wasn't the time or the right Mendoza to ask about it. "I understand."

"Thanks, Wanda. Bye."

The poor woman had looked awful this morning after her interview. Wanda wished she'd made time to talk to her then. Her Fair Havens congregation could have waited for their ashes. Time was fluid for them. She had gone with duty rather than instinct, and that was never a good idea. Elena might know more than either Wanda or Rye would have suspected about the cold case and the current one, and someone might not want her sharing.

15

WHEN THE ICY WIND BLEW RYE INTO HARVEY'S ON Thursday night, it was like stepping into a snug English cottage. The barista was playing the rarely used piano, although she stood up when Rye came in to help with tea and cookies. Wanda was in an animated conversation with Greg and Tony by the fireplace. Elena and Jaz were sitting by the window talking with Camila. Rye put her food down on the table by Camila and began the process of unwrapping her outdoor attire.

When Rye sat down, Camila scooted over and wrapped an arm around her shoulder, giving her a quick squeeze. Rye reached into her pocket to extract a slightly crumpled envelope. Camila took it and pulled out the picture Rye had been carrying around for days now.

Camila glanced at Rye. "Can I show them?"

"Sure."

Camila handed the photograph to Jaz. "That's Melanie, Rye's mother, with Lionel Burgess, the victim of the cold case we were talking about."

Elena glanced at the picture, her hand going to her throat in surprise. "I took that photo." Her eyes welled up. "Mel and I worked together at the courthouse before I married Gerard." Elena accepted the picture from Camila with trembling hands. "This was taken on Founders Day. It was a big deal back then. I don't remember why your dad wasn't in the picture. He was probably on duty."

"You knew Lionel, too?" Wanda asked.

"We were friends from fourth grade on." Tears rolled down Elena's cheeks as she studied the photograph. "He was one of the only people besides me that Melanie seemed to like to spend time with. We went out dancing—"

"My dad hates to dance," Rye interrupted.

"That's why she came with us," Elena replied. "We had a weekly happy hour that we loved. Every Tuesday, your dad would take you out for a special daddy-daughter date. You don't remember?"

Rye shook her head. "I don't remember much of anything before my mother left." She paused. "I did spend a lot of time at the station with my dad, though. He had a little desk for me next to his, and he would bring coloring sheets or stickers for me to work on."

"Maybe that's where you two went. I'm not sure," Elena replied. "I do remember Mel often met up with one of the musicians from the band. What was his name?" She drummed beautifully manicured nails on the table. "I think he knew Mel's sister and was still in touch with Kara."

"Who's Kara?" Camila asked at the same time Rye said, "What sister?"

Elena looked confused. "Your aunt Kara?"

"My mother was an only child." Rye knew this, had always known this.

"At work, Mel had a picture on her desk of her holding Kara as a baby," Elena replied.

Rye felt numb. Around her, people continued to discuss the case, to pass around the photograph she'd brought. It wasn't until Elena spoke again that she looked up.

"That's why I nudged Greg to consider this case. We had our high school reunion this past summer, and there was a time of remembrance for all the students who'd passed on. I hadn't thought of Lionel in a while, but when I saw his yearbook picture up on the screen, I was reminded of everything that had happened. I always wondered whether, if he'd been white, the police would have put more effort into finding whoever did it."

Elena had seemed so uninterested at the last meeting. Now she was blotting her eyes, clearly affected by the loss of her friend.

"Why didn't you tell us it mattered to you personally when Greg first brought up the case?" Camila asked. "You must have valuable insights."

"I wasn't prepared for how hard that podcast would be to listen to," Elena said. "By the time I was feeling ready to share, it was time to go. Then that man stole my purse. It's just been a difficult time."

"You knew my mother and Lionel," Rye said. "Do you think she had something to do with his death?"

"The only evidence linking your mother to the crime is her disappearance," Tony interrupted. "It's just as likely, even more likely, that she ..." He trailed off.

"That she was killed, too," Rye finished for him.

Jaz interrupted. "I'm going to pull rank on amateur criminal investigation. Right now, you are trying to build a case on pure speculation. I know this is personal for you, Rye, and for you, Elena, but we should approach this the same way we have the other cases brought to the meetings."

"Greg, I don't want to overstep," Wanda said, "but maybe we should call it for tonight?"

"No!" Rye exclaimed. "I'm fine. I want to talk about this."

"We need to regroup. Maybe we could meet next week?" Greg offered. "I know…I know, Rye, that this is postponing it a second time, but I think we should take it out of the book club setting and just meet as friends. Anyone who wants to discuss the case can come to our house. No book to discuss, just this." He looked at Tony, who nodded in agreement.

"I, for one, have phone calls to return and I need to get going. I vote for next week," said Wanda, relieved that Bellona was absent.

Camila squeezed Rye's hand. "I'll stay if you want to talk?"

Rye shook her head. "I need to speak to Elena." She pulled on her coat. Elena was already paying her bill.

"I'm heading home, but call if you need me, okay?"

"Thanks Wanda," Rye replied. She grabbed her bag and jogged after Elena, catching her at the door. "Would you mind if we had a quick chat?"

Elena shook her head. "I'm not really up for it tonight. I thought I was, but…I promise we can talk soon." She pushed the door open, and a bitter wind blew in. Rye followed her out, a few steps behind as she tried to wrap her scarf more securely.

A man brushed past her, dressed for the weather. Rye was envious of his neck gaiter, pulled up almost far enough to reach his wool hat. She stopped to retie her boot, and when she looked up, Elena had disappeared. Rye walked to the end of the block where she'd parked and saw that the man had come up to Elena as she reached her car.

She was too far away to hear what he was saying, but she saw Elena reach up to push him away. Rye started across the icy lot as quickly as she could. She slipped twice, ripping her jeans as she went down the second time, and was practically crawling by the time she made it to the car.

Elena was on the ground, leaning against the door, hand to her head. Blood was dripping down her face.

"Elena?" Rye knelt in front of her, already digging her phone out of her pocket. She dialed 911. "Elena, are you okay?"

"I fell," she said, putting her hand up to touch the cut. "I think I fell."

"Did that man push you?"

Elena shook her head, then winced. "No. I pushed him."

"Why?"

"He was asking ... He kept asking—" She wobbled, and Rye pulled open the back door and helped her sit down.

"What did he want?"

"Can you call Gerard for me? I don't have a phone, and I need him to come get me."

"I think I should call an ambulance, or at least take you to urgent care. You have a head injury."

"No, no. I'm fine. I just want to go home."

"Elena—"

"Please," she said, holding her hand against her head. "Just call Gerard."

Rye gave in. She closed Elena's door and slid into the front seat, turning on the car so they wouldn't freeze to death while waiting for him to come.

"You don't have to wait with me," Elena said. "I'm okay here."

"If you don't mind," Rye replied, "I'd feel more comfortable waiting."

"And if I do mind?"

Rye glanced in the rearview mirror. The older woman was gazing out the window, tears running down her cheeks. "Well, then, I'm sorry, but you're stuck with me."

Elena had the radio tuned to a channel playing show tunes. Rye turned it up, and they sat in silence, listening to Dick Van Dyke tell them to put on a happy face.

16

WANDA CLOSED HER COMPUTER. SHE SHOULD KNOW better than to read emails after nine o'clock. It stressed her out and threw off her nighttime routine. As she climbed the stairs to a warm bed and Wink, her cell phone rang.

She glanced at the caller ID. "Hardy? Is everything okay?" He never called this late. He had been brought up with the same phone etiquette she had—neither called before nine in the morning nor after nine at night unless it was an emergency.

"Elena was attacked tonight. Rye stayed with her until Gerard picked her up."

"When? What happened?"

"After book club. Rye said a man approached Elena in the parking lot. Elena got upset and shoved him. Rye didn't see what happened after that, but Elena claims she fell. Hit her head on the ice."

Wanda nearly tripped over all the chew toys that the dogs had abandoned at the top of the stairs. "I'm glad Rye was still there to help. I left right away. I knew she was going to talk to Elena about..."

"About what? The cold case? The one involving my wife? Rye told me you all were discussing it." Hardy didn't sound happy.

"Apparently Melanie and Elena were friends? Or worked together?" Wanda wasn't sure exactly how much of this Hardy already knew. When he didn't say anything, she continued. "Rye didn't know that, and when Elena mentioned Kara—"

"Who's Kara?"

Wanda froze, her cup of tea halfway to its coaster on the bedside table. Rye not knowing that her mother had a sister was one thing, but it had never occurred to Wanda that Hardy might not know either.

"Who is Kara?" Hardy asked again.

"Melanie's little sister," Wanda replied.

"Mel didn't have a sister." Hardy sounded almost relieved.

Wanda had no idea what to say to that. "Maybe Elena was wrong?"

"She must have been." Hardy's tone implied that the conversation was closed. "Any progress in your Suarez snooping?"

"Not much." She refused the bait. "Aside from inheriting her dog, I haven't gotten much traction on it."

"How's Wink taking that?"

"Surprisingly well. Who knew he had a puppy buried deep down, just waiting for a couple of brothers to bring it out? My house has seen better days, but Lance is so happy."

"That's good," Hardy replied. "I talked to him for a few minutes at the concert, and he seemed stressed. I'm glad he has something more fun to focus on. Speaking of which, did I remember to tell you I saw Martina that night after the concert?"

"I don't think so."

"With everything else that happened, I didn't think much of it at the time, but she was upset."

"About the protesters?"

"No. Well, probably that, too. She was on the phone, and I might not have noticed her at all, except she was crying," Hardy said. "I heard her telling someone that she was afraid 'they' had found her."

"They?" Wanda asked. "The protesters?"

"She wasn't more specific, unfortunately."

Wanda took a sip of her tea. "Thanks. I'm not sure what it might mean at the moment, but if I figure anything out, I'll let you know." Her phone beeped. Rye was calling.

"Hey, your daughter is on the other line. Let's talk soon, okay?"

"Sounds good," Hardy replied.

Wanda settled back onto her pillows, allowing Wink to snuggle in next to her, and switched her phone to speaker so she could warm both hands on the mug.

"Rye, are you okay? Hardy just called."

"Yeah, I'm fine." Rye sounded wrung out. She gave Wanda a quick rundown of what had happened. "I convinced Gerard to take Elena to get checked out, and guess who I saw when I followed them to the hospital in Elena's car?"

Wanda knew plenty of people at the hospital, but she doubted Rye knew them, too. "Who?"

"Andy." Andy Soucek was Rye's childhood best friend and a recent ex-boyfriend. They had transitioned from dating back to friendship more easily than Wanda would have expected, and both Andy and his niece Rachel were frequent visitors at Hardy's house.

"What was he doing at the hospital?"

"Visiting his girlfriend."

Wanda paused. "Oh? Also in the hospital?"

"Nope. Crystal is a beautiful, funny pediatric surgeon. Honestly, I want to date her," Rye replied.

Wanda knew Rye was trying to make a joke out of what must have been a tough end to a long night. "Well, that's nice to hear," she replied neutrally. She wondered whether telling Rye that she had just spilled the beans about Kara to Hardy would push her friend over the edge or be a good distraction.

"Apparently, my dad met her already." Ouch. Wanda didn't want to touch that one. "He hadn't mentioned it to me, of course," Rye added.

"I wonder why." Wanda knew full well that there was zero chance Hardy would willingly insert himself into any dating drama.

Rye sighed loudly enough that Wanda heard it over the line. "Probably because he thinks I would be jealous of how happy they are."

"Would you be?" Wanda asked. The idea came as a surprise. Rye had seemed relieved to end things with Andy.

"Not of them, but happy does sound nice," Rye said. "Don't you think?"

"Rye, both of my ex-husbands remarried less than a year after we divorced—one to a very nice man from the UK, and one to an acquaintance of mine who worked, maybe works, at a gym where I can no longer go, having destroyed property there. When I tell you that nothing had been working in those relationships for a long time, it is an understatement. And I have not really clicked with anyone since those not-so-golden days. I do understand. I know what it's like to be jealous of just plain happiness. It's hard to be alone. But you have Claudia."

There was a long silence. "She texted this afternoon. She wants to take a break. Try being friends."

Wow. This really had been a bad day for her friend. "I'm sorry," Wanda said. "That's awful."

"On the scale from meeting my ex's new girlfriend to finding out I might have an aunt, it actually rates fairly low on the list of surprises." She laughed, but it sounded forced.

"Would it help or hurt to know that I spared you a conversation with your dad about Kara?"

Rye laughed again, this time in surprise. "You what?"

"I wasn't thinking, and when he called me tonight it just popped out."

"What did my dad need from you?"

Wanda knew this wouldn't be a good time to mention to Rye that she and Hardy talked a few times a week on the phone. "He wanted to let me know about Elena."

"Hmm."

Before she could say anything else, Wanda asked, "Do you remember anything about your grandparents?"

"Dad's parents? Sure. Grandma Ruth died before I was born. Grandpa Charlie lived over on Marsh Road. He had candy and comic books and would let me watch as much TV as I wanted. I'd sleep over when my dad had a big case, and I never went to bed before two a.m. It drove my dad up a wall when I came home grouchy and exhausted."

"What about Melanie's folks?" Wanda asked.

"I never met them. I thought they were dead when I was a kid. Now I'm not sure. Maybe she was estranged from them."

"You never asked Hardy?"

"I did," Rye said. "He told me her dad had died when she was young, and her mom remarried."

"That's it?"

There was a long silence. "I asked a lot of questions after Mom left. This probably won't come as a surprise to you, but I wasn't one of those children who internalize their problems. I wanted to know everything he knew, everything about my mother, even the bipolar disorder—anything that would keep her from fading away. One day I just stopped asking questions." Rye paused again. "After Andy and I became friends without mothers."

Andy's mother had taken her own life, and at seven years old he had been the one to discover her body. His second-grade friendship with Rye and his grandmother's love pulled his life out of a tailspin. Wanda decided that she should find the school counselor in retirement who'd helped these two children stabilize, stay in school, and grow up to be damaged but very good human adults. She knew that Rye, as blunt as she could be, was also empathetic and observant. Wanda did wonder what had happened to make Rye stop searching for answers. Maybe having a friend had helped. Maybe Hardy settled into a new routine and she adjusted to it. Or maybe she just stuffed all those questions down inside.

"What about now?" Wanda asked.

"Can't we talk about something easier, like who stabbed Martina Suarez in the back?"

Wink stood up and stretched, then jumped off the bed. Wanda could hear his collar jingling down the hall, Lance's door opening and closing, and a thump as Figaro jumped off the bed to meet his friend. Wanda rubbed the warm spot where the dog had been. "Maybe tomorrow. Tonight, I think I need a break from murder."

17

Wanda felt like she and Lance had already fallen quickly into a good routine with the dogs. They each needed a person to walk with, since they tended to follow squirrels in opposite directions. During the two walks (minimum), morning and evening, she had more time than usual with her nephew. He might tire of it eventually, but at least for now Lance was an enthusiastic conversationalist if she didn't try out sermon ideas on him.

Wanda's attention had wandered when he started sharing details of the latest game he and Leslie were playing online, and Lance, to his credit, noticed quickly.

"Earth to Aunt Wanda!"

"I'm sorry, Lance," she replied. "I was thinking about book club."

"Did your mystery buffs solve the Mardi Gras murder?" Lance asked as he attempted to reign Figaro in at the crosswalk.

"Are people calling it that?"

"It was the news headline. 'Mardi Gras murder of reclusive diva.'"

"Poor Martina. She didn't like publicity for her talents. She asked when I introduced her for the service to 'just call me a cleaner, or a singing cleaner. You can skip the opera part.' She would have hated being a spectacle. And no. It didn't come up. Everyone was caught up in a murder that might be tied to the disappearance of Rye's mother."

"Really?" Lance's eyes widened. "Spill."

"No. I shouldn't have mentioned it." Wanda sighed.

"Could I offer you a trade? I actually have some information for the investigation that I know you will be doing into the death of Martina Suarez."

"What? Really?" Wanda looked at him in surprise.

"Really."

"Well? Spill!"

"I was talking to Figaro—"

"As one does," Wanda interrupted.

Lance ignored her. "—and I promised him that we would find out who took his mama away. I assumed you and Rye would be investigating, so I did some research. Did you know Suarez is the five hundred and first most common surname in the United States? It's Iberian in origin."

"Martina was from Mexico via Alaska and went to the New England Conservatory in opera studies. I know that much. She told me."

"Martina did, you're right. But Martina—or at least *that* Martina—has been dead for five years. Breast cancer."

"What?" Wanda stopped abruptly.

"The woman who moved here as a cleaner was born Luisa Suarez. She's Martina's older sister." Lance grinned at Wanda. "And Luisa had a rap sheet for petty crime, theft, blackmail, impersonating an officer…but all of that stopped when Luisa moved in and took care of her sister for the last year of Martina's life."

"How did you find this out?"

Lance rolled his eyes as if to say, *I'm seventeen, of course.* "I pay for services that allow me to check criminal records of the men my mom thought about meeting on dating sites."

Hmm, Wanda thought. Smart. "So, when her sister died, Luisa took Martina's name and identity?"

"And stayed clean. There are no police reports after that point under either name. And Luisa is really Martina. She took the name legally."

Wanda stopped to allow Wink to sniff a bush. "I was at Fair Havens Wednesday, and Andy said Martina sang all the time in the Memory Care unit, but that it was always folk or rock, never opera, which was what Martina—the real Martina—had trained for. I just assumed it was because that was a better choice for the residents."

"I didn't find anything about Luisa's education, which may mean she was a self-taught musician. I doubt many people, even with talent, can teach themselves how to sing opera."

"And, honestly, 'opera' is such an obscure musical genre that most people don't realize that 'great voice' and 'opera singer' aren't just synonyms. But if this is true, and that's a big 'if,' I wonder whether 'Martina' changed her criminal stripes or just found easier targets."

"There's one more thing I found out, and it has to do with church."

They had to wait as another dog came toward them and Wink and Figgy went bananas barking. When the "danger" had passed and the dogs continued their sniff and stroll, Wanda raised an eyebrow at him. "Go on."

"I told you that Luisa changed her name, right? Well, apparently, she also got re-baptized. I wonder why she'd care about that when she'd already made it legal."

"How on earth did you find that out?" Wanda asked with genuine surprise.

"Are you kidding? The church not only has a website and Facebook page, but they have about a million YouTube videos. I watched her get baptized."

"Where was the church?"

"Right here in town. It's Rising Star Baptist, where Josh Gagne is the pastor. Nicole was losing it over him at the Mardi Gras dinner." Lance made a face. There was a soft whining at his feet. Figgy clearly wanted Lance to pull out the ball in his pocket, so he and Wanda hurried down the block to the house. Wanda let Wink off his leash to let him play with Lance and Figaro while she made dinner. It was time to follow through on her promise to Ryan and check up on the clergy, starting with a certain young tech-savvy Baptist pastor.

Wanda's first thought was to invite all the clergy who had been at the service on Mardi Gras over for dinner. Lance might overhear something she didn't, and it would be good to have an extra set of eyes and ears on the gathering.

Then she had a reality check.

If she invited clergy for next Saturday, they would be writing their sermons, and if she invited clergy on a Sunday, they would be exhausted from preaching said sermons. They would say no. She ignored the small voice in her head that said that if they expected her to cook, they'd hunt for reasons to say "no" at any time.

She also didn't have a week to wait. Considering the new information Lance had given her, it was possible that other people were in danger from whoever killed

Martina and stole her keys. Wanda didn't have the luxury to wait until someone dropped her a clue over lasagna and garlic bread.

At any rate, if Wanda got a bunch of clergy together, she would never get the truth out of them. They would listen to each other, and then misremembering would run rampant. These were people gifted at taking a single Bible story and telling it differently every three years for an entire career. A couple of them would feel obliged to include a bad joke. No one would give her anything she could go on.

There was no getting around it. She was going to have to visit every single one of them. It wasn't like she could just pop by and ask them to chat about a murder. She needed a plan. And, as if by divine inspiration, she had one. She knew some of her plans were less godly than others, but this one would work for interviews and actually produce something. She would have to go around asking advice from her colleagues about whether they would support a Pentecost afternoon event where every faith community provided a choir, praise band, soloist, or instrumentalist for an afternoon picnic of sharing.

Naturally, she needed to visit to "test the waters" before bringing it up in the meeting next month. It was just coincidence that the test samples were the group that had been at Mardi Gras, plus Father Paul, who was Martina's spiritual guide. It was the perfect excuse to talk about music and the loss of Martina. She would not mention Luisa. She *would* try to spot a guilty conscience.

18

RYE CHECKED HER WATCH WHEN SHE PULLED UP IN front of Wanda's house. It was earlier than she would normally stop by, but Wanda would definitely be up, and Lance might be, too. Rye knew they were housing a new dog, and if they had been up all night with him, they might try to sleep in. Luck was on Rye's side, though, because as she was pulling out her phone to send Wanda a "U up?" text that she hoped would get a laugh, Wanda came out with Lance and two dogs in tow.

Rye got out of her car and approached the group cautiously. Wink knew her well and was ready for a good ear scratch, tail thumping wildly. The new dog, who Rye guessed wasn't actually called "Figgy Wiggy Li'l Baby," as Lance introduced him, was equally excited, running in tight circles and kissing Rye's fingers.

"It looks like you two have your hands full here," Rye commented as she followed her friends, who were being dragged down the street by the dogs.

"Did I miss a call from you?" Wanda reined Wink in with slightly more success than Lance was having.

"No," Rye replied. "I just wanted to catch up." She squatted down to let Wink sniff her face. "And I needed a little pup pick-me-up."

"Saturday morning breakfast didn't go well?" Wanda asked. It was a tradition Rye and her father had picked up when she moved back home, and she was never allowed to skip it.

"It was canceled for the first time ever," Rye replied. "I woke up to a note from my dad saying he had something urgent come up and that he would be gone all weekend."

"Did you two talk last night when you got home?" Wanda asked.

"No. His car was already gone."

That was strange. Hardy was protective, and the idea that he wouldn't have waited around to confirm that his daughter was in one piece after what had happened to Elena was hard to believe.

Rye finally stood up as Figgy broke away to tow Lance down the street. She and Wanda watched them with mutual affection until Wink pulled hard enough on his leash that they caught up to the pair.

Rye was telling Wanda about the emails she and Mendoza had been receiving as they turned into the park. "It's starting to feel personal," Rye said. "Not just for me, but for the high school community."

"Even Martina's murder was school-adjacent," Lance pointed out. "I mean, the high school is barely five hundred feet from Saint Athanasius."

"I hadn't thought of that, but you're right. And Martina sang at the chorus concert."

"And she was about to sign a contract to become the head custodian at the school," Lance said.

"How did you find out about that?" Rye asked.

Lance glanced guiltily away. "Look! A squirrel!" He pointed, and Figgy charged.

Rye decided she better check network security at Stoneridge, stat. She filed that thought away as Wanda filled Rye in on what Lance had discovered about Luisa's false identity and criminal past.

"Okay," Rye said, "but she's dead. If she was the reason for the attacks on Elena and the problems at school, shouldn't they have stopped?"

"What if whoever killed 'Martina' didn't know what we do and thinks Luisa's still alive?" Lance asked as he came up the hill, struggling to unwrap himself from Figaro's leash, and showing that he had prodigious hearing. Or had bugged them. No. Not possible.

"What do you mean?" Rye asked.

"What if they thought they were murdering the real Martina but then started second-guessing themselves?"

"So you're suggesting we don't even know which sister was the intended target?"

"I'm getting a headache," Wanda said.

"I need coffee," Rye agreed. She stepped out of the path of Figaro, who had scented a chipmunk and was dragging Lance's arm out of the socket to catch up with it.

"I'm meeting with Josh Gagne later this morning," Wanda said. "I can't stand the guy, but he's a gossip, and he did baptize her. If any of the ministers involved in the service know anything, Josh knows it, too."

"That sounds like as good a place to start as any," Rye said. She yawned. "I need to get going. Saturday is all errands all the time. Will you let me know what you find out?"

"Of course," Wanda replied. "You'll be the first to know."

19

"I'VE GOT FIVE MINUTES FOR YOUR PITCH," JOSH TOLD Wanda when he opened the door to his office.

She swallowed her gut reaction to this bald statement. She had once listened to this man talk for forty-five minutes without pause about an Easter event that the interfaith group hadn't even ended up sponsoring. The young pastor must really dislike her, because if he behaved like this all the time he would have no congregation. She wondered whether it was a personal reaction to her two divorces or a response to the welcome and affirmation by Trinity of all gender identities and sexual orientations. She knew from her long ministry that, unpleasant as his attitude was, it could hide a deep history of pain. She wouldn't be put off, though. She had an agenda.

"Rising Star Baptist has the best praise band in town. I would love to have them front and center at PFC Stanley James Memorial Park at one p.m. for the Pentecost service on May twentieth. They would kick off the celebration and be followed by other contributors." She finished with the tried-and-true, "Can we expect your support?"

Josh sighed. "Who else has agreed to this?"

Wanda smiled sweetly. "I came to you first, since I know your musical program is renowned. People will be begging to sign up if they know Rising Star is going to be there."

He just grunted. Wanda felt that if she took any more deep breaths, she might start to hyperventilate. Really, for all his good looks, Josh lacked enthusiasm, a work ethic, and seemingly even a basic level of empathy. She had no idea why he'd decided to go into this line of work, since he didn't particularly enjoy either his congregation or his colleagues.

Or perhaps she was just being mean-spirited. She could use a 'clean Saturday' infusion herself. "You know, Josh, I sense you're in a hurry, but I've been meaning to ask how you've been settling in." She ignored the fact that he'd been hired almost two years ago. "I know it can be difficult breaking into a small, tightly knit community like this one."

"I've had no problems since I got here."

"Oh? Did you have some before you arrived? You came from…Chicago, was it?" Wanda knew perfectly well it was New York. Josh told people every chance he got.

"New York City. Manhattan."

"Of course! How could I forget!" He hadn't offered her a seat, but Wanda sat down anyway. "That must be a big adjustment." Here went nothing. "I heard the other day that Martina Suarez was from New York City, too. Did you know each other?" Wanda was laying on the country bumpkin act thick. She knew New York was not where Martina came from, but her dangling lure seemed to work.

Josh's face heated up. "Of course not! I would never have associated with someone like her!" Then, as if realizing what he'd said wasn't exactly in line with most pastoral handbooks, he tried to backpedal. "I mean, I never met her before I came here."

"But didn't she clean the church? And your parsonage? I could have sworn she mentioned you a few times when she was helping us out at Trinity." The woman had never done any such thing, but it wasn't as though Josh could confirm that now.

"Anything she told you is a lie!" Josh's face was red. "But sin doesn't pay. I prayed for her, Wanda. Just like I pray for you! And, may God forgive me, I baptized her."

Wanda desperately wanted to ask what, exactly, he prayed for when her own name came up, but she knew she would either laugh in his face or give him the teardown of a lifetime, and neither would be beneficial to her cause.

Josh's phone rang, though, the vibration surprisingly loud against the wooden surface of his desk. He turned his back to her, and Wanda took that as her cue to leave. She hoped she could at least linger in the hallway to listen to the call, but as soon as she stepped across the threshold, the heavy door slammed shut behind her.

When she got into her car, Wanda felt fortunate she had picked the much more pleasant Rolf Anderson at the Lutheran Church to visit next. Rolf was beloved by his congregation in large part because he was not overtly gregarious. He sat with sick people and felt no need to talk. He would hold hands, say prayers, and stay for an hour or more to allow the family a chance to run errands or even just get some fresh air.

Rolf told Wanda he would love to ask a family from India if they would perform at the Pentecost event. The daughter was an award-winning ankle bell dancer, and her brother and mother accompanied her with bansuri and sitar.

He also told Wanda that, yes, Martina had cleaned his church regularly, and he had never had problems with her. They had often sat together and enjoyed a pot of tea during her breaks. He would miss her company.

He hesitated before saying, "She was a little curious about my parishioners. It made me uncomfortable, but I ignored the questions, and she took the hint. I imagine a single woman has to be careful which homes she visits to clean."

He let the topic drop then, and after Rolf served her tea and some cookies a parishioner had brought, Wanda left feeling a much-needed sense of renewal.

Colleen had never had problems with Martina, either, though Martina had cleaned the Unitarian Universalist church once a month. Colleen did mention that she rarely saw Martina after the first time she'd cleaned at the church. Like Rolf, Colleen had felt uncomfortable about some of the questions Martina asked her about the survivors' groups that met there, and, in her typically straightforward fashion, had simply invited Martina to attend any of the meetings if she was in need. At first, Martina had seemed excited by the offer, but after attending one meeting she didn't visit again. After that, Martina seemed to make an effort to work at the church when Colleen was not around. She'd even seen Martina turn around and leave before finishing her work once when she discovered Colleen in the sanctuary.

Wanda and Colleen spent nearly as much time catching up as Wanda did trying to investigate, and she didn't turn down Colleen's homemade brownies, even after the shortbread cookies she'd had with Rolf. She left with the promise that Colleen would check in with a few musicians for the Pentecost service, but having learned nothing that would move the case along.

Lana was out when Wanda dropped by the Methodist church, and her admin offered to leave a note with Wanda's request. She left the information about the Pentecost service and asked if Lana would give her a call when she was back in the office.

Her luck improved when she ran into Bruce at the Starbucks down the street from Jordan Baptist. He told her that the church had a rotation of volunteer cleaners, then offered up a barbershop quartet (which he sang in) for her event. Wanda paid for his coffee in thanks and made hers a triple shot. He was so much less loquacious than usual that she said a couple of thank-yous to the Almighty, then wondered whether she'd offended him in some way.

Nothing to be done about it now. She took a deep, happy sip. There was no way she would make it to Saint Athanasius without this caffeine boost. No one was at the counter, so she went back and grabbed a sandwich to energize her and balance out all the sugar in her system.

After lunch, she drove over only to find out that Father Bogdan was visiting a parishioner at Fair Havens. His wife, Agatha, made Wanda a cup of tea. She was beginning to wonder how many cups of hot liquid she could consume before hobbling to the nearest restroom.

"You look like you've been put through the ringer, Wanda. I wouldn't have guessed that soliciting musical talent from our churches would be such a difficult task!"

"Enthusiasm for new events is easy, commitments not so much," Wanda replied. "I've also been checking in to see how everyone is doing after Martina's death. I was the person who suggested her for the Mardi Gras service, and it's been weighing on me."

"I'm sure you met with some resistance," Agatha said. She was a beautiful black-haired woman who shared her husband's Serbian heritage. Wanda hadn't spent time with her alone before. Without Bogdan present, Agatha seemed more confident.

"Why do you say that?"

"Martina was ... Well, she had a way of making herself unwelcome."

"Do you mind if I ask how?"

Agatha looked at Wanda over the edge of her teacup. "I don't like to gossip."

Wanda knew from experience that people who said this usually enjoyed gossiping more than just about anything else. "I'm surprised. No one else I've spoken to has had anything bad to say about her work." *Except for Josh Gagne,* she thought to herself.

"Oh, her work was fine, Wanda. She was an excellent cleaner. Very thorough."

Wanda waited. There was clearly a 'but' coming.

"But she had a way of using her access to look into things that weren't really any of her concern."

Wanda hoped Agatha might say more, since Martina's curiosity had been a common theme to the day's conversations, but the woman just stared back at her, looking like the cat who had eaten the canary.

"Well," Wanda said, standing up. "Thank you for the tea. If you'd let Bogdan know I came by, I'd appreciate the chance to chat with him. He can call anytime."

"Of course. I'll let him know." Agatha showed her to the door and shut it behind Wanda more gently than Josh had, but with a similar finality. Wanda guessed Father Bogdan would not be calling.

She was grateful, at least, that she knew the location of the church restroom.

20

Lance sighed and stretched his arms up over his head as the credits rolled. "I never get tired of that movie," he said, trying and failing to wiggle out from the pile of dogs that had found warm blankets and a prone boy to be an ideal combo for sleep.

"How many times have we watched *The Music Man* since you moved here, do you think?" Wanda finished off her glass of seltzer and stood to collect the Twizzler wrappers and empty bowl of popcorn before the pups woke up and decided to investigate.

"At least three with you," Lance replied. "I fall asleep to it some nights when I need help shutting off my brain."

"I envy that," Wanda said. "I have never been the type who can fall asleep while watching TV. If anything, it wakes me up."

"I can make you a cup of Sleepy Bear tea," he teased. "I wouldn't want you to be up past your bedtime on my account."

Wanda glanced at the clock by the door. It was eleven thirty. She yawned and followed her nephew into the kitchen, having found even more debris from their movie watching. "That ship has sailed."

"I know." Lance filled the kettle and put it on the stove as he fetched two mugs and tea bags. "Thanks for staying up with me."

Wanda looked at him with unrestrained fondness. Her life had gotten so much better since Lance had come to live with her in the fall that the loneliness of previous years was starting to fade into memory.

Tonight, Mickey had called after dinner and asked Lance to come to England over spring break to meet her boyfriend, and a pit had opened up in Wanda's stomach. The only thing that kept her from spiraling was that Lance had been adamantly against the idea and had told his mother so. It turned into a huge fight, in which Wanda had eventually intervened lest Mickey demand Lance uproot himself immediately as a balm to her stung pride.

"How are you feeling about the fight with your mom?" Wanda wished she could avoid the topic but knew from experience it was better to let Lance talk things out than stew over them in his room.

He concentrated on pouring the boiling water, but Wanda wasn't fooled. Lance wasn't ignoring her—he was giving her question the consideration it deserved. Sometimes she wondered how this old soul had squeezed itself into an adolescent frame. Then she'd see him blowing spitballs with his friends over pho, and she would remember that everyone had the capacity for depth and silliness. Lance was just well-balanced for his age.

"Better," he said eventually. "I know I'll need to call her back tomorrow, and I'm dreading that, but I'm sure I'm right about this one."

Wanda knew that, for years, Lance had been the adult in the relationship with his mother, and she did her best not to encourage that behavior or allow him to replicate it with her. Sometimes, though, Lance's experiences with Mickey came in handy.

"Do you want to go see her?" she asked. "I mean, minus meeting the boyfriend. Because I would come with you. I could run interference."

"Thanks, Aunt Wanda, but I already have plans with Nicole and Leslie over break. We're working on the play. You'll never guess. I wrote a part for a comfort dog." Lance handed her a steaming mug. "Also, my break is two weeks away. Do you know how expensive tickets would be? And you know Mom wouldn't be paying for them."

Wanda considered that. "She'd pay for you."

"Maybe. More likely, she'd find a way to convince you it was your idea, and then you'd end up with the bill."

Wanda groaned. "You're probably right." She wasn't going to tell him that she guessed the new guy would be saddled with that expense.

"I'm going to hit her with the numbers tomorrow, and I'll tell her that if she's still there in June after school is out, I'll come then."

"That's fair," Wanda replied. "If there's one thing Mickey can't stand, it's spending her own money, so your logic seems sound."

Lance stared down into his cup, idly swishing the tea bag around. "Would you come with me then? You know—whenever I go?"

Wanda smiled. "A trip to England with my all-time favorite nephew? Wild horses couldn't keep me away."

He stood and gave her a half hug, wrapping one arm around her shoulders with a squeeze, then dropping a kiss on her head. "Thanks. I'm going to take Figgy and Wink out for a last pee, okay? I'll see you in the morning."

"Nope. I will be preaching," she said. "Unless you're ready for the first Sunday in Lent. Satan will be there."

"You know, Aunt Wanda, your sermon talents would make you great at creating video games."

Wanda laughed. "I'll keep that in mind! It's always good to have something to fall back on."

21

RYE WANTED TO TALK TO HER FATHER. USUALLY, WHEN she was struggling, she dealt with it herself. She was used to doing things on her own, and it felt natural not to share until she had made a decision, but this Sunday morning—well, early afternoon—she was lonely and sad and hurt. She wanted her dad to tell her it would all be okay, even if he couldn't guarantee anything.

So, of course, this was when he'd decided to be out of town. Rye didn't bother to lock the door to the barn apartment she had renovated after she'd moved back from Texas last year. After pulling on a sweater over her pajamas, she let herself into the main house, knowing that, at the very least, he would have good leftovers in the fridge. Sure enough, he'd left fried chicken, mashed potatoes, and gravy neatly marked, along with butterscotch pudding—breakfast and Sunday dinner rolled into one. Rye fixed herself a heaping plate and took it into the living room. Hardy didn't subscribe to any streaming services, but he did have a loaded TiVo, and Rye watched a mindless episode on HGTV while she ate.

She tried to call Hardy but got his voicemail twice. By the third time, Rye was beginning to pace the small room and regret her second bowl of pudding. Her father was never unreachable. She could be, but not him. Never him.

Rye was on the verge of calling Ryan to see if he had some way to track Hardy's phone when the doorbell rang. She shoved her phone in her pocket and went to see who it was. Elena Mendoza stood outside holding a small stack of books.

"Elena?"

"Oh, Rye, hello." Elena had a small bandage on her forehead, but otherwise she looked well. "I was dropping off these books for your dad. He and I were talking about cakes at the Mardi Gras dinner, and I told him I had a few cookbooks he might like." She peeked around Rye. "Is he here?"

"No," Rye replied, reaching out to take the books.

"Oh. Maybe I can leave a note?" Elena slipped between Rye and the doorjamb. "Is the kitchen back here?"

"Yes, but—" Rye followed Elena through the swinging door.

"I just wanted to explain a few of the bookmarks to him. I'd love to jot down the information." She sat down at the table and crossed her legs, looking at Rye expectantly.

"I think he has some paper in his office," Rye replied. "Can I get you anything? Water? Tea? Pudding?"

"I'm fine, Rye, thank you though."

Hostess duties fulfilled, Rye went in search of pen and paper. She came back a minute later with a sticky note and pencil.

"Oh." Elena looked disappointed. "Do you have anything larger? If I try to write all of this down on that little scrap, he'll never be able to decipher it."

"Sure." Rye went back out, and after a fruitless search of Hardy's spotless office, she finally pilfered a few pieces of paper from the printer.

"Will this work?"

Elena was standing at the window, looking out at the backyard. "That's perfect." Elena set to work, filling almost two full sheets in expansive cursive.

Rye sat across from her, watching the older woman write. She tried to imagine Elena and Melanie together. Elena and Gerard Mendoza had an enviable marriage, of which Rye had a front-row view. Now that their eldest daughter went to Stoneridge, Elena would often come to pick her up, the three younger girls in tow.

Rye enjoyed seeing them together—even their bickering often made her laugh—but at the moment, in this quiet kitchen, she felt the stark contrast to her own childhood. Even when Melanie was around, this house had never been boisterous. Both Melanie and Hardy tended toward quiet, thoughtful conversation and activities that were productive. Rye could hardly imagine her mother going out with Elena for anything as frivolous as weekly drinks at a bar forty minutes away.

Elena must have felt Rye's gaze on her, because she looked up and tucked her notes inside the top book. "Have you talked to your father about Lionel's murder?"

Rye shook her head. "Not much. I asked him about Kara, but he insisted my mom was an only child. Are you sure that the baby in the photo was her sister? Maybe it was a friend's child?"

"I don't think so. The baby looked a lot like her—the same eyes—I remember that. Your mother had such striking green eyes, didn't she?" Elena smiled.

Rye frowned, trying to remember. She had plenty of memories of her mother, but she couldn't recall the exact color of her eyes. None of the pictures she had of Melanie were close up or crisp enough for Rye to know for sure what color her mother's eyes were. Rye's eyes were golden brown, like her father's.

"I guess I don't remember."

"No?" Elena seemed surprised. She tilted her head, studying Rye. "You look a lot like her, but you have Hardy's coloring. And his freckles. My girls are like that, too. Sara looks just like Gerard, and Olivia looks exactly like my sister, but the other two are a complete mix of us."

"I don't think I look much like either of my parents." Rye glanced at a picture on the fridge, one taken at the lake last year of her and Hardy. "Well, maybe I have my father's smile."

"I think you have a lot of Hardy in you," Elena replied. "Melanie was...delicate. Not weak, but have you heard those jokes about women wishing they could be prescribed the Victorian cure of a trip to the seaside for malaise? Mel could have used that. She always seemed to be pining." She smoothed over her already impeccable French twist. "We were young. Who knows what she would be like today?"

"Who knows," Rye echoed.

"I thought when she got back from the treatment center she would stop running off, but whatever they did apparently didn't help enough."

"What treatment center?"

"Do you remember her disappearing? Not the last time, not after Lionel ..." Elena paused, then cleared her throat. "Were you old enough to remember that she had left before?"

"Of course. Every few months she would pack her little suitcase and take a trip," Rye said. "I asked my dad once why we couldn't go with her."

"What did he say?" Elena asked.

"Nothing." He had just cried, but she wouldn't tell Elena that.

Elena looked at her with a mix of sympathy and something more—maybe pity. "Your mother tried to get better. I know she wanted to, for you. It was the depressive side of her illness that so often claimed her."

Rye's phone rang then. It was her father. "Elena, thank you—I hate to rush you, but I have to take this."

"I just remembered one thing I needed to add to my notes. Do you mind if I let myself out?"

Rye had already answered the phone. She gave Elena a thumbs-up and walked into the living room. "Dad?"

"Hey, hon. I'm sorry I missed your calls earlier. The cell reception here is pretty spotty."

"Where are you?"

"Virginia."

"Why?"

"When your book club started talking about Lionel Burgess's case, I decided to ask Ryan if I could look at the old case notes. He couldn't show me everything, but it was enough."

"What do you mean?" Rye asked. "What did you find?"

"There was only one suspect in Burgess's murder, a man named Reuben Emerson, but the police never had enough evidence to officially charge him. There were connections. They were known to go to the same bar.

Lionel was a patron, and Reuben was the bass player in a band that played there regularly. A witness told the police she had seen them leave together the night Lionel was killed."

"But there wasn't anything to trace Emerson to Burgess's house?"

"Nothing definitive."

"Who else could it have been?" There was a long silence on the line. Rye finally worked up the courage to ask. "Could it have been Mom?"

"I don't think so, but when I was looking over the reports again, I had access to something I didn't have back then—internet records, and plenty of them."

"So? The police would have had access to records."

"True, but they weren't looking for what I was," Hardy replied. "Reuben Emerson was born and raised in Roanoke, Virginia."

"Okay." Rye waited.

"Your mother also grew up in Roanoke," Hardy replied. "And it's a big city. It could be a coincidence. But I decided to check it out. Emerson still has family down here. I decided to pay them a visit."

"Why would they invite you in?"

"They wouldn't. But I went to their church this morning, and his mother invited me over for lunch when I told them I was new to the area and looking for a place to worship."

"So you lied."

"I embroidered the truth. There's plenty of that in churches." He paused. "Don't tell Wanda I said that."

"Which part of what you told her was the truth? That you're moving to Virginia? That you're religious?"

"Fine," her father said. "I lied. But it worked. His mother had me over, and when I told them where I was from, she told me they had a son who lived up there—showed me pictures and everything. It's definitely Reuben Emerson," Hardy continued. "The father is in hospice care at home, and he was in bad shape, but the mother told me they were 'waiting on a miracle.'"

"What about Mom? Have you found out anything about her?" *Like where she grew up? Or if she really did have a sister she never told us about?*

"Not yet. I'm going to stay another day and see what I can find out."

"Okay."

"There's something else. When I went back to the motel and started looking through the notes on Lionel, I remembered he worked at the DMV. Rye, he could have forged records for your mother. It wasn't as difficult to push forms and paperwork through as it is now that so much is digitized."

"What are you saying?"

"If Melanie wanted to create a new identity for herself, she was well-positioned to do so."

"Why would she need to?" Rye asked. "It's not like when she left us you went out searching for her and demanding she come back."

"Rye, I don't think she got a new identity to leave us. I think when I met her, it was already in place."

Rye sat down on the edge of the coffee table. "But…why? What was she hiding from?"

"I think the question might be who was she hiding from," Hardy replied. "And later…was she hiding you, too?"

Rye felt a lump in her throat. "Dad? I miss you."

"Did I mention I'm calling from the road?"

22

WANDA AND FATHER PAUL WERE ON "AFTER-SUPPER"
terms. They had been newbies in town the same year
and had found a way to support each other when older
pastors hadn't been interested in socializing, or at least
in socializing without a spouse and kids. It involved a lot
of talking and laughing and bottles of wine.

NOW THEY WERE THE OLD-TIMERS.

Wanda sat outside Saint Joseph Church with a lovely
bottle of merlot. Given that the admin had promised
her a soloist for Pentecost, there was only one reason for
Wanda to see Father Paul after hours.

When she started going to meetings, she had decided
to avoid friendships that centered around alcohol. It
wasn't reasonable, and it wasn't sustainable, but it had
been a safety blanket for the first two months of her
sobriety. She had plenty of friends who did not abuse
alcohol, but she cut herself off from them because they
knew her best with a drink in her hand.

Tonight, she had to address herself in the rearview
mirror before knocking on Paul's door. "He's your friend.

You can tell him. Now, let's solve a murder." She grabbed a bottle of ginger beer for herself.

The priest himself came to the door, which meant Mrs. Walsh was gone for the day. When he opened it, his face was pre-wrinkled with compassion that transformed instantly into a huge smile.

Wanda laughed. "Expecting trouble?"

"Always! Illness, death, parish problem that can't wait until tomorrow, church on fire, you name it. As a matter of fact, you are trouble of a completely different kind."

"Don't quote John Lewis!"

"I didn't say 'good trouble.' You, Wanda, are more like temptation."

"Tell me you didn't put me in this morning's sermon?"

"No. I try to stay believable in my illustrations. Come on in." He stepped back and ushered her inside.

The entrance to the colonial-style rectory had an office to the left with a desk, a leather chair, and three comfortable green wingbacks for guests. Through the double doors on the far side of his office, there was a meeting room with a fireplace, a large oval table, and plenty of less comfortable chairs.

Wanda had spent considerable time in both of those rooms for private and group meetings. Tonight, Father Paul ushered her through the door into his apartment on the right. It had a living room with a big TV abutting the eat-in kitchen. There was a battered brown sofa, a scarred coffee table (probably both leftovers from the church fete), a beautiful, well-worn red Persian carpet, and another of those green wingback armchairs.

The effect was a little Christmas-all-year-round, which appealed to Wanda. She sat in the chair, unsure she'd be able to get up from the sofa with her modesty intact.

Father Paul descended into the sofa. She had made a good choice. "Not exactly a man cave, is it?" he asked.

"Not with Sister Boniface on the screen, nope."

He chuckled, probably having forgotten that he paused the episode rather than turning off the television. He turned it off now. "Sorry about that. It's not G. K. Chesterton, but neither is the current Father Brown, and I don't complain."

She smiled in agreement. "I come bearing a gift!" Wanda held up the wine. She needed to get this part over with quickly.

"I can never resist a gift. As evidence, the very chair you've chosen—a hotel ordered them in blue, and when they arrived in forest green, the company replaced them for free." He leaned forward conspiratorially. "We have fifteen here in the rectory, at least that many in various church members' homes, and an additional twenty—"

"—in the women's shelter and the warming space attached to the food pantry. I've seen them there," Wanda replied. "They're quite comfortable."

"Yes, they are. Two glasses?"

"Wine glass for you and a bottle opener for me."

He went to the kitchen and came back again, opened the two bottles, and poured before he spoke. "I hope your temperance does not mean you're taking medication for an ailment?"

"No. It means once or more a week I say a prayer for serenity, courage, and wisdom."

"Wonderful," Father Paul said. "You know I am no teetotaler, but ..."

"But, like everyone else, you knew I shouldn't drink. My favorite musician, my favorite funeral director, and my favorite nephew actually shared their opinions."

"Let's hear it for Tony, Luke, and Lance! And on behalf of all the clergy in town, our apologies."

She wrinkled her nose. "That obvious, huh?"

"When you were sad."

"And angry, and happy, and lonely, and…and if you were going to ask…" She showed him a rainbow-painted four-month chip. "You know these things have an Amazon thirty-day return policy? Talk about lack of faith."

"Or confidence that you'll be getting one for month five."

"You know, I sometimes think the sacrament of reconciliation makes Catholics sunnier."

He laughed. "This is a delightful merlot, and while I love the company, I expect you want to talk about the reason you've come—Luisa Suarez, who went by Martina?"

Wanda hid her surprise. "There's no rush, Paul. It's nice to have a chance to catch up."

"And we'll do that properly once you've solved this case," Father Paul replied stoutly.

Wanda was relieved by the change of conversation. As much as she wanted a chance to chat with her friend, time was of the essence. "Was she your parishioner?"

"Yes, although we didn't see her often on a Sunday—she worked, you know. Very busy. But after Father Bogdan rebaptized her…and then Josh Gagne, for good measure…"

"Two rebaptisms, but not from you?"

"I couldn't do that. She was baptized in body and spirit once. She could choose to receive a new name, and many people do, but baptism is not repeated. Both Bogdan and Josh must have felt comfortable doing it, and I had no legal or ecclesiastical right to stand in the way." He sighed sadly. "I wish now I'd said something. Maybe I could have spared her that horrible death if I'd convinced her to be honest about her past."

"Did she tell you in confession, or is there anything you could share that might help us find the person who killed her?" This could be a sensitive area, but Wanda was aware that asking directly was the only way to find out.

"I knew a lot about that young woman. She did not share in the confessional sense, but only in asking 'advice for a friend.'"

Wanda looked at him with surprise. "A loophole?"

"I trust you'll only tell this to those for whom it's critical to the investigation, but Luisa—for clarity's sake, I'll call her by her given name—seems to have been under suspicion for blackmail. She told me that she had a 'friend' who had been successful at it for a very long time, and that her friend was finding herself in hot water more and more frequently. There was never enough proof to convict."

"Blackmail?" Wanda asked. "That's a serious crime." She thought of how many of the clergy had seemed less than enthusiastic about Wanda's suggestion to have Martina at the service. How many of them might have been influenced by knowing about Martina's second line of work? "There's no doubt blackmail is a motive for murder, Paul."

He simply inclined his head. "Some of the things she talked about would be motive enough, Wanda, but I'm not sure you're asking the right question."

"And what is that?"

"Who else has been repenting recently?"

Wanda sat forward in her chair. "Do you know who killed her?"

"Rarely does a murderer walk into a confessional and share his or her crimes, especially since most people suspect priests are mandated reporters these days." He paused and took a thoughtful sip. "But they may come in asking forgiveness for 'doing unspeakable things,' or for 'witnessing terrible acts,' and I suppose that could suggest some…involvement."

"You can't tell me who, of course."

"I cannot," Father Paul said. "And I would not want to. I think I can share that I have received quite a few confessions from people who did not grieve her loss. That might speak to her using blackmail, but nothing more."

Wanda considered this. "Thank you, Paul. You've opened a couple doors for me to explore."

"Despite her past, I liked Luisa. Her life was not an easy one, even if she might have found a way to make far more money than she could use in a lifetime. Her sister's death was a crushing blow, you know. I don't believe she ever fully came to terms with that grief and loss." He studied Wanda intently, the glass resting on his knee. "I want her killer brought to justice, Wanda, and I trust you to do it."

No pressure there. "I'll be back soon to ply you with Scotch and a game of chess, but for now I leave you to Sister Boniface."

Paul gave her a hug that enfolded Wanda and made her feel loved and cared for. He held her longer than was necessary, and Wanda knew this was his way of apologizing for not having been as bold as Tony, Luke, and Lance about her drinking.

When he let her go, she put on her coat. "You'll keep me posted about when the funeral is?"

"Yes. It will be a week from the day the sheriff's department releases the body. I'll be sure Luke calls you."

"He got married, you know." Wanda didn't know why she'd blurted that out. She felt her cheeks redden.

"I heard that. I haven't met her yet. Irie Belafonte, yes? How are they doing now that they're back here?"

Wanda was embarrassed to admit she hadn't gone to see them. After she had received the postcard about Luke's wedding, she had put him and his new wife out of her mind. Well, maybe not completely out of it, but Wanda had set the information on a back burner to give herself time to adjust. Luke and Irie had now been back long enough that she was bordering on rude not having stopped by to congratulate her dear friend in person. "I need to get over for a visit. I've been so busy, I forgot they flew in a few days ago."

Paul squeezed her hand and gave Wanda a forgiving smile. "When you do, give them my best and tell Irie that Saint Joseph Church would love to welcome her."

"I will," Wanda promised. She'd have to make that call now, because if there was one person she knew with a firm grasp on promises, it was the man in front of her. And she owed him for so much more than just tonight.

23

WANDA'S NIGHT WASN'T OVER YET. WHEN SHE GOT OUT of the car, making her hundredth resolution since New Year's that she was going to clean it—recycle the seltzer cans, vacuum every last dog hair out of it, collect the various Tupperware containers separated from their lids—she saw a man at the door talking to Lance.

"Lance," she called. "Is everything all right?" As she moved closer, she recognized the visitor. "Bruce?"

"I'm sorry to come by so late. I'm sure you've already had a long day," Bruce replied. As a fellow pastor, he should know better than anyone that after nine was for emergencies only.

Wanda ushered Bruce into her office while Lance gratefully escaped upstairs. She didn't offer him coffee, even though she had observed that coffee really was a holier Baptist beverage than Welch's grape juice could ever be. "What's on your mind?" she asked.

"I talked to Josh this evening about the musical interfaith event you were proposing, and I got the feeling from my young colleague that you were making the rounds on your own particular expedition." He paused and studied her, but Wanda schooled her face into pastoral impassivity.

"Oh?"

"The rest of us are well aware of your investigations over the last year, and with a death taking place at one of our committee's events, we're in agreement that you must be looking into it."

"Oh, we are really hoping to have—"

"Perhaps that's true," Bruce interrupted. "But you were also snooping about Martina Suarez."

Wanda couldn't decide if she could come clean or if Bruce was fishing. She settled for a pleasantly bland smile. "Honestly, Bruce, since I was already visiting folks, it made sense to ask. I certainly wasn't expecting Josh to be so sensitive about the topic."

"How well do you know Josh?"

Wanda shrugged. "He's not my biggest fan. We don't exactly grab lunch after church meetings."

"I thought as much. Josh's background…well, his father and grandfather are well-known evangelists."

"Really?" That might explain why he was so rude to her. Evangelist preachers weren't well-known for their open-minded politics. She had never seen him be outright rude to the other women in the group—not that he went out of his way to chat with them—but he wasn't nearly as hostile toward them as he was with Wanda.

"They travel as speakers for events. He mentioned that his grandfather used to have a public access show, and his father was on it for years when Josh was young. Now, his parents and his brother lead inspirational gatherings to renew the faith of small churches and convert non-Christians, as well as offer workshops on church evangelism and church growth. Not Baptist. Their circuit is more independent churches."

"Why isn't Josh part of the family business?"

"He was thrown out. I don't know why or exactly when." Bruce picked up one of Wink's squeaky toys—a well-chewed bunny carrying a cross that one of Wanda's more sacrilegious friends had purchased—from the corner of her desk. He studied it for a moment before setting it gently back down. "Now he's an ordinary pastor of an ordinary church. It seems like the best thing in the world to me, but his sights are set higher. I suspect he would like to prove himself to his family with some extraordinary church growth."

"Whatever he did can't be too terrible," Wanda said. "He passed his background checks."

"You and I both know that conservative churches have much different expectations about behavior." Bruce shook his head. "I know he hoped Martina Suarez was going to be part of his rise to prominence. He plays guitar and keyboard but is nothing special. As we all know, Martina *was* special. And that's the current recipe for success in evangelism—male speaker with a female singer."

Wanda thought of Josh approaching Nicole and felt an inadvertent shiver. "What happened?"

"He told me that Martina left the church the minute he brought it up. Wouldn't even clean for them anymore—nothing."

"Given his situation with his family, that makes me suspicious. Do you think he propositioned her? Made some sort of unwelcome advance?"

Bruce shook his head. "Absolutely not. He wouldn't do anything to compromise his plan."

"Many people are brought down by those sorts of indiscretions. It could have been a moment of weakness—"

"No. Not Josh," Bruce said firmly. "If you knew him like I do, you'd know his church means everything to him."

Wanda tried to think of a single warm, fuzzy thing Josh might have said about his congregation and came up blank. "If you say so."

Bruce stood stiffly. "I'm just asking you to cut him some slack. He's had a tough time of it, and he could use our support."

"I'll do my best," Wanda said. She remembered the sanctimonious tone Josh had used when he'd told Wanda he prayed for her and resisted rolling her eyes.

Bruce slipped into his jacket and shook her hand. He might not be evangelical, but he was old-school. "I appreciate you seeing me so late."

"Next time you come by, I'll brew a whole pot of coffee, and we can sit down and chat."

He smiled. "That would be nice, Wanda. Luckily, tonight, my lovely wife will have our bedtime coffee ready when I get home so we can unwind together."

"Decaf, I presume?"

Bruce smiled. "Sacrilege! I would never!"

Wanda was laughing as she let him out the door.

24

IN THE MORNING, SHE STOPPED AT HARVEY'S FOR A BAG of croissants. The honeymooners had returned from Jamaica a week earlier, and Wanda had been performing avoidance tasks right up until she got into the car. Her coat closet had never looked so organized...the cabinet under the sink in the bathroom...the garden shed. Of course, when she wasn't procrasti-cleaning, she was arguing with herself that it was too early to visit.

Luke would have a backlog of paperwork from Ian Stuchell of the MacTavish Home in Lowell, who handled all the legal work and coordination of services while Luke was gone. They would also be unpacking Irie's things. Wanda considered it and discovered that, no, that thought didn't upset her. Good.

She guessed Irie Belafonte was "she," although the name could be either gender. Wanda had checked. Jamaican, maybe meaning "peace and harmony," maybe "positive and powerful," maybe Rastafarian, but also could be Hawaiian or Japanese. Baby name sites were strange. Wanda had looked up everything about the first name because she did not want to do an internet search on the woman herself. That would feel invasive and probably be inadequate, if Wanda's own online profile was any clue.

She arrived on autopilot and hopped out of the car quickly so no one could accuse her of lurking. One or both of them must have been looking out the window. Luke was out the door of the cottage and enveloping her in a huge hug.

Wanda hugged him back. She burst out, "I'm so happy!" and knew it was true. She let him lead her to the front door, where Irie was wiping her hands on a dishcloth. Irie held out her hand, a gesture accompanied by the soft jangling of her bracelets. She offered Wanda a tentative smile.

Wanda opened her arms. "May I?"

The smile bloomed, and Irie radiated warmth. She enveloped Wanda in a generous embrace.

"Welcome," Wanda said. "I'm so happy to meet you."

Irie looked her up and down, not with judgment, but as if she were memorizing the details of Wanda's face and form. "I am the happy one," Irie replied, her accented English sweet, with a hint of laughter beneath. She stepped back to usher Wanda inside. "Luke has told me so much about you. I hardly believed some of his stories, but now that I meet you I see he was telling me the truth. I can already tell you are a woman of great conviction in a petite package."

Wanda had never been called petite in her life— shorty, half-pint, and even pocket-sized had all made the rounds, but never the more genteel petite—and it endeared Irie to her immediately.

Not much had changed at Luke's, but the home seemed cozier. They had moved the table from the cramped dining room into the kitchen, where it was pushed beneath the window. Dishes still sat by each chair, which explained how Luke had spotted her so quickly. On the shelves that lined the hall through to the living room, Wanda saw a new bowl of shells and several herbs in colorful pots that warmed the space.

Wanda held up her bag. "I'm not much of a cook, but I hope you'll consider this an introduction to Harvey's, the best bakery in Massachusetts, and probably New Hampshire and Vermont, as well."

Irie whisked out three clean plates. Three cups of coffee followed close behind. Wanda noted the bag of beans Irie had left out on the counter. Jamaican Blue Mountain. She had always wanted to try it. She took a sip and sighed with delight as Irie tore open the white bag and took a pain au chocolat with relish.

"Delicious…" and "I love this…" came out of their mouths simultaneously, and Luke laughed.

"This croissant is so good, and you can see I love my croissants," Irie replied. She was maybe an inch under Luke's six feet, round and beautiful. There was a little gray in her box braids, several ear piercings with hoops, a collection of beaded bracelets, and a small silver cross.

"This is just a small gift to welcome you to town. Luke has been one of my dearest friends for years now, and it makes me so happy to see you two together."

Luke was silent, but those long Italian eyelashes were wet. He had unconsciously reached out to hold onto Irie's hand when they'd sat down. He gave it a squeeze now.

Wanda smiled at him, then noticed Irie wore the widest gold wedding ring Wanda had ever seen.

"Perhaps a little much," said Irie, watching Wanda's eyes rest on it.

"It's absolutely perfect," Wanda replied honestly. Luke held out his hand so she could admire his, made of the same bright gold, but slimmer.

"I wanted something I wouldn't need to take off when I work," he told her.

Wanda could see the ring had something engraved around the edge, though not what.

He slid the ring off and handed it to her to examine. "Out of many, one people," she read, before handing it back to him. He slid it back on, smiling at his new wife as he did so.

"You know I've had a winter place in Jamaica for over a decade, and when I first went down there on vacation, it felt like…like my heart had found its true home," Luke told Wanda. He looked down at his ring, then at Irie. "Irie and I met about five years ago when I was able to stay for a few months. We were friends for a long time after that. Her family welcomed me—her community—and then I felt…"

"Like you had come home," Wanda supplied. "But to a person, instead of a place."

Luke looked at her. "Exactly."

"You must have felt this way, to understand so well," Irie said.

"Not with either of my ex-husbands, no," Wanda replied with a laugh.

"With Lance," Luke said. It was not a question.

Wanda smiled. "In just a few months, my nephew has made me feel more at home than I have my whole life."

They demolished the pastries as they chatted, until Wanda wanted to take her belt out a notch. They finally moved to the sofa. Wanda looked out at the small garden where families often went to sit and be quiet.

Distracted, she just missed squashing a large Maine Coon cat, who sat up as she landed on his paw.

Luke came over and scooped the cat up. "That's our new friend, Bembe. He's ten and eats a lot and talks even more. No one would adopt him, so Florence asked me if we would take him home."

Wanda was suddenly grateful that she wasn't as good friends with the supervisor at the SPCA as Luke was. A soft touch, she would have adopted every unwanted pet Florence Baine sent her way.

"If I know anything, you and Rye are investigating the murder of Martina Suarez," Luke said without further preamble.

Wanda was surprised for a moment, before realizing that of course he would know. The woman's body was in his morgue. "We did find her."

Irie broke in. "I am so sorry. I am sure that was, and is, very hard."

"Yes, it is. Thank you. My friend and I—"

"—have solved three murders. Luke told me," Irie said solemnly.

"And I have a clue for you," Luke said proudly. It was a dramatic shift from the way he'd felt last spring when she and Rye investigated Niels Pond's murder, but Wanda would take information where she could get it.

"I'm all ears."

"The body was released to me yesterday. The coroner is done with it. They haven't yet found someone to release the body to when the investigation is finished," Luke said. "It would be a kindness if you could extend your investigation to see if there is anyone who may want to witness her burial."

Wanda let that sink in, knowing how right it was, how right he always was in his tender care for those who had died. And he would pay for everything himself. Always. She nodded. "We'll do our best."

"The coroner's report says the angle of the blade was overhanded, and that it's suspected the blow came from a person the same height or shorter than the victim. She was almost fivefoot ten, so that could be many people. The blade was at least ten inches long and serrated." Luke paused. "There was no sign of struggle. Is that helpful?"

Wanda was thoughtful. "You're sure it was serrated?"

"Yes, of course. Everything is documented."

"The knife I saw next to the body was a chef's knife from the kitchen," Wanda said. "The blade was smooth."

Luke shook his head. "Then it wasn't the murder weapon."

"The murderer took the real knife and left that one behind," Wanda said slowly. "That means the murder could have been premeditated after all."

"Or someone left a bread knife out on the table," Irie pointed out. "The murderer could have used that and then taken it away."

"In either scenario, the police don't have the murder weapon." It irked Wanda that Ryan hadn't shared that detail with her, although she knew he was right not to. It would be a key piece of information in an interrogation of a suspect.

"If we were playing a game of Clue, would I have given you the last piece of the puzzle?" Luke asked hopefully.

"I wish," Wanda replied. "This case is more complicated than 'in the church with a missing knife,' but I do appreciate the two-from-the-end piece of the puzzle." She stood, and Irie joined her, giving Wanda another hug before escorting her to get her jacket. As

Irie opened the door, Bembe dashed out between their legs, and Irie quickly sprinted after him.

Luke watched as his wife expertly cornered the cat and picked him up. He looked down as Wanda pulled something from her pocket.

"This is my four-month chip," she said. "I want you to have it."

"I couldn't—"

"Of course you could. Someone just reminded me that I'm going to get a five-month chip very soon. I couldn't have started down this road without your tough love," Wanda said. "You took a big risk telling me I had a problem, and it might have ended our friendship."

"But it didn't."

"No, it didn't," Wanda replied. "Not even a secret wedding could do that." She patted him on the shoulder as he choked on a cough. Wanda turned as she started down the steps. "But maybe let's keep the big reveals to a minimum, for a few months at least?"

"I'll make that promise if you do."

25

RYE WAS JUST FINISHING UP WITH TWO JUNIORS WHO had gotten into a fight during PE when the office administrator, Sophie, called her.

"Yes?" Rye asked, her gaze focused on the remediation plan they were reviewing. This was the third time these cousins had been in her office in a month, and calls to their families had only served to show Rye how deep the animosity went. She didn't want to be refereeing extended family drama at school, but she also couldn't have them whipping basketballs at each other's heads and following up with fists while in class.

"Sorry to bother you, but the sheriff is here to see you."

Rye rubbed her temples. "Okay. I'll be done in a minute." She hung up with a sigh.

"Oooh, Ms. Rye is in trouble!" Carrie Owens sang.

"The police are here to pick you up?" Carrie's cousin Mary asked. "Sounds like you might need this more than we do." She tossed the remediation plan on the desk.

"I need you both to sign that, and have your parents sign it, too," Rye said. "And remember I have a call with them next week, so if they haven't heard anything about this, I'm going to know."

"Unless you're in jail," Carrie said. She stood up and grabbed her bag, bumping her cousin.

"Don't touch me!" Mary growled back, giving Carrie a shove.

It probably would have broken out into another fight, but Ryan picked that moment to open the door. Rye had to admit he cut a commanding figure, and his glare was enough to send the girls grumbling to class.

"What an unexpected treat." She sat back down behind her desk.

He closed the door. "I left you four messages, Rye."

"And I'm at work. I've had meetings nonstop all morning. I was planning to call you back on my lunch break in half an hour."

"How many times have you been to the police station?"

"Ever, or this week?"

"You know you need to come in to sign a witness statement for the mugging."

"Have you found the person who ran off with Elena's purse?"

"Not yet."

"Did she tell you anything about the person who confronted her in the parking lot? Her second threatening experience in as many weeks?" Rye rested her chin in her hand.

"Also no, if you mean the one that she did not report and that you did not report and that I would know nothing about if Jaz Malone hadn't been in that book club of yours?"

Rye gestured to the piles of papers on her desk. "Well, I didn't see much in either case, and I'm buried in work right now. I'm sorry it wasn't my top priority, but at least Elena must have given you something to go on?"

"Rye, you are giving me a migraine."

"I didn't do anything!"

He sighed. "Exactly. I shouldn't be chasing you down for a signature. That's not in my job description."

"So why are you here then?"

"Because I know if I sent anyone else, you'd use your witchy powers of distraction, and they would leave your office more befuddled than when they entered." Ryan pulled out a stack of papers. "So I brought the station to you." He dropped them on her desk and pulled a pen out of the cup on her desk.

"Fine." Rye was fully aware her tone bordered on whining. "But the Uber Eats guy just arrived, and I'm going to grab my lunch first."

Ryan growled. "I swear to God, if you aren't back here in sixty seconds—"

She tossed him an all-white Rubik's cube a student had gotten her as a gift.

"What's the point of this thing?" she heard him grumble as she left the office.

She smiled at her admin. "Lunch time! I got you an egg salad sandwich. I hope that's okay."

Sophie's face lit up. "I brought a peanut butter and jelly I made from two ends of a loaf of bread and an apple that has traveled between here and my house three times already. You are an angel."

Rye grinned and walked out to pick up her food. The drivers usually swung into the circle in front of the building, and Rye always tried to beat them out of their car.

One of her former students was dropping off today. "Hey, Ms. Rye! Long time, no see."

"Hey, Max!" She gave him a quick hug. "How's it going?"

He smiled. "Dash and I just got an apartment downtown. It's pretty nice. Pet-friendly, so Tikka Meowsala is settling in."

It was hard not to smile when a six-foot-five former high school linebacker whipped out a picture of his beloved orange tabby, but Rye managed a straight face. "That's wonderful!"

He leaned in. "I don't want to be a snitch, but I came in through the back parking lot—just force of habit, you know—and I'm pretty sure some guys are smoking or something."

"By the tech wing?" That was the usual spot. School cameras didn't have a great shot of the mechanic's doors, but the teachers over there were usually on top of it.

"No, by the community garden. Near the playground. That's the only reason I mentioned it. I don't want those little kids breathing that stuff in."

The school had a small daycare center and had since Rye was a student. Teenage parents could drop their children there for free during the school day, and, in exchange, they worked a few two-hour shifts a week.

"I'll go check it out. Thanks, Max. It was good to see you. Don't be a stranger!"

"I won't."

Rye tucked her lunch by the door and headed around to check out the situation. She would have to circle back with security to make sure they prioritized fixing the cameras over here. Someone had smashed them last week. As she rounded the corner, she wondered if the culprits were the same people she saw right now—not smoking, but spray-painting the side of the school.

The man closest to Rye—and it was definitely not a student, she could tell that by now—had painted a huge swastika over the door leading to the math wing. The other was working the garden boxes over with a crowbar, though to what purpose, Rye couldn't imagine, since it was the middle of winter and no offending vegetables could be seen.

She hadn't even had a chance to speak when the second man saw her and ran toward her, swinging the crowbar and yelling obscenities. Rye disarmed him with almost embarrassing ease and had him on the ground as the second man advanced on her. His head was shaved. Under his jacket, he wore a crisp polo that had gotten smudged with paint. She let him get close enough to try to grab her, then ducked under and wrapped his arm painfully behind his back. The first attacker started to stand when Ryan strode around the corner, furious.

He stopped, assessed the situation, and pulled out his handcuffs while calling the incident in. On spotting the uniform, Crowbar popped up and started to run. Rye let go of Spray Paint, twisting his wrist hard once more and shoving him toward Ryan before taking off after the escapee.

He was fast, but her father had been relentless about cardio training since she moved back to town, and Rye was in the best shape of her life. She took a flying leap and tackled him as he reached the street, slamming her knee into the concrete hard enough to bring tears to her eyes. She sat on him until the first squad car pulled up a minute later and Jaz and Tyler got out to take him into custody.

"She's been pinching me!" the guy protested as they tried to load him into the car.

"I have not!" Rye exclaimed, although she had, in fact, been giving him painful little digs.

He lifted up his sleeve to show a red mark where her nails had broken skin. "See? I'm pressing charges!"

"Against me?" Rye exclaimed, on her feet and in his face. "After you defaced school property and attacked me, completely unprovoked?"

He sneered at her, then spit at Jaz, who had taken his arm and was steering him into the back seat. "Get your dirty hands off of me!"

Rye lost it. She grabbed the front of his shirt. He was only saved from a punch to the face by Tyler pulling her off of him.

"Rye! What do you think you're doing?" For once, Tyler's face was devoid of its golden retriever smile.

"You can't assault a man in police custody." Jaz's eyes bore into Rye. The pain in them was evident.

Ryan came up behind her. "I need you to follow Officer Malone and Officer Phennen back to the station so I can take your statement . . . *all* of your statements."

"But my phone is inside." Rye's knee was also in agony, and she thought longingly of her tuna sub.

"You should have thought of that before confronting two assailants on your own." Ryan stalked off.

Rye sighed. "My license is in my office, too. And my keys." She called after Ryan. "Can you make sure Sophie gets her lunch?"

He waved a hand to acknowledge he'd at least heard her. Rye walked around to the passenger door to find Tyler already standing there.

"You're riding in back today," he said. To his credit, he at least appeared to be sorry about that.

"Don't make me handcuff you," Jaz said as she slid into the driver's seat.

Rye glanced at the man beside her, who glared sullenly back. "No promises."

26

At Jaz and Tyler's insistence, Rye had to wait in the interrogation room for Ryan to get back to the station before she could debrief. She knew parents had been notified in triplicate—via phone, text, and email—that there had been an incident, but Rye's only channel to this news was an intern popping in to give her limited updates.

After a phone call to Hardy's voicemail to let him know what had happened, she'd been left alone in the chilly room. Her initial gratitude that her friends hadn't handcuffed her to the table to teach her a lesson wore off, and Rye got very bored. Tyler had assured her the chance of any charges being pressed was minimal, but Jaz made it clear that vigilante justice was not going to be tolerated on her watch. Apparently, that included pinching *and* threats to cowardly bullies.

After two hours in an empty room, Rye had absorbed the lesson. She neither wanted to make this place part of her normal routine nor wished to lose her job over something as minor as getting in the last word.

Not that she regretted anything. In fact, she spent the first hour wishing she had pummeled both men into the ground. She knew that since they hadn't been armed, charges against them would be minor—defacing public property, maybe.

She spent the second hour of her confinement wishing she hadn't skipped breakfast. Her blood sugar drove her from hangry to lethargic. When Jaz finally came in and took a witness statement for the mugging, Elena's confrontation, and the morning's altercation and said she would process them and give them to Ryan to review and sign, Rye didn't resist.

She was dozing on the metal table when Ryan came in to escort her to his office. In her dream, she watched her mother smuggling large unwieldy bundles—bodies, Rye realized—into the back of a pickup truck. Rye rode with her for miles, neither of them speaking, until a hand shaking her shoulder woke her up.

Rye blinked back tears. She hadn't dreamed of her mother for years, had forgotten that somewhere in her memory were the contours of Melanie's face, the shape of her hands on a steering wheel. She wiped her eyes quickly and followed Ryan into the relative warmth of his office. Jaz handed her a cup of tea as she passed—not hot water from the station, but spicy chai from the shop Jaz's husband owned down the street. Rye stopped and gave the woman a brief, tight squeeze and a whispered "sorry" against her ear. Jaz smiled. A knot that had formed in Rye's chest loosened.

Rye settled into her now customary seat across from the sheriff and took a sip of her tea. She expected a barrage of anger, a diatribe on everything she had done wrong this morning. Instead, he leaned back in his chair and rubbed his eyes. "How are you doing?"

Ryan looked like hell. He had dark circles under his eyes, and his skin was pale. His stubble was coming in peppered with gray, a reminder that this man wasn't the youthful deputy who had antagonized her in high school. Or whom she had antagonized—her memory was fuzzy on the details.

"I've been better," she replied. "How are my kids?"

"You haven't checked your phone?"

"I left it at school, remember? Aside from a call to my dad when I got here, I haven't heard anything."

"There was video taken." Ryan handed her his phone. "Many videos, in fact."

In the first, she could see a few people using spray paint to make art over the racist graffiti. They had hoods and masks on, but Rye knew who they were—Thiago Ramos, Jamaal Joshuason, and Rey Boulanger—all gifted artists who frequently ended up in her office. They were good kids, and Rye was working to help their impulses catch up with their intentions. There was no way she would admit to knowing their identities if anyone asked.

In front of them, what seemed like the entire student population was yelling and holding up signs. She saw everything from "Black Lives Matter" to "F&*% White Supremacy." Rye's gaze was immediately drawn to that second sign, held up by Lance, curse-censored and all. She remembered a conversation she'd had with him last month about why some protesters chose to do that— local news stations had strict rules about profanity. Her favorite sign was drawn by a senior, Simone Jackson. It read, "We are ~~SCARED~~ SACRED!"

"They're protesting?" Rye checked the hashtag attached to the video to see more photos and posts from her students.

"Your students are furious," Ryan replied. "First the concert protest, now this."

"I can't believe it." Rye handed Ryan back his phone. "I thought we'd be fending off parental complaints while finding a way to put more security in the budget."

"Why do they need more security? They have you." Ryan handed her his phone again. This time it was a video of her tackling the perpetrator. "One of the paras was coming back from lunch and caught the whole thing. She sent it out to the entire school—parents, students, staff—everyone has seen it. I wouldn't be surprised if you're the star of the news cycle."

"That's ridiculous. The kids should be front and center. I can't believe they've organized a protest." Rye put the phone down. "I'm so proud of them."

"I guess they're trying to live up to your example."

Rye felt a shiver run down her spine. "Is this your way of telling me that I set a bad example for my students by approaching those men?"

"I don't have to say it. You just did."

"I thought it was going to be a couple of kids smoking. I was planning to write them up and send them back to class!"

"And when you realized that wasn't the situation, why didn't you come get me?" Ryan asked. "I was in your office, remember?"

"I had about five seconds between assessing the situation and the first attack. Besides, my dad has been training me in hand-to-hand combat since I was nine years old. My whole life, I've been surrounded by people who would step in and do what I did without hesitation."

"So why didn't you go to the academy?" Ryan asked. "If you had, this would be a very different conversation."

"I did," Rye said. "I just...I didn't graduate."

Ryan leaned back in his chair, surprise spreading across his face. "Why not? You're certainly smart enough. I'd have thought you would be at the top of your class."

"Careful, Ryan. That was almost a compliment."

"It was meant to be."

Rye sat with that for a minute. "I didn't like the culture. My dad, the officers here in town that I grew up with—it was different." She shook her head. "I got ulcers from the anxiety. I couldn't sleep." Rye sipped her tea. "I was so messed up I ended up dating an addict, and I didn't even notice."

"She's the one who died?"

"How did you know about that?"

"Hardy talked about you all the time. When she was convicted for vehicular homicide, I think I was the only person he could tell about it."

"Because of your mom," Rye said. It wasn't a question. When Ryan had run for sheriff after Hardy retired, it had come out that Ryan's mother had been a drug addict, and he and Tyler had lived with her in their car for a year during their childhood. After she died of an overdose when Ryan was seventeen, he had taken care of his brother outside of the foster care system. Hardy's support had won people over on Ryan's behalf, and although he wasn't as personable as Hardy Rye had been, he had become well-liked for his commitment to the community.

"Hardy never told me you went to the academy," Ryan said.

"He doesn't know. I told him I took a gap year before I went to Rice."

"Why not? He would have been proud of y following in his footsteps."

"But I didn't, did I? I became a teacher

Ryan tipped his head in acknowledgment. "A teacher who kicked some serious butt today—not that I in any way condone your actions."

"Sure." Rye's head hurt. She wanted to sleep, although she knew what she actually needed was food. She didn't like being around other people when she was like this. Low blood sugar made her maudlin.

"You would have been an asset to this department if you'd followed through with your education," Ryan said. "But don't forget for one minute that people are watching. Those students are paying attention, and if you're reckless, even for a good cause, don't be surprised when they act that way too."

"Maybe I should encourage them," Rye replied.

"I think that's your father's plan. I hear he's been training up a justice-minded army of tweens in his back garden."

"Not all of us are that young." Rye looked him over critically. "You could stand to join us for a few sessions. You might like it."

"Spar against you? No, thank you. You fight dirty."

"I do not!"

He slid photos across his desk of a couple of bruises her fingers had left on Crowbar's back. "Pinching? Really, Rye?"

"My father taught me to use every advantage I had," she countered.

27

WANDA SAT IN HER OFFICE STARING AT THE DESK. She had not fully absorbed the news she had heard about the high school, first from Lance and later from the media. It wasn't the only time something like this had happened. The synagogue had been targeted a month before, and she knew Imam Abbas got a sickening number of threats weekly.

Stone Ridge was not immune to the nationally rising number of racial incidents. Wanda wondered whether Rye's actions today would make a difference to the atmosphere, positively or negatively. She sent a silent thanks to Julian of Norwich, who'd said, 'All will be well, all manner of things will be well.'

Wanda knew she needed to focus on work, which she had let slide too much, given the season. On her desk was a sermon outline for the second Sunday in Lent. It was hard to top the devil's temptation of Jesus. She would play with the Hebrew Bible story of Abram married to menopausal Sarai. She would take the idea of him being told he would have descendants like the stars in the sky and both of them receiving new names. She figured everyone in the pews would know what wanting a new name or a fresh start felt like.

Of course, it had nothing to do with Luisa Suarez.

There was also a request for a wedding at the church sitting in front of her. The couple's names: Lara Alesci and Bellona Pond. Wanda looked down at the note Lisa had scribbled on a sticky note: 'Will bring their own officiant.'

Bellona Pond was a pain in the … Wanda had finally gotten over the request that she not officiate at the funeral for Bellona's husband, Niels, last year, but really? Wanda knew Bellona was not religious, but Lara was a member of the church and almost always in the pews on Sunday. The women had kept their relationship quiet for a long time, but when Lara told Wanda that Leslie and her brothers were on board with the women making it official, Wanda had been thrilled. She was less thrilled about this second request to vacate her own church for Bellona Pond's sake.

In fact, the request ticked her off. Wanda was tempted to tell them to take their officiant and go find a lovely garden if they didn't want to use the church *and* the pastor who had bent over backward to help them through a tough time. Instead, Wanda approved the request.

Lisa tapped on the door and poked her head in. "Do you want fresh coffee and scones?"

Wanda perked up at the appearance of her very own angel. "You have no idea!"

Hardy was in the outer office putting cream and sugar in his coffee and arranging his homemade scones on a plate.

Lisa had her coat on. "I'm taking Lily to the library for Paws to Read. She loves getting to snuggle with the therapy dogs they bring in."

"You know, you could have a dog of your very own," Wanda suggested. "Lance and I are taking care of—"

"You think I'm going to be the one to pry that dog out of Lance's embrace?" Lisa laughed. "Besides, an extra mouth to feed with medical bills to boot. No, thank you!"

As Lisa left, Wanda could hear the organ opening up all the way from the sanctuary. Some portentous music for the Lenten season. Tony would balance it with something beautiful and light on the piano.

Hardy was holding up a coffee cup toward her. She could see he had cautiously turned off and unplugged the pot. Always safe.

"Yes, please," she said. He knew how she liked her coffee—a splash of milk and a packet of stevia.

Hardy followed her into the office and sat down in his favorite spot, the chair next to the window. "I need some help."

She started to poke gentle fun, but one look at his face told her it was not appropriate. Wanda decided to take a bite of her scone and let him continue on his own.

"I'm angry with Rye."

Wanda waited.

"What she did this morning—"

"What you've trained her to do?"

Hardy looked up in surprise at her very unpastoral response. So much for remaining professional and allowing him to share his feelings without judgment.

"You're looking at me like someone who didn't see you and your daughter have a target-shooting contest last weekend. Or didn't experience, with the bruises to prove it, what it feels like to be on the receiving end of your defense training," Wanda continued. She had planned to be neutral. It was not going well.

"A man attacked her with a crowbar!"

"I'm not trying to joke about what you're feeling, Hardy, but aren't you a little proud of her?"

"Of course I am! Did you see that video?"

"I did. And do you know what I saw?" Wanda paused until she was sure she had his full attention. "I saw my friend witnessing a hate crime and having zero tolerance for it. She possessed the skills necessary to intercede, and, honestly, those men didn't give her a choice about how to handle it. They attacked her, and she responded with force, just like you taught her to do." Wanda shook her head. "I wish it hadn't happened, but since it did, I'm proud of Rye. She put herself between those bullies and students like Lance, and Nicole, and Leslie."

Hardy leaned forward and rested his face in his hands. "I hadn't thought about it like that." After a moment, he continued softly, "I just didn't realize how scared I would be, seeing her threatened like that."

Wanda stood and went to give him a hug, propriety be damned. He leaned into her, arms wrapped tight around her waist.

Eventually, Hardy pulled back and found the box of tissues to blow his nose. Wanda grabbed her own wad of Kleenex and dropped into the chair beside him.

They both sat there silently, reclaiming their public faces.

"I just want her to be safe." Hardy looked at Wanda, and she could see a shadow of the young man who had been left alone with a heartbroken daughter to raise.

"That's the one thing we're never promised with the people we love," Wanda replied. "We love them despite that, because the alternative is to be alone."

"I've tried being alone," Hardy said with a wan smile. "I didn't like it."

"No. You're built for big love," Wanda agreed.

He looked at her, his face as open as she'd ever seen it, as though she had mentioned something that had always existed in his heart but he'd been too busy to recognize.

"I would have had ten kids if the option had been open to me," he said.

Wanda smiled. "Me, too. A house chock full of chaos, mess everywhere I looked."

"A joyous noise." Hardy stood up and reached out a hand to pull Wanda to her feet. "A wild rumpus."

They were standing close enough for Wanda to see the freckles under his eyes. Hardy pulled her closer and kissed her on the cheek, his nose pressing against her skin for a moment longer than his lips did. Then he hugged her again, less desperately this time, his hands warm on the small of her back. Wanda leaned into him with a sigh and rested the same cheek against his chest. She could feel his heart beating, the tempo quick, though the circles he gently traced on her back were slow, measured.

When they both pulled away, Hardy pushed a strand of hair behind her ear, carefully avoiding her hearing aid. "Thanks for listening," he said. "I'm going home to hug my daughter."

Wanda watched him go. She went back to her desk, to the scone and the cooled coffee. She might have stayed staring at them a lot longer, but her phone buzzed with a text from Lance that he had arrived to pick her up.

She wrapped a second scone in a napkin for Lance and put it in her bag, then made sure to take the rest of the treats down to the sanctuary. Her pastry quotient for the day was used up. She waved and pointed at the plate she was leaving for Tony, although he was deep in rehearsing Nicole in "I Told Jesus It Would Be Alright if He Changed My Name" with Roberta Flack stylings. That would put some energy into this week's scripture. Yes, everyone could use a new name at some point.

LANCE WAS WAITING FOR HER IN THE CAR. HE BEAMED. "I'm right on time! And I saw Hardy on the way out. He said he brought homemade scones." He plucked the napkin out of her outstretched hand through the window.

"Wanda!" It was Elena Mendoza. She had just pulled into the church parking lot.

"Hi, Elena. What's up?" Wanda sincerely hoped it was nothing important.

"Have you seen Hardy?" Without waiting for an answer, she went on, "They found the baby from his Mardi Gras king cake in Martina's apron pocket!"

"What?"

"It has Hardy's fingerprints on it." Elena was practically vibrating as she shared this news. "I thought you ought to know. I mean, it's all over the news—not the part about it being from his cake, but no one else brought one, so it must be!"

"It's on the news? About the fingerprints?"

"Well, it has to have them, doesn't it? And I know you and Rye are investigating, but I wasn't sure if you'd heard, so I came right over. I didn't want to tell Rye. I know how close she and her father are."

She had a feeling Elena wanted to talk longer, but Wanda didn't have it in her. "Thank you for letting me know. When I get home, I'll give Rye a call and make sure she's okay."

She wasn't sure what else to say. Was Elena implying Hardy had something to do with Martina's death? Just because of a plastic baby?

"Hey, Aunt Wanda? I have to get home to meet Leslie and Nicole," Lance called from inside the car.

Elena peered in at him and waved. "I'll let you get going then," she said, stepping back from Wanda's car.

Wanda wished her a pleasant evening and slid into the passenger's seat, allowing Lance to take them home. "Nicole is practicing with Tony right now for the choir tonight," she said after a moment's thought.

"And Leslie's having dinner with her brothers. I could just tell you needed an out."

Wanda looked over at her nephew. "You are a gem."

"I know."

"Are you going to ask for a big favor now?" Wanda was only half joking.

"No, that was a freebie. When I'm buttering you up, you'll know it."

Wanda just shook her head and leaned back, closing her eyes. She could still feel the comforting beat of Hardy's heart and the warmth on her back where his hand had been. She needed to call him, and Rye, to make sure everything was okay. She wished she could freeze time instead and just enjoy something good for a while.

28

HARDY WASN'T WAITING IN THE PARKING LOT. MUCH as Rye had been dreading her father's tirade, she had been expecting him. Ryan had told her that he was waiting. She stood behind the police station scanning for his car, knowing her own vehicle, wallet, and phone were still at school. She turned to head back up the stairs to call a cab and bumped into Ryan coming down.

"Where's your dad?" He glanced around as though Hardy might jump out from behind a bush at any moment.

"Your guess is as good as mine. I'm still minus a phone."

"Need a ride?"

"Depends. Are you going to make me sit in the back?"

"Only if you insist I run the sirens."

Rye smiled. "That was one time. And I'm pretty sure you liked it." Rye allowed Ryan to lead the way to his car. The inside was immaculate. What she wouldn't give for a ride with Tyler and Jaz right now. They always kept snacks in the glove box.

"You were my boss's daughter. I wasn't given much choice in the matter."

"Are you kidding?" Rye replied. "My dad never let me run the siren."

"I didn't let you run the siren either," he said, as he pulled out into traffic. "I pressed the button for three seconds."

"Good memory."

"I used to do it for Tyler back in the day," Ryan said, slowing at the crosswalk. They watched as a woman and her dog meandered across the street.

Rye's thoughts flew back to a few weeks before her high school graduation. Ryan, new on the force, had picked her up from a party. She hadn't been drinking that night, but the friend who drove her was, and Rye hadn't been able to find the girl's keys. Rye had tried to call her dad at home, but no one had picked up. The only other guess for where to find him was the station, but he hadn't been on duty. Ryan had answered and, to his credit, had come to get her immediately.

Of course, he'd done so with sirens blaring and lights flashing, scaring everyone but Rye into fleeing the scene. It hadn't made her popular for the rest of senior year, but Rye had been beyond caring at that point. She was already counting the days until her escape.

That night, though, they'd had fun. Ryan had graduated from the academy the year before, and there was still a wildness in him that had disappeared during his years under Hardy Rye's mentorship. Of course, even then, to Ryan, "wild" meant taking the cruiser through the drive-through with his boss's daughter in the front seat and running the siren briefly. And, in hindsight, maybe it had been.

For a month or so after that, she and Ryan had enjoyed a friendship based less on animosity and more on shared interests. They had bumped into each other at the shooting range twice, and Hardy had even allowed her to join the new police recruits on a long run. She wasn't sure, then or now, whether he had meant it as a punishment or prize.

It wasn't until a few days before she left town that she had ruined everything. Rye had been helping out at the farmer's market, selling raffle tickets for the sheriff's department. She had made an offhand joke about Tyler's lackluster grades that had shifted her friendship with Ryan completely.

"Rye? Earth to Rye?"

Rye shook her head and sat up. She had…phased out? Dozed off? She hadn't noticed that they'd arrived in the school's staff parking lot. She rubbed her eyes and stretched. "Sorry about that."

"You were snoring," Ryan said as he turned off the car.

"I don't snore."

"You were." He pulled out his phone and held it up. He had taken a video of her, and sure enough, little snores.

Rye blushed. "Well…sorry."

"It's fine. I just needed proof because I knew you'd try to deny it."

"You know me well," she admitted.

He looked at her, a strange expression on his face. "I thought I did." He paused for so long, Rye started to reach for the door handle. "I wrote you off a long time ago, you know." He sat back and stared at the steering wheel. "And I'm sorry. None of us should be judged by who we were at eighteen."

"You probably could have been. I mean, you were already a responsible surrogate parent enrolled in community college classes."

"At eighteen? No. I was ..." Ryan trailed off. "No."

"Well," Rye said, "if it's any consolation, by the time we met, you seemed like you had it all together."

"I was twenty-three years old, taking care of a high school sophomore who was on the verge of dropping out. Your dad was as intimidating as anyone I'd ever met before, and I was drowning."

Rye glanced over in surprise. "Really?"

"Yes, really. I got reprimanded for spending time with you, too," Ryan replied. "I was furious at the time. You bugged me, but you also made me laugh. You made me feel like maybe I hadn't missed out on everything after all."

Rye scrunched up her face in confusion. "Why did you get reprimanded for that?"

He looked at her. "Seriously? I was twenty-three."

"So?"

"So, everyone thought we were flirting, and you were in high school," Ryan explained slowly. "Not exactly a good look."

"I was eighteen!" Rye said indignantly. "And we weren't flirting. We were ... friends."

"Tyler told me you apologized to him a while ago."

Rye studied her hands, chagrined. "But you deserve an apology, too. I didn't appreciate your situation then, and I was ... I should have known Tyler was off-limits."

"Yeah."

"It really hurt to lose you as a friend, though," Rye continued. "I know why you didn't keep in touch—or maybe I didn't know, because it was more complicated than I realized—but I do now. I lost you and Andy in the same month, though, and it was…hard."

"You chose to leave, you know," Ryan replied. "You could have stayed, tried to fix things."

"Like you said, I was eighteen. I wasn't sporting a fully developed frontal cortex yet."

Ryan actually laughed at that. "Fair point."

Rye sat back. "As part of this full disclosure, I feel like I should tell you I've been helping Wanda look into Martina Suarez's murder."

"I know."

"And the book club has been investigating Lionel Burgess's murder."

"And your mother's disappearance," Ryan replied. "Yes, I've heard."

"Are you angry about that?" Rye wasn't sure why it mattered so much to her, but it did.

"Honestly, I'm not even surprised. I might even be a little impressed that you've managed to embroil yourself in two cases stretching so far apart with everything else you've got going on. Personally, I don't know how Claudia puts up with you."

Rye swallowed hard. "Easy. She doesn't."

"Oh. Oh. I'm sorry." To his credit, he looked it.

"It's for the best. In my experience, no partner is more interesting than a good case," Rye said.

Ryan tilted his head. "That's true." He looked her over. "You really would have made a great cop. You're dysfunctional in all the right ways."

"I could kick your butt, that's for sure," Rye said, opening the door as the skies opened up and cold rain began sheeting down.

"And that is what you call instant karma." Ryan didn't offer her the umbrella Rye could see in the back seat.

She gave him a double thumbs-up and began walking toward the school, already soaked through.

"When you call Wanda to tell her all this, don't forget to mention who apologized first!" Ryan called after her.

Rye turned around and switched fingers. She waggled them at him until he drove out of sight.

29

29

WANDA WAS ALREADY WAITING AT HARVEY'S WHEN Rye arrived five minutes late the next morning. She stood up to give her friend a hug and was surprised that the usual short squeeze was much longer today.

"How are you doing?" Wanda asked.

"Can we talk about something other than me?" Rye grabbed the cup of coffee Wanda had ordered and filled it to the brim with milk. "I'm not looking forward to facing work today. Have you seen all the videos?"

Wanda thought she'd probably seen more than Rye had, since Lance, Leslie, and Nicole had been Chromecasting them to the TV all evening. She settled on a nod, pushing a plate with a warm piece of spinach quiche in front of Rye. Her friend needed it more than Wanda did today.

"Want to talk murder instead?"

"Always."

Wanda took a sip of coffee and cleared her throat. "We have a current murder victim, and we have a cold case murder victim."

"Not to mention my mom's disappearance."

"Lance did some digging. We knew that the Martina Suarez we met was born Luisa. Martina—the real Martina—was the one who studied opera at the New England Conservatory. She died from breast cancer five years ago. Luisa moved to Boston to take care of Martina. This is newer—after her sister died, Luisa came here, legally changed her name, and got baptized twice, once by Father Bogdan, who would do anything for anyone, which I have on the highest authority."

"God?"

"No! Agatha!" They both laughed. "The second time was by Josh Gagne."

"I guess they don't call them Baptists for nothing," Rye replied. "Why on earth would she get baptized twice?"

"Your guess is as good as mine. And Luisa asked Father Paul over at Saint Joseph to do it as well. She attended his church, so it made sense."

"But he said no?"

"He doesn't believe in the practice. One baptism per soul was essentially what he told me." Wanda paused to take another thoughtful sip of coffee.

"Makes sense to me. What I don't understand is how she made the jump from caregiver to impersonator? And why?"

"Luisa had a criminal record. Maybe she wanted to make a fresh start."

"You know what's really odd? She went to all this trouble to take her sister's name, but she didn't go out of the way to hide that she was taking it—not really." Rye wiped chocolate off her fingers. "You told me Lance watched her baptisms on YouTube, and at least three different pastors would have been witness to it, if you count Father Paul. Why would she do that? She was legally Martina. Why draw attention to it?"

"She didn't tell them she was anyone but Martina. Rebaptism is often a statement of someone trying to let go of the past. She probably just asked for baptism as 'Martina,' a woman changing her life. Other people might just think she was a chronic church switcher. It's a thing. Not ours. My United Church of Christ theology is in some ways as far from Roman Catholicism as you can get, but I would say no if I felt a baptism request was being made just for an emotional boost."

"If you say so."

"I do. But anyway, it was also Lance who found out her criminal past included blackmailing, and I got…additional confirmation."

They sat in silence considering this. "Lance told me Luisa sang in a band nearby years ago. That's probably why she moved to central Massachusetts after her sister's death. Lance found their Myspace page, if you can believe that."

"So you think she wanted to try to get together with her old bandmates?" Rye asked incredulously.

"Maybe." Wanda picked up her phone. "Bone Digger? No. Bone Whisper? That doesn't seem right."

"Bone Dreamer?" Rye asked, startled.

"Yes, that's it! Do you know them?"

"My mom loved them. There's still an old band poster up in my dad's office. The bar they played at was local. I asked Dad about it once, and he said she liked to go hear them play."

Wanda put down her coffee. "Did your mother go out a lot at night?"

Rye shook her head. "Not that I remember."

"So what are the odds that Bone Dreamer is the band she used to go see with Elena and Lionel?"

Rye already had her phone out. "I'm texting Elena now." She tapped her fingers, waiting for a response. "Oh, shoot! I forgot she lost her phone. I guess I could text Gerard. That feels strange, though."

Wanda nodded. "Let's keep your boss out of this if we can. I can try to call her at home later. Keeps it completely free of your job, too." She wiped her mouth. "Have you talked to your dad yet?" She hoped Rye didn't notice her slight flush. She was fishing to find out whether Hardy mentioned anything about almost kissing her. If he hadn't, Wanda sure wasn't going to.

Rye shook her head. "When I finally got home, he was in a mood."

"You should probably make peace with him before he uses every egg in the county to bake his way to emotional equilibrium."

Rye had to laugh. "Fine. After work, I'll talk to him."

"Wait, Rye. Did he mention anything about the baby?"

"What baby?" Rye put down her phone and gave Wanda her complete attention.

"He didn't tell you that the police found Martina...Luisa...with the little plastic baby from his King Cake?"

"No. Where did you hear that?"

"Elena stopped by the church yesterday to let me know. Ryan didn't say anything about Hardy when you were together yesterday?"

"Nothing."

"I definitely think I should be the one to call Elena, then. She's intersecting both of these cases, and I want to see what her reaction is when I speak to her," Wanda said. "If you do it, you risk getting in a mess with Gerard.

Besides, she told me yesterday, and I don't see how she would have known unless—"

They both looked up as the bell on the door jingled. Ryan and Tyler Phennen walked in, dressed for work. Wanda made eye contact with Tyler and waved enthusiastically. He waved back and strolled over to chat.

He was practically glowing when he got to them. "Have you talked to Ana yet today?" he asked Rye.

She shook her head. "Why?"

"Hold on." He pulled out his phone and sent a text. He got a response quickly, then turned to stare at Rye's cell, which vibrated almost immediately. She picked it up and opened a message from Ana. It was a photo of her hand, a brilliant opal on her left ring finger.

"You're engaged?" Rye looked up, a grin spreading across her face. After a rough week, this was welcome news. She stood up and gave Tyler a hug. Wanda did the same, taking Rye's phone to admire Ana's ring.

"I got permission to tell you, but Ana wants to share the story of how it happened if you don't mind waiting?" Tyler asked.

"I'll see her later today, and she can give me all the details!"

"It might be much later," Ryan said, appearing at his brother's side. He gave Tyler's shoulder a squeeze, but his gaze was on Rye. "Hardy has been brought in for questioning. I thought you might want to go see him when you're done here."

"Is this about the baby?" Wanda asked.

He looked at her in surprise. "You know I can't talk about it." His tone was almost apologetic. "I don't want him in there any more than you do." Ryan was having trouble meeting Rye's eyes, and he turned back to Tyler.

"Pick up the coffees we ordered, Romeo. We better get going."

Rye gathered up her things. "I have to go. Gerard told me to take the morning off, but I scheduled a couple of meetings at school. If I hurry, I can at least check on my dad before that."

"Meetings will wait," Wanda said. "If you hear anything—"

"Why don't you just meet me there?"

Wanda grabbed her coat. "Okay, but I'm going to bring a distraction."

30

RYE HAD ALWAYS FELT LIKE THE POLICE STATION WAS comforting and familiar. She knew the halls, rooms, and stairwells, not to mention what view was visible from every window. Rye knew which officers were friendly, who was just drawing pay and waiting for the weekend, who would dismiss her as the (now former) boss's daughter. For the most part, though, it was a good crew. Both Hardy and Ryan had seen to that, leading the force with integrity and high expectations that trickled down.

Today, though, Rye realized what the station must feel like to the majority of people who came there. It was a place people only entered when something terrible had happened to them or because of them. Her father was inside with former employees, with his friends, and she could only imagine the humiliation and fear he must feel.

Rye heard a bark and turned to see Figaro pull out of Wanda's grip and dash up to her, planting two muddy paws squarely on her shoulder. His tail wagged wildly, and his tongue lolled out of his mouth in a happy grin. Rye couldn't help but bury her face in his soft fur, giving him ear rubs and whispering, "Good boy. You're such a good boy," though he was clearly not well-behaved at all. She didn't care—not about the dirty shirt or the rough examination of her nose with his tongue. All that mattered was the pure sense of joy emanating from him.

When Wanda caught up, having untangled herself from the leash and collected the bag she'd dropped when he yanked her arm, she wrapped a hug around both of them, then pulled the dog down to sit. "I don't think he'd make it through the training to be a comfort dog here," she said, giving Figaro another pat on his head.

"Good. He's perfect, and I never want you to give him up."

"I don't think Lance could bear it if I did." Wanda turned and walked up the steps with Rye. "And, you know, I could never bear to break that boy's heart."

"Like you haven't already become Figgy's mama?" Rye collected their visitor tags from the front desk and led them toward the elevator.

"Let's take the stairs," Wanda suggested. "Figgy tends to pee when we ride elevators, and I'd rather not spend time cleaning that up right now."

Wanda let the dog pull them up two flights and then over to Tyler and Jaz's desks to say more congratulations and hello. Rye walked straight to Ryan's office and knocked. There was no answer, which meant he was observing the questioning or doing it himself. Probably the former, since he was likely to have recused himself because of his long-standing relationship with Hardy.

Rye tried to remember who was new enough to do the job. No one she could come up with was senior enough to be taking part in a murder investigation. She flopped down on the chair by Ryan's office to wait. There was a glass-paneled door that led to the interrogation rooms, but Rye had learned the hard way that even she couldn't get away with going back there unescorted. She waited, leg jiggling and stomach clenching around the quiche she'd consumed.

Wanda came over and tried to sit with her, but Figaro was not interested in taking a rest when there were so many good smells to explore, so she had to settle for checking in with Rye each time they made a round of the floor.

Wanda had just brought the dog back in from a pee when Ryan led Hardy out. They were followed by a woman Rye didn't recognize, who she realized must be Detective Jameela Sachar. She'd heard Jaz and Tyler talking about Sachar when she was hired a few months ago, but Rye hadn't had a chance to meet her.

Rye took the opportunity to study the woman as she chatted with Ryan. Detective Sachar was a striking woman in her forties, sharply dressed in navy wide-legged trousers and a cream blouse, her black hair cut in a tidy bob. She gave Rye and Wanda a brief, searching look, then reached down to feed the dog a tiny milkbone she must have slipped from her pocket before hurrying off down the hall.

"I feel underdressed," Wanda whispered to Rye.

Rye rubbed her hands on her pants, self-conscious of her scuffed leather loafers and paw-printed sweater.

"Is Hardy free to go?" Wanda stood up as the men drew closer.

"He is," Ryan said, "but can I get a word with the three of you first?"

They followed him into his office. Hardy and Wanda sat down across from Ryan, Figaro settling at their feet, while Rye chose to stand.

"So?" she asked after they had gotten settled. "What's going on, Dad?"

"Ryan came by this morning to tell me that during a subsequent search of the church for Ms. Suarez's laptop, her apron was discovered behind a stack of chairs in a closet in the back of the sanctuary," Hardy began. "Inside, officers found the baby from my king cake, with my fingerprints on it, wrapped inside a napkin."

"So?" Rye asked. "You made the cake. Of course it would have your fingerprints."

"It was wrapped inside this." Ryan pushed an evidence bag across the table. Wanda leaned over to pick it up.

On the napkin, someone had scrawled, *Hardy Rye— how much???*

"Did you know Martina?" Wanda asked Hardy.

He shook his head. "I remember her trying to speak to me when I was picking up my food, but it was so noisy I couldn't hear her. After about three tries, she gave up. I figured I would find her later and ask what she needed, but I forgot. I went to watch the parade and then went home."

"And, before you ask," Ryan interjected, "we have plenty of witnesses who place Hardy at the parade during the projected time of death. He was almost comically over-alibied, in fact."

The two men shared a look. It must be an inside joke, Rye thought. "Then why is Dad here for questioning?"

Ryan glanced from Hardy to Rye. "We needed to be certain that Hardy wasn't a victim of Luisa's blackmailing scheme."

Wanda laughed out loud, then clapped a hand over her mouth. "Hardy?" She stared between the two men as though she didn't understand a joke they were both in on.

"Martina was running a blackmailing operation in town," Hardy said. "As I understand it"—at this, he looked at Ryan—"a few people came forward after her death to say that 'friends of theirs' were being blackmailed by her. It was in the news."

Wanda and Rye glanced at each other. Neither of them regularly watched local news, and they rarely read the paper, either. It was a shockingly obvious oversight on their part, especially this week, and neither wanted to admit it in front of Hardy and Ryan.

"Oh, yeah, of course," Rye said, giving Wanda a tiny we'll-talk-about-this-later shrug.

"This note could have been in reference to how much money she thought she could get from him," Ryan said.

"What could she possibly blackmail my father over?" Rye asked.

"Did she think you had something to do with Lionel Burgess's death?" Wanda asked. The podcast had only come out a month ago. It was certainly possible that Martina had listened to it, although why she would have jumped to that conclusion, Wanda didn't know.

"Or Melanie's disappearance," Hardy suggested. "Ryan spoke to Elena Mendoza, who confirmed she had talked to Martina about the cold case on the night of the murder."

Ah, Elena again. "Why?" Wanda asked.

"I can't share that. This is an active investigation," Ryan reminded her.

"There's nothing stopping us—me—from asking Elena, though." Rye was already on her feet.

She grabbed her bag, but Wanda caught her arm. "You have to get to school." She could tell Rye wasn't convinced. "I'll let you borrow Figgy for the day if you let me take this one."

Rye snatched the leash, pulling the dog awkwardly up onto her lap to let him give her face kisses. "Can I bring him to work?"

"No," Hardy said, firmly taking the leash back. "I need him more."

Figaro, a good judge of character, didn't hesitate. He jumped off Rye's lap and sat down patiently next to Hardy.

"Smart dog," Ryan noted.

Rye just stuck her tongue out at Ryan and stomped from the room so she wouldn't be late to her job as role model for the young and impressionable minds at Stoneridge High.

31

Wanda decided not to call ahead. Usually, she used her steering wheel as a prayer mandala, but today she reached into her glove box for the rosary Father Paul had given her years ago and prayed the Prayer of the Savior, followed by three Hail Mary's.

An elderly woman Wanda didn't recognize answered the door. Gerard must be back at work.

"Good morning. Is Elena here?"

The woman looked her up and down, and, after apparently deciding Wanda wasn't a threat, she opened the door further and ushered her into the living room. Without a word, she turned and stumped down the hall to the back of the house. Wanda sat down on the edge of the lush sofa.

Elena came in. Wanda expected her to look tired, but she was dressed for work, makeup on and hair done.

"Wanda? This is a surprise," Elena said. "I hope everything's all right?"

Wanda put on a pleasant smile. "I'm doing well. I was so sorry to rush off yesterday. Have you recovered from your injuries?"

"Oh, yes. My mother-in-law has been here to take care of me, and now I'm feeling great and ready to go back to work." She raised her voice for this last part and then leaned in. "She spends the day cursing at me in Spanish and cleaning the house to the point that none of us can find anything. She's a decent cook, but I'm ready to have my kitchen back."

"I can imagine." Wanda had a great relationship with her second mother-in-law, but her first had hated everything Wanda did, said, was. "I just came from seeing Hardy. I know I had to cut you off last night, and I wanted to make sure you didn't have anything else you needed to tell me."

"Are you two close?"

Wanda wanted to be honest, but there was something in Elena's tone that made her hesitate. "Well, Rye is a friend of mine." That was the truth.

Elena sat down on the chair next to Wanda and leaned forward so she could lower her voice. It made it much harder for Wanda to hear her without fiddling with her hearing aids, but she settled for watching the other woman's lips while staying absolutely still. She would seek forgiveness later, but, honestly, she resented having to work this hard with someone who knew her well enough to know better.

"Hardy Rye has everyone fooled," Elena said.

"What are you talking about?"

"He killed his wife."

Wanda didn't know what she'd expected Elena to tell her, but it wasn't that. "What?"

"Melanie Rye? Lionel Burgess? He killed them both. The reason no one was ever arrested in either case was because the department covered it up. They didn't want one of their own to be revealed as a murderer."

"Why do you think that? Do you have evidence?"

"Melanie, Lionel, and I went out together every week. We always went to the same bar on the same night so Melanie could talk to this one guy in the band. They would go off together for a while, and she would come back before we left so I could give her a ride home. It gave me time alone with Lionel." Elena blushed. "I was always hoping he would see me differently if we had more time together." Wanda wasn't sure what to say to this, but Elena continued, starry-eyed. "He was the best dancer, Wanda. He would sweep me out onto the floor, and it was magical!"

"You were in love with him?" Wanda asked gently.

"I've never told anyone that," Elena said. "I know he preferred men, but I was head over heels. Young love is very powerful, isn't it?"

"It's certainly been the motive for many crimes," Wanda said without thinking.

"That's right! Now you understand why I know Hardy must have been responsible," Elena declared. "Melanie had a history of disappearing—we all knew about it—so it wouldn't seem suspicious. The timing of Lionel's death is too coincidental not to be connected."

Wanda could hardly believe what she was hearing. "But you don't have any evidence?"

"A gut feeling," Elena said. "That's why I knew, when Martina was killed, that this might be the only chance to make him pay for what he did so long ago."

"What are you talking about?" Wanda felt like she was on a Tilt-a-Whirl. Every time she got her bearings, she was thrust in the opposite direction. "What did you do?"

Elena leaned in. "I may have snooped around a bit when he wasn't home."

Wanda was horrified. "You broke into his house?"

"Of course not! Rye let me in. She had to take a call, and I just took the opportunity to look around," Elena replied defensively. "I didn't find anything, unfortunately, but—"

"What did you think you would find?" Wanda interrupted. Had Elena really thought Hardy would have kept some record of a crime just hanging around his house?

Elena seemed to realize that Wanda was not on her side and stood up. "You don't understand, Wanda. In one day, I lost two friends, and neither of their cases were ever solved. You've done far more this year to solve the murders of people you barely knew. When do Lionel and Melanie get their justice?"

"You're right," Wanda replied. "It's not fair. Their families and friends deserve closure, but you can't fabricate evidence. You can't point the finger at Hardy without proof. How would you have felt if someone had done that when Jonathan Thorne died in November? What if I had accused Gerard on nothing more than a feeling and a desire to see the case closed?"

Elena was silent for a moment. "It would have destroyed us," she said quietly. "He was already devastated to have lost his friend."

"And how do you think Hardy felt about losing his wife?" Wanda asked. "I'm not certain of many things, Elena, but I believe in his integrity. He has put himself up for scrutiny on your say so, but I think you know that was a cruel thing to do." Wanda stood. "I've never known you to be anything but a kind and loving person. I hope you'll do the right thing here."

Wanda quickly excused herself. She sat in her car, parked down the street, watching her friend—her friend, for heaven's sake—head out to work. Soon after, the old woman came out to the porch and sat in a rocking chair, mug in her hand.

She looked peaceful. Wanda was jealous.

32

After the meeting at the police station, Rye decided she was not fit to be a role model for anyone, much less a bunch of teenagers, and called to take the rest of the day off. Sophie, apparently unfazed by all the drama, efficiently changed Rye's appointments.

After about an hour, though, Rye was irritable. She felt tired, but when she lay down she would think of something that needed doing and pop up. By two o'clock, she had fixed the leak in her shower, organized the clothes she wanted to donate, and scrubbed the kitchen floor.

What she really wanted to do was text Camila about going for a run to absorb some of this kinetic energy. Of course, her friend was still at work, and Rye was supposed to be taking this time to mend fences with her father. She sorted her pile of mail and changed the sheets before dragging herself next door. Uncharacteristically, she found her father in his recliner, watching TV in the middle of the day.

"Rye, if you keep pacing in front of the television, I'm going to banish you from Taco Tuesdays for a month!"

Hardy admonished her, shifting in his recliner to try to catch a glimpse of the basketball game behind her.

Rye plopped down on the couch and watched for at least ten seconds before she was up again. "I just don't understand how you're not upset about this! You were taken into the station for questioning about a murder just because the victim had the plastic baby from your King cake? It's ridiculous!"

"I've solved murders with less," Hardy replied, his attention still clearly elsewhere. "And if you were in Ryan's position you would follow up on every possible lead, too, especially if it reflected on an officer."

"I wouldn't suspect one of my oldest friends of murder, if that's what you're implying."

"You suspected Claudia, then continued to date her even while she was under suspicion for Jonathan Thorne's death last autumn," her father pointed out.

The breakup was too fresh for that barb. "I knew she hadn't done it."

"No, you hoped she hadn't because you liked her. And I'm sure Ryan hopes I have nothing to do with this case because we've been friends and colleagues for a long time. He still has to do his job, though."

"And you'd be disappointed if he did anything else," Rye said, irritated. She'd heard some variation of this line from her father many, many times before.

"I don't know why you're so upset. I heard through the grapevine that you and Ryan were on better terms these days." Although Hardy's gaze was still on the television, Rye knew his attention had shifted to her.

"Did Wanda tell you that?"

"Lance, actually," Hardy replied with the shadow of a grin.

"How did Lance hear?"

"I assume from Wanda. By the way, Claudia came by yesterday to pick up those pot pies for the PTA thing she's helping to organize."

Rye had completely forgotten about that. Claudia was a teacher liaison with the PTA, and one of the winter fundraisers was an alumni fun run and luncheon. They held it every year, even in drifts of snow, and people seemed to love it. Everyone gave generously. It was a huge boon for the arts department. This year, Hardy had volunteered to provide part of the meal, and he had been filling the freezer in the garage for a few weeks now. Rye was supposed to drop the food off at school this week to be stored in the culinary classroom freezer, but it had slipped her mind.

"Did you forget?" Hardy looked over at her, eyebrow arched.

"I did."

"You also forgot to mention that you two broke up. Claudia gave me quite an earful."

"I've been a little busy."

"What's going on with you and Ryan?" Hardy's segue, as always, was perfectly on point.

Rye flopped down on the couch again. "Today? I'm mad at him."

"Yesterday?"

"I apologized for hurting his feelings fifteen years ago."

Hardy glanced over at her. "Did he accept?"

"Sort of. I think so?"

Hardy snorted. "Glad to see my skills in diplomacy have been passed down to you."

Rye ignored him. "Speaking of feelings, I haven't seen any new women around here for a while."

"We're not talking about my love life right now."

"We're not talking about mine, either."

"So you aren't dating Ryan?"

"Of course not! Why? Are you dating Wanda?" Rye retorted. Hardy blushed. Rye was certain she had never in her life seen her father do that. "Wait—are you?"

"No!"

"But you want to! You like Wanda!" Rye exclaimed. "How long have you liked her? Does she know? Have you kissed? Is that why you're always cooking new dishes now, so you have an excuse to see her?" Rye jumped up. "That's totally why! I can't believe I didn't see it!"

"Rye—"

"I wonder why she hasn't mentioned it to me."

"Prudence Rye!" Hardy could be heard in the next county.

Rye blinked in surprise. Her father never called her Prudence, not since she'd asked to go by Rye after her mother left. "What?"

"She doesn't know." Hardy looked mortified that Rye had figured it out.

"Are you sure?"

"Yes. Of course I am."

"Because you're so observant?"

"Observant enough to know whether Wanda feels the same way, yes."

Rye started to laugh. She couldn't help herself, and once she started, she couldn't stop. Everything that had been pent up for the last few weeks seemed to pour out of her. She couldn't catch her breath, and her laughter began to sound more like wheezing than mirth.

When she finally caught her breath, she noticed her father looking on with pure annoyance. "Dad, you wouldn't know if a woman was interested in you if she wrote a novel documenting her feelings. Every girlfriend you've ever had has just sidestepped her way into a relationship with you. I'm not sure you even liked half of them—you just didn't want to be rude when you realized they were keeping a toothbrush in the bathroom."

"You're rude enough to the women I've dated for both of us," he replied.

"I'm sorry. Would you like me to give any of them a call and ask them back?" Rye put her hands on her hips.

"Can we just go back to you worrying about whether or not I'm the prime suspect in Martina Suarez's murder?"

"No! You like Wanda! We have to talk about this!"

"We do not."

"Are you going to ask her out?"

"Rye!"

She studied her father's face. He was looking anywhere but back at her. "You're scared."

"Of what?"

"Of her not liking you back. Of her turning you down, and then you both lose the friendship. Of how much it would hurt to put yourself out there for someone you actually care about."

Hardy was silent. His eyes drifted back to the TV, and Rye could tell he was finished talking to her about this.

"Dad—"

He stood up abruptly. "I forgot that I have an archery lesson with Rachel today. Andy and Crystal are coming, and I need to make something for them to eat." He hightailed it into the kitchen, the swinging door gently closing behind him.

"Fine, be that way," Rye said to his empty chair. She wasn't going to hang around and make nice with Andy's new girlfriend, at least not today. She would go in— No, school was over. This was an endless day.

But maybe Wanda was home. Not that Rye would spill the beans, but there was no reason she couldn't find out exactly how wrong her father was.

33

WANDA WASN'T HOME, BUT LANCE WAS, AND HE happily put aside homework to let Rye in. Figaro and Wink had been sleeping together on the couch, but as soon as she walked in they both bounced up, ready to play.

"Want to take them on a walk with me?" Lance asked after he and Rye had thrown the monkey toy enough times that the dogs had knocked over a lamp, a pile of library books, and a glass of water from the coffee table. "I can't take both of them alone yet. They tend to work each other up, not to speak of tangling the leashes."

"I noticed." Rye laughed as the normally docile Wink jumped and begged for more attention. "Sure. I can walk."

Lance grabbed the leashes, and they stepped out into the windy afternoon. Figaro was pulling hard away from the route Rye knew Wanda and Wink usually took, but Wink seemed game to follow, so Lance and Rye fell in line behind them.

"How's your play going?"

"It's been fun," Lance said. "My mom sent me to theater camp when I was in middle school. I hated performing, but talking about the scripts was interesting. Leslie has been helping me with the dialogue, and Nicole tries to play every part for us so we can see how perfect she would be if she were cast."

"Doesn't Ms. Ramirez handle the casting?" Rye asked.

"Usually, yes. But she said since it's my play, I could sit in on auditions and help."

"That sounds great." Rye untwisted Wink's leash from Figaro's. "I can't wait to see it. What's it about?"

"It's a ghost story about a girl in high school who's getting bullied. She begins to dream every night that she's following a ghostly figure—an old woman—with a dog. After a few nights of this, Annie is woken by the sound of a dog barking, and when she looks out her window she sees the same figure walking across the lawn below."

"Sounds great!" Rye said. "I'm already intrigued."

Lance was practically jogging at this point to keep up with Figaro. "It's not exactly Shakespeare, but it's more fun than I was expecting."

"Where's Figgy going, do you think?" Rye had scooped Wink up to run after them.

"No idea," puffed Lance. "He's determined, though."

They trailed Figaro for another few blocks until they reached a small dog park. He slowed and sniffed around the gate, then glanced up at them, wagging his tail. A woman with short white hair came over, a boxer trailing behind.

"Figgy! Love! Long time no see, buddy." She leaned down and gave the dog scratches behind the ears. Figaro's tail thumped enthusiastically. She gave Rye and

Lance an appraising look. "Who are you? Martina didn't say anything about getting a dog walker."

Rye paled, and she felt Lance shifting uncomfortably beside her. "Lance, why don't you let Figgy play?" She glanced at the woman. "He likes your dog?"

"Oh, yes! He and Harrison are old friends." The woman allowed herself to be led to a bench while Lance pulled a ball out of his pocket and started throwing it for the dogs.

"That's nice." Rye smiled, watching them run back and forth across the brown grass. She thought Wink would want to join them, but he curled up by the bench and rested his head on her foot with a sigh. "We didn't know about this place."

"Martina didn't tell you?"

Rye turned to the woman. "I'm sorry to have to be the one to tell you this, but Martina died. Lance and my friend Wanda have taken custody of Figaro since Martina didn't have any family."

"Oh my goodness." Tears welled up in the woman's eyes, and she fumbled in her pocket for her tissues. "I had no idea. What happened?"

"You didn't see the news?"

"I was on a cruise. I just got back yesterday. I didn't bother to pay for the Wi-Fi, since there's no one here I can't go without talking to for a few weeks." She blew her nose. "I'm just heartbroken for that young woman. She was so kind to me, even watched Harrison when I went into the hospital last year."

"You were good friends?" Rye hadn't seen anyone react to the news of Martina's death this way, and it made her feel better. No one should leave the world without at least one person to mourn them.

"We'd meet up here after work a few times a week, bring tea or wine and watch the dogs play. She's been good company for me since my husband passed."

"I'm so sorry for your loss."

"May I ask how she died?"

Rye had no desire to tell this grieving woman the truth, but she had to. "She was murdered."

The woman gasped. "What happened?"

"The case is still open, unfortunately."

"They haven't caught the person?" The woman looked deeply shaken, and Rye felt awful that she had brought this news to her.

"Oh, Martina—what did you do?" the woman murmured. She blew her nose again. "I suppose that's why there's one of those lockboxes on her door. I stopped by last night to see if she and Figgy were coming to the park, and I thought it was odd."

"A lockbox?"

"For a key. You know, like real estate agents use? The police must have put it there, don't you think?"

Rye nodded. "I'm sure they did."

The woman watched Lance dancing around with the dogs. "I'm glad Figgy has landed with such a good-hearted young man." She wiped away another tear. "You can always tell the good ones, can't you?"

Rye disagreed in principle, but the woman was right in this case. "He's one of the best."

"I notice he has Figaro on a leather lead. That dog will snap it within the week, you just wait. Then he'll lead Lance on a merry chase!"

"The dog was a surprise," Rye said. "Lance went out and bought a few things quickly."

The woman looked at Rye oddly. "Why didn't the police give you Figgy's things? Martina had everything for that dog. I'm sure they don't need them for their investigation."

"Oh, I don't know," Rye replied. "I don't think Wanda and Lance knew Figgy had . . . stuff."

"Martina had done a lot of research—only the best for her Figaro." The woman smiled sadly. "Maybe you could call the sheriff's department and see if they would let you pick up his things. Martina lives—lived—just there." She pointed to a modest blue house on the edge of the park.

A chance to look through the victim's things? It was worth a try, at least.

"Thanks for your help," Rye told the woman. "And, again, I'm sorry to have to share such sad news."

The woman patted her hand. "She's not the first friend I've lost. Grief is a frequent companion these days." She stood up and whistled. The boxer dropped the ball and raced over. "It was nice to meet you."

"You, too. I'm Rye, by the way."

"Rye, I'm Pen—it's short for Penelope—though no one called me that except my mother." It was clearly a joke she'd made many times before, but it hit Rye hard.

She watched as Pen put a lead on Harrison, then picked up her book. "If you ever wish someone would call you Penelope, let me know." Rye pulled a business card out of her pocket and handed it to Pen. "Just ask for Prudence."

THE LAST THING RYE WANTED TO DO WAS CALL RYAN and ask for a favor, but as soon as Lance heard that Figaro could have his own toys and bed and blankets, he wouldn't let it go. Rye had not built up willpower against the pleadings of a boy and his dog, so she reluctantly pulled out her phone and called the station.

Tyler answered. "Sheriff's department. This is Officer Phennen speaking."

"Hey, Tyler, it's Rye."

His voice warmed. "Oh, hey, Rye!"

She got the impression he'd raised his voice, and she had a brief image of the rest of the office gathering around while he put her on speakerphone. Lance was looking at her oddly, and she realized she had frozen. "Yeah, hi. Um. Lance and I are out with Figaro—you know, Martina Suarez's dog? And Figgy led us to the dog park by the Suarez house."

"He led you there?" Tyler sounded skeptical.

"He pulled us," Lance shouted in the direction of her phone, as Rye waved him off.

"He practically ripped Lance's arm from the socket trying to get here," Rye said, "and we met one of Martina's neighbors with her dog. She told us that Martina had spent a lot of time choosing Figaro's belongings and that we might want to pick them up."

"I see."

"She said she saw a lockbox on the front door when she dropped by to visit, and that you might be willing to allow us to retrieve the dog's things. She's just back from vacation, so maybe you haven't met her."

Rye could hear Tyler talk to someone in the office, and then Ryan was on the line. "You think I'm going to let you go into the victim's house? Have you lost your mind?"

"It was never a crime scene! Your officers have presumably already been through the house and removed anything suspicious. There's no reason to believe the killer wanted something from her home, so I can't see why it isn't reasonable for us to pop in for five minutes to collect a few things to make the dog you guilt-tripped Wanda into taking home more comfortable."

"I don't know what you think you're going to find. The dog was left in a closet when she was at the service."

"Really?" Rye looked down at the happy, well-adjusted dog at Lance's feet. He didn't seem to have suffered from neglect.

"That's where he was found," Ryan replied. "The neighbor must have it wrong. It was a man, so it was different from the woman you met."

"Ryan," she said, doing her best to keep her lecturing tone in check. "Could I please have permission to take Lance into the house briefly to check? We won't touch anything that doesn't belong to the dog."

After a minute, Ryan must have handed the phone back to his brother, because Tyler, in a sanctimonious tone, replied, "Let me get that lockbox code for you, ma'am."

Rye gritted her teeth. She was going to have to let that "ma'am" go this time. "Thanks, Tyler."

"Of course, ma'am. Happy to help." There was a pause. "The number is five-eight-zero-one-seven"

Rye repeated the digits aloud so Lance could type them into his phone.

"And just so you know, that code will be changed," Tyler told her.

"Tonight!" Rye heard Ryan yell faintly.

"The code will change tonight. Got it." Rye hung up before Tyler could throw another *ma'am* her way.

"Let's go," Rye said, stuffing her phone in her pocket and allowing Figgy to pull them toward his old home. "Before they change their minds."

34

WANDA GLANCED DOWN AT HER PHONE. RYE HAD SENT her a long text, the gist of which was that she and Lance had gotten permission to go into Martina's house to pick up Figaro's belongings. As a longtime dog owner, Wanda knew that would be more work than Rye expected. Having been friends with Rye for almost a year, she also knew Rye would not limit her exploration to pet supplies when the opportunity to snoop fell into her lap.

Wanda sent a thumbs-up emoji and pulled into a space next to Saint Athanasius. Father Bogdan had called and asked her to stop by, and she could tell, even over the phone, that he was upset. She had canceled her other appointments and driven over immediately.

Wanda tried the door to the social hall, but it was locked. Father Bogdan didn't have an outside door that led to his office, so she walked around to the front and was surprised to find that door unlocked. She peeked into the sanctuary in case Bogdan was in there, but a quick scan told her it was empty.

Wanda walked down the dimly lit hall to the church office. The door was ajar, so she went in and across to the pastor's study. It was slightly open, as well. She gave a loud knock before peeking in. Father Bogdan sat at his desk staring at a laptop. He looked disheveled, a sight Wanda had never witnessed, even when they were leading vigils together outside in snow and rain. He always managed to maintain a look of crisp dignity, but today he sat slumped over, his shirt and hair rumpled, giving off the impression he had kept a different kind of vigil all night in this very spot.

He startled as she looked in. "Wanda! I didn't expect you so soon." He made an effort to smooth his collar into place, and she didn't have the heart to tell him it wouldn't make much difference when his cardigan buttons were misaligned.

"You sounded troubled, Bogdan." She hung her coat and purse on the rack by the door and sat in the chair closest to his desk. She occasionally left off the honorific for her friend when they were casual. This did not look casual to her, but it did look like he needed tenderness.

He closed his eyes briefly, and when he opened them he seemed to sag further into himself. "I have listened to many people open their hearts to me, share unspeakable tragedies, bear witness to pain no one should ever suffer, and I thought, foolishly, that hearing those confessions had made me strong enough to bear whatever might befall my own family." He paused then for so long that Wanda almost spoke. Only years of training kept her silent. "It didn't. Wanda, I tell you, I was not prepared for this."

"For what?" she asked gently. What could be so troubling that it had brought this normally straightforward, jovial man to be almost poetic in his despair?

"This," the priest replied, gesturing at the laptop. "This computer belongs to my wife."

"And why do you have Agatha's computer?"

"I shouldn't have taken it. I know I shouldn't. I've never subscribed to the idea that a husband has a right to know what his wife does—not without her express permission—but she's been acting so strangely." His finger traced along the edge of the keyboard. "She's had nightmares. She's been agitated with me and downright rude to parishioners. I even heard her speaking harshly to the children in the choir, and I've never known her to even raise her voice while in the church before. The fact that it's happened multiple times in a few weeks–" His voice cracked. "It's not like her."

"Okay." Wanda didn't want to spook him. Agatha had seemed feisty when Wanda had stopped by, but she didn't know Agatha like Bogdan did. If he thought she was acting oddly, Wanda believed him. "What did you think you might find on her computer?"

He shrugged helplessly. "I'm not sure. Evidence of an affair? I couldn't really believe that, but…doctors' appointments for terminal disease? Anything that might give me a hint to why she's been so angry and distant."

"What did you find?"

Father Bogdan turned the computer around. Wanda put on her computer glasses and read the email he had up on the screen. When she was finished, she closed the computer gingerly and slid it back across the desk.

"Is that the only one?"

He shook his head, face bleak. "Not even close. I've looked through at least fifteen so far. She was being blackmailed by Martina Suarez. It's been going on for months."

This was it. Concrete evidence tying Martina not only to blackmail but to the building where she was killed. "Are the emails explicit? Do you know what she was blackmailing Agatha over?"

He nodded. "At least three mention the cause. The rest are 'requests.'"

The door slammed open then, and both Wanda and Father Bogdan jumped. Agatha stood in the doorway. She looked from her husband to Wanda to the desk where the computer sat open.

There was no mistaking the device. Agatha had pasted stickers all over the cover, even using alphabet letters to spell out her name. It reminded Wanda of something a tween would do, and she was suddenly struck by the age difference between the couple. Wanda couldn't help but wonder if whatever Agatha was protecting had taken place when she was in her adolescence.

"I see you found my computer. I've been searching for it since last night," Agatha said. "Remember, Bogdan? I asked you if you'd seen it?"

He looked guilty. "I know you did."

"And you lied to me. You said you had no idea what had happened to it, and that maybe I had carelessly misplaced it. Isn't that what you told me?"

"It is," he replied softly. "I've been worried about you recently. When I ask if anything's wrong, you always say no." He looked down at the screen. "That's a lie, isn't it? Something is terribly wrong."

"You had no business going through my personal accounts!" Agatha's voice rose.

"Look at you!" Bogdan stood up now, gesturing to her. Agatha was pale and drawn, as though she hadn't slept in weeks. "I thought you must have cancer and didn't want to tell me, that you were protecting me from something we should face together."

"This isn't something you can help me with," Agatha said. "You should have just left well enough alone!"

"Why?" Bogdan's tone was anguished. Wanda knew he loved his wife, and she had always thought it went both ways. They seemed so lighthearted and joyful together. Today, though, Agatha looked haunted. "Why won't you let me help you?"

"You can't help with this. There's nothing you or God can ever do to absolve me of what I've done."

Bogdan stepped forward and wrapped his young wife in his arms, allowing her to crumple there. Wanda stood, unsure of what she should do. Call the police? Probably. But what if Agatha hadn't done anything legally wrong? Maybe hers was a moral quandary, in which case, Wanda should leave these two to talk it through.

Her decision was made when a crash resounded outside the office.

35

Rye had already collected three dog beds, two porcelain bowls, and enough toys for ten dogs when Lance called to her from upstairs.

"What?" Rye yelled. "I can't hear over the sound of money being wasted on this animal!"

The dog in question was going absolutely bananas. He hadn't stopped jumping on and off furniture since they had arrived, and Rye didn't worry about his trying to escape as she brought armloads to the car she'd jogged back to get. He was clearly going to have to be dragged out of here when they were finished. Wink had kept up with him for as long as he could, but eventually he had flopped down on the couch for a nap.

"Come up here!" Lance yelled back, enunciating to be heard over Figaro's yips of delight.

Rye dropped a pile of monogrammed blankets on the floor by the stairs and headed up. The stairwell was lined with photos of Figaro and his person—Rye could never decide if she should call the woman "Martina" or "Luisa." There were photos from trips around the country, of the dog in a life jacket out on the water, at a rooftop deck in

New York City, sniffing cherry blossoms in D.C. At the very top of the stairs, there was one frame not devoted to him.

It had space for ten photos. In each shot, there were two nearly identical girls, although one was clearly taller in the pictures of them as children. The haircuts and clothing styles changed, but the smiles remained the same. Here were Luisa and Martina before the real Martina's life was cut short.

The glass was smeared, and she wondered whether Luisa had brushed these photos with her fingertips every time she walked up and down the stairs. Rye had done that for a long time after her mother disappeared. Her mother's picture had been a talisman of sorts, a reminder that the woman was flesh and blood at one time, not just a frozen image that would fade.

"Rye?" Lance popped his head out of a room at the end of the hall. "You've got to see this."

She followed Figaro to the open door. "What did you find?"

Rye stared around her in dismay. The room had been destroyed. "Please tell me you didn't do this."

"Of course not!" Lance's tone was only mildly offended. "After I checked the bathroom and the guest room, I came in here. Everything was torn apart."

"Did you touch anything?"

"What do you think?" he scoffed.

Rye knew she should call Tyler immediately and report this, and she would. Right after she took a look at the closet.

Rye stepped gingerly around the piles strewn across the floor to peek inside.

Figaro started to growl as she stuck her head in. Both Rye and Lance looked at the dog, startled, but he didn't stop until she backed away from the door.

The clothes were pushed aside, and several pairs of shoes were lined up on the floor beneath them.

"Find anything?"

Rye appreciated that he hadn't tried to join her. Lance was a big puppy himself, always tripping over his own feet, especially when he got excited. "Not yet."

She was glad she had gloves in her pockets. She pulled them on and eased open the first drawer of the small bureau. The top drawer held socks, then underwear, then what Rye could only identify to Lance as "a woman's . . . necessities"—and she wasn't talking about sanitary products.

The bottom drawer stuck, but when Rye knelt down and wiggled it open, she discovered that was because it had been jammed full of packets of photos and what looked like old journals. She glanced through the top one, but there was too much here for her to look through with Lance and the dog in the next room.

Rye glanced up as she started to stand, then knelt again to get a better look. Above the bureau was a gold crucifix attached to a large, intricately painted wooden panel. From where she sat below, Rye noticed that the thick slab extruded from the wall at a slight angle. She stood and tried to remove it from the wall. At first, it stuck hard, but after a minute of gentle prying it popped off. Behind the crucifix, there was a small hole in the drywall.

"Rye? What are you doing?" Lance asked. "We should call the police and let them know about what happened here."

"You do that." Rye reached inside the hole, which was barely large enough for her wrist to fit through. She fumbled around until her fingers brushed against something soft. She couldn't pull it out until she'd removed her hand, pushed the bureau aside, and positioned herself directly in front of the hole. From that angle, Rye was able to extract a small, heavy bank bag from its hiding spot. She unzipped the top and peered inside to see several fat rolls of cash. She slid her hand into the hole once more to be sure she wasn't missing anything, but it was empty.

She lifted the crucifix to rehang it. It was heavy, and seams ran down the back of the wood. When Rye pushed on one side, then the other, she felt a click. The back panel slid open, and a little red book fell out. She opened it gently and read the first page. The print was tiny, but the words were explosive.

"Lance," she called as she extracted herself from the closet, but he held up a hand, already on the phone. "Are you okay waiting here by yourself?" she whispered.

"Hold on a second," he said into the phone. "Where are you going?"

"I need to talk to Wanda, to warn her."

"About what?"

"You'll be fine here, right?" Rye replied, avoiding the question.

"A squad car is heading over."

Rye bolted for the stairs. She felt a twinge of guilt as she passed the picture of sisters again. The past may be precious, but the present was full of danger.

By the time she reached her car, she had called Wanda and texted her. She was about to drop the phone onto the cluttered seat beside her when it rang. "Wanda?"

"No, Camila," her friend replied. "Were you waiting on a call?"

"I was. I am. I just found something…" She trailed off.

"What? Something about your mom? Or Lionel?" Camila sounded intrigued, and Rye couldn't help but smile grimly at her enthusiasm.

"No. I've been helping Wanda look into Martina Suarez's murder—"

"Of course you have!"

"And I found out something big. Lance told me he thought Wanda was at the Greek Orthodox church, and I'm worried. It might be nothing, but she isn't picking up her phone. And I'm hitting every red light!" This last part was declared angrily at the blocked intersection in front of her.

"I'm at school right now. Do you want me to walk over and check on her?" Camila asked.

Rye knew that her friend rarely "walked" anywhere and that she could probably be at the church in under a minute. Rye was easily five minutes away—maybe more if the traffic didn't open up.

"It could be dangerous, Camila."

"I'll be careful."

Rye could hear the sound of the heavy metal doors closing and knew Camila was already on her way. "Seriously, Cam—"

"Rye, I can handle this."

"Please, just be careful."

"I will. I promise." Camila ended the call, and Rye laid on the horn.

36

AGATHA MADE IT TO THE DOOR FIRST, BUT WANDA and Bogdan were not far behind. The sight unfolding before them stopped them in their tracks, in large part from the sheer absurdity of it. Reverend Josh Gagne was holding a laptop above his head with one hand while trying to fend off Rye's friend Camila at the same time. He elbowed her in the belly, and she backed off for a moment, probably unused to being attacked by clergy.

"Josh, what are you doing here?" Agatha asked. Her back had straightened, the weepy woman from a moment ago replaced by someone much more collected.

"I thought you wanted your computer back," he replied angrily. Camila was circling him, and he was clearly distracted.

"Bogdan had it. He's read it."

"Then what is this? You left it at my place."

"It's Martina's computer, you idiot."

He looked down at it, and in that moment, Camila dashed toward him, head down. Josh evaded her, but just barely.

"We can't let him destroy that computer!" Wanda shouted. "Secure the door! That computer may have the only evidence of Luisa's blackmail!" The moment she said it, she regretted it. Neither Agatha nor Josh had thought that through. It was clear from their expressions.

Camila either didn't hear Wanda or chose to ignore her directions. She took a runner's leap and tackled Josh to the ground. The computer went skittering across the floor.

"No!" Josh yelled, and tried to shove Camila off of him so that he could grab it. She was stronger than she looked, though, and he could only inch along the floor, Camila straddling his back, her hands yanking back on his collar.

Wanda didn't hesitate. She jogged past them and scooped up the laptop. It was only when she turned around that she realized Agatha had reemerged from her husband's office and now held her own computer under one arm and the point of a serrated knife against Bogdan's back.

"Agatha!" Wanda stared at the small woman, shocked. Had she brought that into the office when she confronted them? What had she been planning to do with it if Josh hadn't shown up?

"If you think I'm stupid enough to hang around here waiting for the police to arrive—"

"What are you doing?" her husband asked. "This isn't you!"

Josh laughed from where he remained pinned. "Isn't it? You didn't know your wife was an accomplice to blackmail, not to mention a murderer?"

"I didn't kill her, you did!" Agatha replied angrily. She pulled up her sleeve to show a still-red scar along her forearm. "And even if I had, it would have been in self-defense. She stabbed me! I left the knife she used for the police to find her fingerprints!" Agatha jabbed her finger in his direction. "You were the one who killed her."

Josh bucked hard, surprising Camila and throwing off her grip. He dragged himself to his feet. Eyes unfocused, he took a preacher's stance. "That corruptor has been blackmailing me since I got here. She only got what she deserved!"

Wanda felt sick. "What could she possibly have had on you that was so awful—"

"I know," said a voice from behind Agatha. Wanda whirled around. Rye was standing there, holding up a small book. "You didn't find anything on her computer, did you?" she asked Agatha, pointing at the laptop Wanda still held. "Because Luisa was old-school."

Josh lunged, but Agatha and Bogdan were between them, and his sudden movement caused Agatha to drop her own computer and lurch toward the younger man. She swung up, only managing to slice at his arm before losing her grip on the knife. It clattered to the ground, and Josh grabbed for it, but Wanda and Camila got there first. Camila bared her teeth at Josh and growled when he tried to yank her off the ground.

"Try it," she said. "I dare you."

Josh didn't have time to try anything. Wanda had grabbed Agatha's laptop and swung it back and forth, landing glancing blows on both assailants. They staggered, and Bogdan took the chance to dive into the office and lock the door.

"I'm calling the police!" he yelled.

"They're already on the way," Rye said.

"What is that, exactly?" Wanda asked, nodding toward the book Rye held while continuing to hold the laptop like a cudgel.

"A Luddite copy of all of Luisa's blackmail victims, including how much money they had paid her and descriptions of the evidence she has against them."

"Where's the real evidence?" Camila wiped away some blood from her nose.

Rye held open the book and showed them a small key taped in the front. "A safe deposit box, I'm guessing."

"And in the book itself?" Wanda kept her gaze on Josh and Agatha.

"Record of Josh's payments, of course. There are other names you probably know in here, Wanda, but at least two of them have 'No' written next to them in red ink— I'm guessing that means they didn't allow her to use what she had against them."

"She never got a dime from me," Agatha said, slowly sitting up, hand pressed against her head.

"Under your name, it says, 'information only,'" Rye agreed.

"Information?" Camila repeated.

"She was giving Martina information about her husband's parishioners," Josh said, rising to his feet, his hands balled into fists. "And his colleagues."

"It's not my fault you were caught sleeping with a fifteen-year-old girl when you were twenty-two," Agatha said with something more than disgust in her tone. "Or that you were disturbed enough to make a sex tape."

Josh leapt on her, his hands going around Agatha's neck. Camila jumped onto Josh's back as Rye struggled to pull Agatha out of his grasp, slowly peeling his hands off the woman.

"We were in love!" he screamed as Camila yanked backward hard enough that he had to release Agatha.

"What do you know about love?" Agatha sneered, her hands massaging her neck.

"More than you!" Josh was struggling to dislodge Camila. Rye pushed Agatha aside and landed a punch to Josh's gut, allowing Camila to pull his struggling form all the way to the ground.

Wanda wasted no time getting an iron grip on Agatha's arm, knowing the woman would bolt as soon as she saw the chance.

"Let go of me!" Agatha struggled, but Wanda managed one of the moves Hardy had taught her recently, getting Agatha's hands locked behind her. She knew from experience it was painful to pull against the hold, and sure enough, Agatha quickly went slack.

Father Bogdan opened the door and peeked out. Seeing that both Josh and Agatha were subdued, he stepped cautiously into the hallway. "Agatha," he said softly, "what could Martina possibly have known about you that would lead to all of this?" He spread his arms wide as if to encompass everything from the murder to this very moment.

When Agatha didn't reply, didn't even look up at her husband, Rye answered for her. "She was already married when you married her. She has a grown son, too."

Father Bogdan looked shocked. "But you always told me you didn't want children."

Agatha's face was a mask of despair. "I got pregnant when I was fourteen. My parents sent me to live with my grandparents until I had the baby, and then they kept him and I went home to finish high school."

"Are you her son?" Camila asked Josh, her eyes wide.

"No," he scoffed. "This isn't a soap opera."

"Too bad," Camila said. "Then it wouldn't be real."

"My son died a few years ago," Agatha explained.

"Your other husband killed him?" Camila suggested.

Rye gave her friend a look, and Camila made a sign to show she was zipping her lips.

"My other husband was his father. Filip never knew about the baby, though. When I came home, we started dating again, and when I was eighteen, we got married."

"How did you get here, then?" Rye asked, at the same time Wanda said, "Why did you marry Bogdan?"

"Oh…oh, no," Father Bogdan murmured. He sagged against the wall.

"What?" Wanda asked.

"Your brother?" he asked weakly. "The one in the nursing home?"

"My husband," Agatha confirmed.

Camila audibly gasped. "It *is* a soap opera!"

"Your husbands know each other?" Rye asked.

"I've been visiting Filip Nikolic for years now, since Agatha and I first started dating. She told me he was her older brother and asked if I would come and pray over him."

"How…" Rye trailed off. "What?"

"Filip sustained a head injury when he was in Afghanistan. While he was recovering here, he had a stroke and never regained strength in his left side. Speech is still very difficult," Bogdan said softly. "His memory is also poor."

"It's not like I ever introduced either of you as my husband," Agatha said. "Filip was no longer able to work or live at home. I was only twenty-three when it happened, and after taking care of him for a few years I was ready to remarry."

"So why didn't you just get a divorce?" Rye's tone managed to suggest she thought Agatha was either the stupidest person she'd ever met or the cruelest.

"Because," Wanda said slowly, "then she wouldn't have been able to share in her husband's military benefits."

"It wasn't just that," Agatha replied hotly. "He had no other family. If we'd gotten divorced, he would have no one to make medical decisions on his behalf."

"Why didn't you just tell me?" Bogdan asked. "I would have understood."

"But you wouldn't have married me," Agatha replied. "You couldn't have. Your church wouldn't have allowed it, and you would have rejected even the idea of being involved with a married woman, even if that marriage was only in name."

"Instead you lied to me for all these years?"

"If Martina Suarez had never come here, never found out, we would have been happy. She destroyed everything she touched."

"No," Bogdan said, looking up as the door at the end of the hall opened and officers streamed inside. "No one forced you to lie to me, Agatha. What Martina Suarez did was illegal, but what you have done—you have to live with that guilt on your own." He turned and walked into the office again, closing the door behind him.

As Tyler reached the group, he looked from Rye to Wanda to Camila, then to the closed door. "Is he a threat to himself? Do I need to break it down?" He was clearly prepared to do so.

"No," Wanda replied. "He's just not quite ready to face what comes next."

37

BEFORE THE POLICE TOOK JOSH AND AGATHA AWAY, Father Bogdan came out. Whatever prayer he had prayed had given him at least temporary calm. He kissed the woman he thought of as his wife gently on the forehead. He murmured a prayer with her before she was taken away.

Wanda's debriefing with Tyler didn't take long, but she waited for Bogdan, sensing her friend might not want to be alone. Detective Sachar spent over an hour with him. When he came out of the office, he asked Wanda to pray with him.

They went into the sanctuary. After a prayer in a language she didn't understand but an emotional depth she recognized from prison and hospice, they sat in silence. Incense lingered in the air, and the room felt warm, but Wanda wasn't sleepy. She was focused on her breathing, using a meditation technique she had been practicing at home. It usually took her a while to sink into it, but today her body and mind craved that quiet place to heal.

Wanda hadn't known Agatha well, but she was familiar with the feeling of betrayal that came with uncovering secrets a spouse had been keeping. Everything that had once felt good and clean became tainted, at least for a while. In Bogdan's case, it would probably be increasingly difficult to separate which memories were true from which were just an act.

Wanda couldn't imagine the scope of what Agatha had done—introducing her two husbands—leading her current husband to believe that her first was a blood relation? Camila hadn't been entirely wrong. This was soap opera territory. But Wanda did know the humiliation of having an entire congregation privy to a marriage falling apart.

On top of doing that, Bogdan would have to handle the repercussions of Agatha's violation of the congregation's trust and adhere to whatever decision they made about his possible resignation. Wanda knew he loved Saint Athanasius, poured his heart into it and the community, and she hoped desperately that he would be spared that second loss.

"I love her," he said, breaking the silence at last. "We could have straightened it out together, figured out a way she could care for Filip and marry me."

"But?" Wanda was absurdly glad that Bogdan spoke of his love in the present tense. Still, she knew there was a 'but' coming.

"I'm not sure I can forgive her for using information about my parishioners to save herself. Agatha learned those things as my partner. That was her blackmail price—not money, but secrets that had been entrusted to her—and she paid it."

Wanda reached out and patted his hand. "I'm worried you might not forgive yourself."

"I'm not sure I will, either," he replied. "I should have known, should have suspected something, if not in the years of our marriage, at least in the last few weeks. She helped to cover up a murder, even participated in it, and I didn't notice. I didn't realize someone had been blackmailing her. I should have known all of this, Wanda. She is my beloved, whether she still considers herself mine or not, and I knew nothing."

"I have always considered you to be a man of exquisite character," Wanda replied. "You think the best of people, and you love them unconditionally. If you didn't see those things, it's because Agatha has been taught and expected to hide her true self since she was fourteen years old. How long did she keep the secret of her son from you and Filip? How much did that single year of her life twist and change the way she shared herself?"

"She's not evil," he said stoutly.

"No," Wanda agreed. "She's not. She was abused and probably blamed. Confused as a child, she grew into a woman with a lot of secrets she needed to keep to survive."

"If she were not my wife, I would offer her forgiveness immediately," Father Bogdan said.

"We know it was a series of terrible choices, but she's still a child of God."

"She is," he agreed. He was crying.

Wanda waited silently while he wept. When his breathing finally slowed, she dug into her purse and handed him a packet of tissues.

"You have no control over what she thinks or does," Wanda advised him. "You can ask forgiveness from your congregation, and you can do your best to heal from this. Maybe that looks like showing up for her trial, or like continuing to visit Filip, who will be alone now. Maybe it looks like taking on more shifts at the soup kitchen to atone or getting a divorce to unburden yourself. Well, not a legal divorce, since you were never married, but a church severance service. What you can't do is change Agatha."

He sighed. "I know."

"If you ever want to talk about it, I'm here," Wanda said. "But you might also call Father Paul. He was widowed young, before he became a priest, and he's gone through so much since then. It's a rare thing to find a priest who understands marital love and loss and who also understands the weight of parishioners' secrets. He could be a good friend right now."

"Thank you. I will," he replied. "Maybe not today, but soon."

With that, Father Bogdan got up and left the sanctuary. She could hear his footsteps retreat down the hall. They were firm, but his sweater was still misbuttoned and his eyes red.

She said a final prayer, although she knew the answer already. Colleen would get a call soon about visiting Agatha while she was incarcerated to offer her counseling services. Wanda felt angry and grief-stricken on Bogdan and Luisa's behalf, but she couldn't—wouldn't—give up the impulse to offer healing to the woman who had been so damaged as a child.

She spared a minute to wonder what had happened to Luisa herself before all these things began. She, too, had been damaged. Wanda guessed it was the reason she had steered clear of Colleen's parishioners. After Luisa had gone to the first rape and sexual assault survivors meeting, she'd backed off what seemed to have been a plan to blackmail the survivors. No matter what else, this woman who thrived on blackmail had understood that these folks were already damaged enough.

DEATH IS DISCUSSED 227

a woman who thrived on blackmail had made more than a few folks with already damaged reputa...

38

"ARE YOU SURE YOU'RE DOING OKAY?" RYE ASKED Camila as they walked down the road back to the school.

Camila was practically bouncing as she walked. She had been calm during her interview with Jaz and had happily let the EMT check her out. Aside from a bloody nose, she hadn't sustained any injuries, and she'd been joking around with Tyler while she waited for Rye to finish her interview.

"I didn't mean for any of that to happen," Rye said.

"I know. I told you, I've been taking self-defense lessons—"

"Classes are not the same thing as being threatened in person," Rye protested.

"—with your father," Camila finished. "I've been taking lessons with your father."

"What?" Rye stared at Camila. "When? What?!"

"Claudia and I both were, for a while."

Rye put her hands over her eyes and forced herself to take a deep breath. "I need more information, Camila."

"After Jonathan was killed in November, I convinced Claudia we should take self-defense classes, and she mentioned that your dad was teaching a couple of people. I reached out to him, and he said he would be happy to help."

"Why didn't you ever mention this?" Rye asked, wondering why Hardy had never said anything either.

"Claudia quit after two sessions. I liked it, so I kept going."

"Is that why you two are fighting?" Rye asked, recalling how the women had acted at the Mardi Gras supper.

"No."

Rye waited for more, but apparently Camila wasn't ready to share. She glanced behind Rye, who turned to see Ryan standing there, holding an umbrella.

"I'm freezing, and I want to go get changed to take Tyler and Ana out to celebrate their engagement," Camila said. "We can talk later, okay?"

Rye watched her walk away. She started when Ryan appeared at her elbow.

"She's my best friend, you know," Ryan said, offering Rye a place under his umbrella. "After Tyler."

"Really?" Rye hadn't known that. She considered Camila to be one of *her* best friends.

"Really. After Ana and Tyler started dating, the four of us had dinner together all the time. Sometimes at Ana and Camila's apartment, sometimes at our house. I think they were happy to meet siblings who were as close as they were." Ryan rubbed at the stubble on his chin. "Eventually, Tyler and Ana wanted more ... privacy, but Camila and I kept hanging out."

"I don't think I realized you had women ... friends," Rye replied.

"There's a lot you don't know about me."

Rye tried not to let that sting. There had been a time when Ryan had counted her among his best friends, even if she hadn't been wise enough to appreciate it at the time, and his department hadn't approved of it. "What about Wanda?"

He laughed. "No. Wanda and I have always been a little too complicated to be...comfortable."

"It's always been weird to imagine Wanda and you dating." Rye's nose wrinkled at the thought. "And that was on and off again for a long time."

"Mostly off. We made a strange couple. Even then, not really comfortable." He waved as Tyler and Jaz drove out of the parking lot. Detective Sachar pulled up to the curb. "I think she's a happier person now, don't you? With Lance?"

Rye thought of what it felt like to walk into Wanda's house these days—the mess, the noise, the teenagers sprawled around eating enough that Wanda had caved and gotten a Costco card—and grinned. "Absolutely." She zipped up her jacket and pulled her hood on. "Are you?"

Ryan pulled his sunglasses off his head and wiped futilely at them before sticking them into the pocket of his shirt. He gave Rye a wan smile. "Happy enough."

"That's good." Rye hoped he wouldn't ask her the same question. It felt a little early in this rebuilding stage to announce that she was absolutely miserable. "Thanks for coming so quickly today. Wanda wields a mean laptop, but—"

The horn honked once. It was a polite reminder, and Ryan took it. "That's my job," he reminded her, then took off toward the squad car, his long legs eating up the distance almost as quickly as Rye was completely soaked through. Maybe a sheriff should offer someone who has solved a crime an umbrella? Just a thought.

She headed to her own car. She needed a cup of tea and a bowl of homemade ramen, and Rye knew one person who would be happy to provide both. She texted her dad and instantly got a thumbs-up in reply. Rye was starting to warm up already.

THE NEXT MORNING, SHE ANSWERED TEXTS FROM Wanda and Hardy and left the others unread. She had a full docket of both students and parents, and it felt good to be busy with ordinary problems. At lunch, she had a Zoom session with her therapist, and while it didn't fix everything, it was a relief to lay everything out to an impartial third party.

Rye ate her yogurt and trail mix in the break between meetings. By the end of the school day, she felt mostly human. When Camila showed up at her door as she was packing up, Rye didn't even jump to the conclusion that Camila was angry with her about everything that had happened—perspective bought for the low, low price of her one-hundred-sixty-dollar "lunch break."

"Hey," Camila said. She stood by the open door. The main office behind her was dim and quiet. She held up her phone, which had a long crack down the middle of its screen. "It turns out I left the fight with more than a bloody nose, and this is going to be more expensive to fix."

"I'm happy to pay for the replacement. If it weren't for me, you wouldn't have been there."

"You don't need to apologize," Camila said. "But I am wondering if I should start cashing in on that guilt. I do need another person for the Muddy Waters Relay in April."

Camila had a knack for finding races that were not just about the running. Rye shuddered to think what component water might play in an early spring race. "I'm not sure I feel that guilty. My shoulder still aches from that fall I took when you forced me to sled down a hill of sheer ice." Rye came around the desk, slinging her bag onto said shoulder. "Standing in line at the Apple store while you get a replacement phone is penance enough."

"Especially since I don't even have an appointment," Camila replied gleefully. "It could be hours!"

Rye groaned dramatically as she followed Camila out to the front doors. "We're stopping for snacks first, then. I can't face those geniuses on an empty stomach."

"Do you want Cinnabon or one of those hot dogs wrapped in a pretzel?"

"Obviously both," Rye replied.

They were still adding to an absurd list of foods for their imaginary food court order when they passed Lance waiting on the curb.

He waved at them before turning back to his phone, but Rye stopped. "We're headed to the mall, and I'll be passing your street. Want a lift?"

Lance checked his phone again. "Sure. Do you have a minute before we go?"

"Of course."

He held up his phone. "I don't know if this is spoofed or real, but someone is livestreaming from the student parking lot."

Rye took the phone from him and studied the video. She started walking quickly, then broke into a run. Lance, with his long legs, and Camila, who could have easily outpaced her, kept up without trouble.

"What is it?" Camila asked.

Rye didn't answer. She just moved faster through the cold air, rounding the corner in time to see two sophomores spray-painting the back of the school. A third was making the video, and he turned the camera on Rye as the three of them descended on the group.

"Jacob, Bradyn? And Andre, of course." Rye noticed that Lance was also recording, and Camila was already on the phone to the police. The wall had been covered with swastikas and slurs Rye wouldn't repeat even inside her own head.

These three were always together. They played on the tennis and golf teams, and all of them had parents with military backgrounds. One—Bradyn—had an uncle who'd gone to school with Rye. Facebook had kept her informed that Scott McKay had joined a militia after he'd graduated. She hadn't seen him since...since he'd come after her with a crowbar.

Of course! Rye hadn't recognized Scotty in the moment, but as she stared at Bradyn now the family resemblance at seventeen was unmistakable. How had she missed that?

She'd suspended Bradyn right after winter break for cheating in two classes. His parents had been furious and demanded the suspension be struck from his record, but Rye had refused, and Mendoza had backed her up.

She tried to think back to Elena's mugging and to the man who had followed her that night after book club. Had that been Scotty, too? Maybe, but Rye couldn't have sworn to it. Scotty had friends, though, and none of them had been the kind of boys you wanted to be caught alone with at a party. She doubted they'd grown into better men.

The other two boys' families that were much more covert in their ideology. They belonged to a country club that was notorious for being so white that even employees had to fit a certain profile. She had no doubt that Andre and Jacob would have been down for any form of revenge Bradyn suggested, just for the fun of it.

Jacob lazily wrote another expletive on the wall. Rye knew his parents had more money than God, and if they wanted to make recordings disappear, they had the influence to make it happen. She hoped Lance was live streaming.

"Jacob's mad because Nicole wouldn't go out with him," Lance said. Rye glanced at him, but he was focused on the guy in front of him.

"I'd never be seen with that dirty little—"

"I was there when you asked her out, and she laughed in your face." Lance took a step toward him, but Rye put a restraining hand on his arm. "It was two days before the concert."

"She'll come around if Jake decides he wants her." Andre grinned. "Maybe I'll drop in on that nasty blonde she's always hanging out with, too."

Lance was on them before Rye could stop him. She and Camila dove into the fray, wrenching the boys apart, but there were only two of them, and four to separate.

And the toughest one was Lance.

39

By the time a squad car pulled up, sirens blaring, everyone was in rough shape. Rye and Camila agreed to take responsibility for Lance's punishment from the Stoneridge perspective for throwing the first punch while the other three were taken in for inciting the fight and defacing the school. Lance sent a link to his video to the police so they could confirm what had been said and done. Those brick walls had seen more activity this week than in all the years since they were built added together.

"I told Wanda I'd watch out for you at school," Rye said as the three of them trudged back to the faculty lot.

"Think she's going to kick me out?" Lance looked a lot more vulnerable than Rye expected. She knew this was far from being his first fight, so it wasn't that.

"Wanda?" Rye replied in surprise. "No way. She would never let you go."

Rye looked up to see Elena Mendoza arguing with a tall, wiry man with salt-and-pepper hair and a close-cropped beard.

"Who's that?" Camila put a hand up to keep Lance from moving toward them. It was clear the discussion was heated, and although Elena was not a particularly small woman, the stranger towered over her.

Rye glanced at Lance. "Stay here." He gave her a mock salute but backed up. A black eye was blossoming, making him look somehow tougher and younger than usual.

"Hey, Elena!" Rye called as she and Camila quickly crossed the distance to her.

Elena seemed to freeze when she saw Rye. The man did, too.

Camila glanced around the circle before asking in her usual blunt fashion, "What's going on? Elena? Are you okay?"

"You are the spitting image of Melanie," the man murmured. He had gone white as a sheet.

Rye opened her mouth to respond but couldn't think of what to say. Camila squeezed her hand. Rye's brain finally seemed to catch up. "What?" She wondered if she'd gotten hit on the head harder than she thought during the fight.

"I'm Reuben," the man said, as if that explained everything.

"Reuben Emerson?" Her father had met with his parents in Virginia, and now he was here? It couldn't be a coincidence.

"He's a murderer," Elena replied angrily, and Rye could see now that the older woman held a can of mace at the ready. "You think I don't recognize you? You were at that bar every week, playing bass and buying drinks for all the girls. I only ever saw you go anywhere with Melanie, though."

Reuben shook his head. "I didn't kill anyone. I swear it."

"You were the only suspect to Lionel Burgess's murder—" Rye started to say, but Elena interrupted her.

"You're trying to deny the affair? It was obvious! Everyone in the bar knew it. And one of them must have told her husband about it. That's why he murdered her and then pretended to go hunting for her killer!"

"I'm confused. Do you think I slept with her or killed her?" Reuben seemed—not amused, exactly, but at least resigned, and certainly not panicked about being called out for murder.

"Neither! You killed Lionel! That's it—you killed Lionel!" Elena had tears in her eyes. "He must have tried to convince Melanie to stop seeing you, or maybe he saw some confrontation between you and Hardy Rye, and you thought he would go to the police. I don't know, I don't know whether you or Hardy ended his life, but I know you're both responsible for his death!"

"Lionel was my boyfriend," Reuben replied softly. "I didn't kill him. Hardy didn't kill him. My father did."

"Prove it!" Elena said, waving her mace at him.

He held up his hands in surrender, then slowly reached for something stuffed into his back pocket. He pulled out a newspaper and spread it on the hood of the car. On the front page was the initial article about Martina Suarez's murder.

"This is Luisa Suarez," he said. "She and I played together in a band called Bone Dreamer for a couple of years. We had a regular gig at the Pour House. Mel used to come see me, and she brought her friends. Usually you"—Reuben nodded to Elena—"but also Lionel."

"Okay," Rye said, just to say something. Her brain felt like it was short circuiting.

"Lionel and I started seeing each other. It was casual. I wasn't out yet, and he was, so we didn't talk about it," Reuben continued. "Luisa found out."

"So?" Camila asked.

"Luisa, for as long as I knew her, made money on the side blackmailing people. It started as a way to make some cash, and then it just became a way of life for her. One night, she got drunk and showed me this book where she listed all of her 'clients.'" Reuben shook his head. "After that, she threatened me. Told me that she would out me if I didn't keep quiet."

"So what?" Elena challenged.

"It was a different time," Reuben replied. "And my father was a deeply conservative religious man—in fact, a violent man with a conservative religious agenda. I knew he would disown me, or worse, if he ever found out that I was dating not only a man, but a Black man."

"He did find out, though," Rye reasoned.

Reuben nodded, reaching up to rub the back of his neck. "I guess Luisa overheard me warning Mel and Lionel not to come to the bar while my father was visiting. She thought she could make extra money by blackmailing him, too. She would keep quiet about me if he paid up." He cleared his throat. "Instead, he decided he would kill Lionel when he had the chance. While he was at Lionel's, he saw a photo. It was a picture of me with Melanie and Kara."

"Kara? My aunt?" Rye asked.

"You don't have an aunt," Reuben replied. "Kara is your sister."

All three women froze.

"My what?"

Reuben reached out as though he wanted to take Rye's hand, then seemed to think better of it, and let his arm fall to his side. "Melanie was my stepsister. Our parents got married when I was twelve."

"What?" Elena looked aghast. "And you two were…" She couldn't even finish her sentence.

"So you're Kara's father?" Camila asked. She'd held out as long as she could, but this was too good.

"No, I'm not Kara's father," Reuben said with disgust. "Mel's age-appropriate jerk boyfriend got her pregnant when she was sixteen, and then he told her to get an abortion. He didn't want to deal with any of it. When she refused, he broke up with her, and, worse, he told my father." Reuben looked at Rye. "He beat Mel to within an inch of her life when he found out about the baby. I don't know if he was just punishing her or if he hoped she would miscarry. Maybe both."

"But she didn't," Camila pointed out.

"My stepmother called me. I was living up here at the time. She asked me to come get Melanie. She was afraid my dad would kill Mel if I didn't hide her."

Lance was clinging to Rye's arm at this point. She had no idea when he'd crossed the parking lot to join them, but she couldn't have shooed him away if she'd tried. "What happened? Couldn't he have followed her up here?" Lance asked.

"He could have. My stepmother sent us to stay with her cousin Nora in Colorado. Nora was the ultimate pioneer woman—she had a huge garden, canned everything she grew, lived off the grid, even worked as a midwife—and, most importantly, my father had never met her. When she'd heard Margaret was going to marry a far-right conservative, Nora cut ties. They had never been close, but when Mel got pregnant, Margaret immediately thought of her."

"She hid you and my mother?" Rye asked. "Just like that?"

"No questions asked," Reuben replied. "I'd still make my weekly calls to my father, and I'd visit, pretending I had no idea what had happened to Mel."

"What about the baby?" Camila asked.

"When Kara was three, Mel and I moved here with her. I wanted to get back into music, and Mel just didn't like country life. We didn't have much money between us, but Melanie found a job right away, with you." He said this to Elena. "She'd changed her name legally already and had all the documents she needed. She was no longer Melanie Emerson, but Melanie Saunders. She cut her hair very short. It was the same color as yours," he told Rye, "and she darkened it for a while after we moved. Until she met your father."

"But why didn't she tell Dad about Kara?" Rye asked. "He wouldn't have cared. He wanted to have more children."

"Your mom had done drugs with her boyfriend, and she kept doing them even after she found out about the baby. She stopped drinking, but she had pills he'd given her before they broke up. When she got depressed, she would take them. Kara had behavioral problems that were overwhelming us. The nursery school we sent Kara to kicked her out, and both of us worked full-time. We couldn't afford a nanny, and obviously, there would be no family help. Her pediatrician recommended special therapists that we couldn't afford. A few months after we came back here, Melanie begged Nora to take Kara again. We couldn't give her a safe home. Nora was willing to at least try."

"Why didn't my mom go with Kara?" Rye asked.

Reuben rubbed his hand through his hair. "Nora asked her not to. She said she couldn't handle a child and Mel. Melanie's depressive episodes were too difficult, and Nora wanted to focus her energy on raising Kara."

"So she just gave her daughter away," Rye said. "Started fresh with version two-point-oh."

"Mel loved both you and Kara so much," Reuben replied, his tone harsh. "She was young and scared, and she did what she thought was best for Kara. And it was. Nora was able to help Kara by paying for everything she needed. She gave her a wonderful childhood. She's a lovely woman."

"Does she know about me?"

He nodded. "I told her a few years ago. I didn't have any way to contact you. I'd never met your father or seen where you lived. I refused to ask Mel's married name. She didn't want to give me information that could get beaten out of me."

Elena had deflated next to them, but now she spoke up. "But what happened to Melanie?"

"I don't know," Reuben said softly. "My father came up here for an unplanned visit. That's when he actually met Luisa and she tried the blackmail. One night, he found Lionel and me at my place above the bar. Melanie had been there, too, but, by chance, she was out at the store when he arrived. Dad started screaming at me, and Lionel got out of there as fast as he could. My dad followed him home. I had to wait for Melanie to warn her, and I didn't get to Lionel fast enough. By the time I reached his house, my father had started beating him the same way he used to go after me and Mel. I tried to get between them." Reuben was crying now. Elena was, too. "He shoved me back. I must have lost consciousness for at least a few moments, because when I came to, he was standing over Lionel's body holding a bookend. It was a gift I'd given Lionel for his birthday. My father had bashed him in the head with it as Lionel was trying to get to the phone to call the police."

"Why didn't you call the police?" Elena asked through her tears. "You could have gotten Lionel justice! He was a good man." She turned to Rye. "Did you know he ran an underground shelter for victims of abuse?"

Rye shook her head. That must have been what the clothes and diapers were for. She'd forgotten about the pictures of Lionel's home, but now that she thought about it, she could imagine that big house being a safe haven for so many, including her own mother.

She had imagined trafficking when, really, she'd been looking at evidence of compassion.

"My father told me he found out everything about Kara," Reuben told Elena. "He'd hired a private detective. He knew where to find her. If I told anyone what had happened, he promised he would kill her."

"Maybe he was lying," Elena argued, but the fire had gone out of her.

"Other kids have dads with tempers. Other kids come from ultra-conservative religious families. Other kids are beaten. But my father hired someone to track down his wife's grandchild to use as leverage against me," Reuben said. "He was so far gone that he would have killed a child to keep his secrets."

"How did you ever survive all that?" Camila asked. She, of all of them, had looked past the unanswered questions and hurt and come to the heart of it—that Reuben had stood in the middle of so much evil and tried his best to protect the people he loved.

"I drank myself nearly to death," he said. "I went back and lived near my father and stepmother to make sure he never followed through on his threat. A few years ago, he was diagnosed with mouth cancer. He could barely speak after that. I took it as a sign, stopped drinking and moved back up here. Started working with a youth music program that reached out to underserved communities. I speak Spanish and English fluently, and I can play just about any instrument I pick up, so they were happy to have me, and I was happy to find work that kept me motivated to stay sober."

"He survived that cancer, but he was sick again," Rye said. Hardy had tracked him down just last week.

Reuben pulled out his phone and showed her an obituary. "He died two days ago. My stepmother thought his condition was stable, but she woke up to find him gone." He started crying again. "I'm finally free."

Blue and red lights cruised up to them. Jaz got out of the car and came over to stand by Reuben. The three teens were still in the back of the car, with Tyler keeping an eye on them.

"This is not how a February thaw should be spent," Jaz said. "I got a call from a teacher heading home that there was something happening out here. What's going on?"

Elena ignored her. "Why should we believe any of this? You could be making it all up!"

"To what purpose?"

"We have Luisa's book," Rye said. She glanced at Jaz, and her friend gave an affirmative nod. "If she didn't have more than one volume, the police can verify what Reuben said."

Elena seemed to deflate. "So Reuben wasn't stalking me?"

"Of course not!" He seemed genuinely perplexed. "Why would I do that?"

"You show up after all these years, when we finally decide to look into Lionel and Melanie's cases—what should I think?"

"I live fifteen miles from here," Reuben said. "I came today because a friend from my Bone Dreamer days saw the news that Luisa had been killed. The funeral hasn't been scheduled, but the director at the funeral home let us have an informal wake this afternoon. I was the only one there. His wife listened to all my stories." He smiled. "Plus, I wanted to meet my niece."

"How did you know I would be here?" Rye asked.

"You're YouTube famous right now for taking out those guys at the school the other day," Reuben replied. "Even I've seen the videos."

"But you've never met me."

"I did, once. When you were baptized," Reuben said. "But, honestly, I'd recognize you anywhere."

Reuben pulled out his wallet and handed Rye a well-worn photograph he had inside. Mel was sitting on an old couch holding Kara in her lap. Rye had never seen a picture of her mother at twenty, but Reuben was right. If Rye pulled up a picture of herself at the same age, they would have looked like twins. She handed it back to him with tears pricking her eyes.

"I was never baptized. My parents didn't go to church."

He shook his head. "Your father wasn't there. Mel didn't want him to know she was superstitious that way. It was just us and the priest."

"You're Rye's godfather?" Camila asked.

He nodded. "Prudence Margaret Rye," Reuben said. "Not exactly a common name."

Rye felt bruised and tired. "I need to go home. But, Reuben, I met someone who wants to be at the funeral, so you won't be alone. She was Luisa's next-door neighbor, and she has some happy memories. I'll let Luke Fairchild know."

Reuben reached into his pocket and pulled out a card. "Thank you. I'll understand if you never use this, but if you want to, I'm around." He handed it to his niece. Turning to Jaz, he asked, "Would you mind if I followed you over to the station so we could look in the book together?" He glanced at Elena. "It would put our minds at ease, I think."

"We'll see what we can do," Jaz said. Reuben and Elena left then. Elena glanced over her shoulder a few times, but Reuben looked back only once, giving Rye a little wave before he got into his car.

"I think I need a rain check on the shopping trip," Rye said after the three of them had been left alone.

"Do you want a lift home?" Camila asked.

Rye shook her head. "Lance can drive me. I need to talk to Wanda and my dad."

Camila wrapped her in a warm hug. Rye laid her head on Camila's shoulder and rested it there for a minute. "I'll text you tomorrow?"

"If I don't answer, try Ana, okay? I'm staying at her place tonight." Camila waved at Lance and headed down the row to her own car.

"Are you really going to let me drive your car?" Lance asked Rye.

"No," Rye said. "I can't take any more stress tonight. But call Wanda and tell her to meet us at my place. Make sure she brings wings. Lots of them."

FOR THE SHORTEST MONTH, FEBRUARY SEEMED TO GO on forever in New England. Yesterday, Rye had stood in this very spot with only a sweater on and learned she had a sister. Today, she was in a parka bringing Lance home again for Wanda because the weather had turned nasty.

She had been thrilled with a snow-delayed opening this morning, since she and Wanda had stayed up way too late debriefing and destressing over wings and Hardy's homemade apple cider. By the time Wanda and Lance left, it had been after midnight and way past Rye's bedtime.

She'd happily slept in until a decadent seven thirty, then showered and bundled up for the below-freezing temperatures. At four, when she was finally wrapping up work, heavy clouds had moved back in, and Rye had been watching rain and snow alternately turn her commute home into a nightmare.

Wanda called to ask if she could drive Lance home, since Wanda didn't want him catching the local bus in this weather. That had turned into a further request to bring Leslie and Nicole home, and Rye had acquiesced. She didn't want them driving on those roads any more than she was looking forward to it herself.

She had navigated to the Pond house, where she was able to drop both Leslie and Nicole. The noise level dropped significantly after they got out of the car, and Rye found she could concentrate better as she made her way to Wanda's.

Lance's phone started buzzing. He looked at her in surprise. "Rye, your dad's calling me."

"My phone is dead. Answer it."

"Hi, Hardy…I'm with her. We…It died…" He glanced at Rye. "She *should* keep a charger in the car. I agree…No, I don't know where Wanda is, but she turns her phone off all the time. She likes the silence." He nodded, although Hardy couldn't see him. "What happened? No. I won't…We'll go to the church first, since she's not answering her phone, check on the dogs, then we'll come right to you…Yes, we'll bring her with us. Officers are waiting at Rising Star?" He grunted acknowledgment twice more, then ended the call.

Rye had to keep her eyes on the road. "What is it?"

Lance's phone rang again. He held up a hand. "Sheriff? Sir. Hardy just reached us. I'm going to tell Rye, then we are going to check on Wanda and…He might…Yes, sir." It was pretty clear that Ryan Phennen had hung up on him.

Rye opened her hands in the eternal so-what-is-it gesture.

"The transport taking Josh Gagne and Agatha Bogdanovic down to Norfolk County for pretrial holding slid off the road when they were taking a shortcut to the interstate. They hit a tree. Both guards were unconscious, but the impact triggered a control button that opens the back automatically so no prisoners will be trapped in a fire from a crash. Josh Gagne escaped. Agatha Bogdanovic stayed with the guards, and I guess she helped them."

Surely Josh Gagne's priority would be to disappear. Only an idiot would try to track down the person responsible for his capture instead of making a break for it, right?

"How far from here had they gone?"

"Not far enough."

41

WANDA SPRINTED INTO THE CHURCH WITH WINK AND Figaro pulling madly on their leads. She could barely keep up as they scrambled down the hall to the front office. Wanda could hear voices, and clearly the dogs could smell the tantalizing scent of warm brownies.

As they careened through the door, the three of them got stuck and popped into the office with a cartoonish crash that caused Irie, Luke, and Greg to look up from their conversation. Wink immediately trotted over to Greg to be picked up and snuggled like a baby while Figaro's tail thwapped loudly against Lisa's desk. Irie knelt to receive kisses and give him ear scratches.

Wanda dropped her bag with relief. "I am getting a full workout with those two! Thank goodness Lance takes care of Figgy in the mornings and when he's out of school. I can't handle that energy all day every day!"

"There's a great new dog park opening up a few blocks from the church," Luke said. "I think it will be ready next month. Maybe you can take them there to get some big running?"

"That sounds nice." Wanda rubbed her shoulder. "When I was a one-dog woman, I didn't have to worry about these things, but now"—she looked fondly at Figaro, who came over and rubbed his head against her leg—"well, this one will keep me young, that's for sure!"

Greg laughed. "Dogs are the best for that."

Tony walked in carrying an armful of sheet music, and Greg stole a kiss before Tony had a chance to set it down. This seemed to trigger the lovebirds, because Irie leaned over and gave Luke a kiss, and Wink hopped down from Greg's arms to snuggle on the big flannel dog bed with Figaro.

"That reminds me," Wanda said, having allowed herself only a brief pang of jealousy. "We're here to meet about a wedding reception with a reaffirmation of vows, right?" She glanced at Luke and Irie. "This will be for Luke's friends and family who weren't able to come to the wedding in Jamaica, and I know you have ideas for it!" She glanced at Tony and Greg. "What about you? You have some wedding plans to share as well."

"We have binders full of plans," Greg replied.

"So many binders," Tony agreed. "Did you bring them in, love?"

Greg held up the plate of frosted brownies. "I remembered the treats…by the way, not good for dogs…but I forgot the notes. They're in the car. I can go grab them."

"You do that," Wanda said, pulling off her jacket, hat, and gloves and laying them on the radiator to dry. "But be careful—it snowed last night, and it rained earlier. With this drop in temperature, the roads and sidewalks are like sheets of ice." She helped herself to a brownie while unlocking the door to her office. Luke and Irie followed her in, and she waved to the seats closest to the coffee table. "I'm going to grab a couple more chairs for Greg and Tony. You get settled. It's strange talking about more than one wedding event, but I'm glad to do it after an unpleasant few weeks."

"Do you need help?" Irie asked.

"I'm good. I have a few lightweight stackable chairs in the sanctuary that are newly padded. I'll be back in a jiff."

She walked down the hall, grateful Tony had left the piano light on so she wasn't fumbling in complete darkness. The chairs were up by the pulpit, having been used by a few choir members on Sunday, and Wanda headed up there, shivering in the drafty room.

She slowed as she picked them up, noticing that the red light for recording services appeared to have been turned on above the front row of pews.

"Wanda." A low voice behind caused her to jump, dropping the chairs in the process.

She turned around to see Josh Gagne standing there, soaked to the bone and wearing a khaki jumpsuit. She'd spent enough time praying with people at Norfolk County in Dedham and the closer Shirley and Lancaster correctional facilities to recognize the Norfolk County pretrial clothing.

"Josh! What are you doing here?"

"You have to listen to me," he said, moving forward and catching her wrist tightly. "You think you know what happened, but you don't! No one does."

Trying to be optimistic, but knowing that Norfolk did not release prisoners in these outfits, she asked, "Did you get out on bail?"

"No. Judge didn't give me bail. She asked for a psych eval. Me, God's servant on earth." He appeared genuinely shocked. "The transport van slid off the road, and I knew it was a sign from God that I was meant to tell my story." His face glowed with something akin to fanaticism. "I'm going to record it, Wanda, and in a holy place. This church is holy, even if it did choose a female leader." He gestured to the sound table set to the side of the chancel platform. "I have everything ready."

Wanda slowed her breathing to remain calm. His hand was like ice, nails digging into her skin, and she noticed he held a car scraper in his other hand.

"I'd rather be forgiven by a real pastor," he said, "but I can't control where God sends me. The crash was only a mile from here, so the Lord must have intended for me to show you the truth of my innocence." His voice was silky, charismatic—the way it probably sounded when he preached on Sundays, without a hint of doubt.

"Josh, you already know I believe that God forgives us all, but no person can really offer forgiveness."

"My parents gave forgiveness all the time, and it freed people from the past. My grandfather gave forgiveness to thousands. My brother Eric gives people forgiveness all the time. And you know what?" He twisted her arm hard. "They knew how to withhold forgiveness, too, and they did it to me."

Looking at his face and the pain in it, Wanda decided to get off her theological high horse. "Of course I'll offer you forgiveness. Your congregation, though—they deserve an apology."

"And I do apologize to Rising Star. I am doing that now," he said earnestly, leaning into the microphone. "I beg my parishioners to forgive me. I have preached repentance for you, and now I repent." He was really on a roll. "I ask forgiveness for the love in my heart that led to my downfall. I ask God's blessings on me, for all of you to hear me, to see me, as I do, as a man on the cross, weeping and begging for God's grace to fall upon me!"

"Josh—" Wanda tried to pull out of his grip using one of the techniques Hardy had shown her, but the pressure was so great, she was sure her wrist would break if she kept trying. "You have your forgiveness. Please, let me go."

"No, Wanda. I need to confess my sins. I need to be free!"

She refrained from pointing out that he was free at a moment when he clearly shouldn't be and resigned herself to letting him speak. Her cell phone was on the desk in her office, and unless Tony and Greg came in the back door past the sanctuary, she was alone.

"You see, I was in love once." He bowed his head, giving the camera a charming, self-deprecating smile that chilled Wanda. "Before I heard my calling, when I was a young man, I met someone. I thought she was a good Christian woman who lived humbly, working as the secretary for her father's construction company. She told me that she was free to do what her heart desired." Josh pushed pause on his congregation and turned toward Wanda with an imploring look. "And she desired me."

"This is what Martina had over you?"

"Not the relationship, no," he said. "Beth told me she was nineteen, and I believed her. I believed her, and I loved her, and when I found out she was only fifteen, I knew she was God's messenger telling me to turn away from sin and commit myself to the church."

"But Agatha said you made a video," Wanda replied, unable to help herself.

He looked disgusted. "Not me. Beth took one, kept it, and after my father paid her family off to keep the relationship quiet, she found someone interested in the evidence."

"But how? How could she have met Martina?"

Josh was calm again. "I introduced them—Beth and the woman you all knew as Martina Suarez." He laughed, and it was a rich baritone. "The devil must have been truly inspired by my moral failings! I knew her from voice lessons, when she was Luisa. We went out after class one evening, and I invited Beth to join us. I learned later that Luisa groomed her, then collected information. She was a devil who lived and breathed blackmail."

"She convinced Beth to give her the recording?"

"After I found out the truth about her age, we broke up. I told Luisa all about it. She was so sympathetic. That must have been when she bought the recording. She bought things that she could use years later. Then Luisa said her sister Martina got sick and disappeared. I thought it was over. I went to New York. Ministry was good. Two years ago, she returned to this area. Rising Star was a great little church, ready to grow, and they knew I'd lived here once. A year ago, I accepted the call. If I'd known she was here, I would have gone somewhere, anywhere else! She even convinced me to baptize her in her sister's 'honor' before she let me know she had the recording of Beth and me together."

Wanda wriggled her wrist, but he kept a firm grip, pulling her closer. She could smell that he hadn't washed recently, and he was sweating now even in the cold, although he still managed to maintain a glimmer of preacher poise.

"If anyone found out, I would have been ruined. God had worked his will on me so many times—too many for me to allow her to take a messenger, a redeemed Barabbas, from the Holy One."

"So you killed her." Wanda delivered this pronouncement flatly, then landed a kick just below his knee that sent him sprawling. His confession was recorded. There was no reason for her to remain his willing hostage.

Wanda scrambled back as Josh followed her, limping. She could tell the sharp edge of her boot must have cut the skin by a thin line of blood visible on his pants.

"I cleansed her spirit!" he called. "I released her from the earthly torment of her sins, and when she was gone I prayed over her that God might forgive. She tried to ruin me and still I gave her that!"

Wanda had recovered her feet and was ready for Josh when he launched himself at her. She just wasn't prepared for the chancel mic wire that tripped them both, toppling them down the three stairs to the floor. Wanda lay there for a moment, disoriented. When Josh loomed over her, his ice scraper raised up, Wanda felt afraid for the first time.

Neither of them saw the hand that swung the hymnal into his head, sending him over to crash unconscious to the stairs.

Wanda gazed up at Irie.

"You said you'd be back in a jiff," Irie explained. "We don't have this expression, but once Luke told me what it meant, I knew something was wrong. You are a woman of your word. You would not have gotten distracted."

Wanda gratefully accepted Irie's hand and rose up. Even after her tumble, nothing seemed broken—just bruised, and undoubtedly sore tomorrow. "Thank you, Irie. You may have just saved my life."

"It's the least I can do for my new friend."

Luke strode in, Greg and Tony at his heels. They took in what happened, and Luke finished his report to the person on the other end of his phone—presumably dispatch.

"Are you okay?" Tony asked, running over to wrap Wanda in a hug.

"I'm fine."

"Maybe we should start covering your ongoing investigations with Rye at book club," Greg said as he checked to be sure Josh wasn't an immediate threat. "You certainly seem to find yourself in the middle of enough of them. And Irie? You pack a mean hymnbook."

"Oh, I don't know if the book club will believe this one," Wanda said.

"And Wanda doesn't need any more encouragement," Tyler replied from the doorway.

"Can I join this book club?" Irie asked Wanda, as Tyler led the EMTs to where Josh lay. "I told Luke I was worried I might get bored here without all the family drama I'm used to, but with you around I think I'll be okay."

Luke and Tony groaned, almost in unison, but Wanda wrapped her arm around Irie's waist. "You're welcome anytime, Irie. Next meeting is a week from Thursday at Harvey's."

"And what book should I read?" Irie stepped out of the way of the stretcher.

Wanda laughed. "It really doesn't matter, since we'll just talk murder anyway!"

42

THE CHAOS FOLLOWING THE PRISON TRANSPORT VAN accident justified Wanda's decision to stay home as the miserable weather pattern held the next day. Her desire to be cozy and covered in dogs had nothing to do with getting trapped in her own sanctuary with an irrational, self-confessed murderer. Nope. Nothing.

It also had nothing to do with the fact that Hardy had been angry with her for drawing Josh out, allowing him to hold onto her when she could have escaped earlier. She had received a long lecture about subduing attackers, and when Wanda had tried to protest that Josh's confession could go a long way toward convicting him, Hardy reminded her that it wasn't her job to elicit confessions from people. There were professionals who did that sort of thing for a living.

Wanda was at least happy to know that Agatha had stayed to help the Norfolk transport crew and had called the crash in on their radio. The police had been searching for Josh, first at Rising Star and then at the nearest churches. Wanda wouldn't tell Irie that the police had already made it to the parking lot by the time she subdued Josh. Irie was so proud of her role in protecting Wanda, and if the police hadn't been fast enough… Well, Wanda was thrilled that Irie had been there, too.

But today! Rain, light snow, ice, more light snow, more ice on power lines, cold rain—all of it making the dogs slow to leave the doorstep and even slower to pee. She had dragged Figaro to the backyard first. On the way out, it had been his usual boisterous dash. The pull back to the house after he'd completed his business nearly dislocated her shoulder.

She was just returning with dog number two, the more elderly Wink, who whimpered and whined and seemed to think she was taking him to the guillotine. How could she betray her faithful friend? She vaguely considered a canine litter box in the basement. No. Just, no.

Boots off. Coat off. Treats given. Time for tea and a warm biscuit with butter and jam. After all, why should the creatures-great-and-small have a treat and she be treat-less? As she filled the kettle, Figaro raced up the stairs. She turned on the gas, listening. The dog had run upstairs as though Lance were here.

It had been so quiet, she hadn't checked. Wanda bounded up after the dog and found Figaro whining outside Lance's closed bedroom door. Wanda knocked. She could hear conversation.

"Lance, are you there? Figgy really wants to get in. I fed and walked him."

"Coming," Lance replied. Then she heard him say, "You're in luck. She's here."

The door opened, and for a minute it was a dog-and-boy bonding moment. Wanda looked around. "I thought I heard voices."

Lance swung his laptop around and showed her a man with gray hair, a short beard, and bright blue, perceptive eyes. Wanda fervently wished she had done a better self-inspection, but she was professionally acquainted with awkward meetings.

"Aunt Wanda, this is Robert Chambers."

Mickey's boyfriend? Wanda gave him her best preacher's smile. "Lovely to meet you, Robert." She wished she could ask Lance to mute the call so she could interrogate him, but she settled on a pleasant, "I didn't know you two were chatting."

Robert laughed. "I made Mickey introduce us. I have a son myself, although he's eighteen and off at university this year. I know he has strong feelings about who his mother and I date, and I figured Lance might feel the same. He graciously agreed to talk to me."

"He's actually pretty cool," Lance said. "He's been helping me with the play."

Wanda felt a twinge of jealousy, followed by fear. Would Lance want to move to England to live with Robert and Mickey? She had just gotten used to her house being full to the brim. She wasn't ready to say goodbye yet.

"Lance was telling me about how he helped to solve a murder?" Robert asked.

Solving a murder, indeed. Wanda flashed a glance at Lance, which he interpreted correctly and winced. "'Solved' might be stretching the truth, but he's a good cyber detective."

"She's right. Wanda does the heavy lifting," Lance replied, clearly trying to butter her up.

"Well, Lance contributes his share in culinary expertise and dog walking."

"Plus, I fix all those problems on your phone," he pointed out.

Wanda laughed. "Yes, you do."

Robert cleared his throat. Wanda thought he looked a bit nervous. "Listen, there was something else I wanted to talk about, and I'm glad you're both here."

"What's up?" Lance straightened in his chair, a look of concern crossing his face. "Is Mom okay?"

"She's wonderful," Robert said. "She's so wonderful that I would like to ask your permission to propose to her this spring."

Wanda wondered if she looked as dumbstruck as Lance did. "You want to marry Mickey?"

"I do, very much," Robert said. "I know this is fast. We've only been together for a few months, but I think, for both of us, we just know. It feels right."

Lance looked shocked but not unhappy. "Have you two talked about marriage and everything it involves?" he asked. "Have you discussed where you'll live, what your finances look like—"

Wanda thought he might be directly parroting something she herself had said a week ago to a very young couple who'd come to her asking to be married quickly and without their families' knowledge.

"We have, yes," Robert said, smiling. "Your mother and I, when we met, became friends very quickly, and she asked me to always be brutally honest with her. I told her I abhor brutality but that honest, direct conversations were my stock-in-trade. I hope to have many years to learn about Michelle, but, for now, I would be honored to call her my wife." His tone was gentle. "But only if you give me your blessing, Lance. If you're not ready, I can wait."

"Can I have some time to think about it?" Lance asked.

"Of course," Robert replied. "If you decide it's a good idea, I'd like to come to the U.S. in April or May to propose. We could have a little party afterward so I could get to know Michelle's family and friends, and they can get to know me. Maybe we even could come at the right time to see *Annie and the Ghost* performed. I bet there will even be a real comfort dog to play the part, if everything Michelle says about her sister's persistence is true."

Lance smiled. "Do you think your son would want to come?" he asked. "I'd like to meet him, too."

Robert scratched his beard, his eyes alight at the idea. "I'll ask him. It's been so long since he and I have traveled together, and it would be nice to have the opportunity."

"He likes my mom?" Lance seemed a little nervous.

"Stephen has come to visit us a few times now, and he and Michelle seemed to hit it off. He doesn't tell me everything, but I believe he likes her."

"Robert, thanks for taking the time to call and talk to us, to Lance especially," Wanda said. "I'd love to chat sometime, too, just the two of us, when you're free."

"And I would love to get to know the irrepressible Winnie!" Robert replied cheerfully.

Wanda shuddered. Mickey had held onto her childhood nickname, but Wanda had shed her own early. The only person who called her Winnie anymore was her sister … and, apparently, her sister's soon-to-be fiancé.

Figaro put his paws up on Lance's lap and whined for attention. Lance grinned down at him and gave his ears a scratch. "I'll call you in a few days and let you know, okay?" he said. Robert nodded, and after a round of goodbyes, they signed off.

Lance spun around in his chair, his eyes wide. "Can you believe my mom might actually get married?!"

Wanda laughed. "I thought you would be more upset, or stressed, at least."

"I was. I'd still like to meet him, and have Hardy meet him. But I've been trying to keep an open mind talking to him, and to my mom, and she's right. Robert seems like a good guy. She's happy, Wanda. Like, really happy."

"The kind of happy to make her fly off to Italy on a day's notice?" Wanda remembered her sister's bad idea that had landed her with this phenomenal kid, at least temporarily.

"No. Like…calm happy. Like the way I feel living here."

Wanda couldn't help it. She wrapped Lance up in a hug and squeezed. "Lance, whatever you decide, whether they get married or not, the fact that you and Mickey feel that way is the best news in the world."

Lance knelt to give Figaro a hug, too. The dog got jealous when affection was spread anywhere he couldn't join. Wink jingled in and hopped onto the bed, curling up in one of the many blankets there. Wanda sighed. This was heaven. She might or might not win the battle with Ryan Phennen about adding a comfort dog to the station, but she could start by letting the dogs she had comfort her.

"Hey, Aunt Wanda?"

"Yes?"

"Is that offer still available? Can I stay with you for as long as I want, no matter what?"

She sat down on the bed and gently stroked Wink's silky ears. "No matter what, Lance, this is your home."

43

RYE AND HARDY SAT ON THE PORCH DRINKING TEA. The wind had died down, though the trees, at least, were still dripping from the cold rain. Rye had brought out the fleece blankets they left in the hall closet for winter nights, and they sat quietly together listening to the droplets land on the roof.

"Have you talked to Wanda about how you feel?" Rye brought her cup of peppermint tea close so she could breathe it in.

"No," Hardy replied. His chair creaked as he rocked, a sound as familiar to Rye as her own breath. "There's been too much going on."

"Like Reuben showing up here?"

"Like that, yes." Hardy didn't elaborate.

"Do you think Mom is still alive? Like, out there somewhere, hiding?"

Hardy squeezed Rye's hand. "No, I don't."

"So you believe she would have come back if she could have?"

"I know she would have."

"When she used to disappear, do you think she was with Kara?" Rye wasn't sure she wanted to know, but she also needed to make some sense of it all.

"Rye, honey, if I knew, I would tell you. Your mother was capable of so much love, but she also struggled with her depression. Her medication didn't seem to help, so she would go off it without talking to her doctor. I'd like to believe that when she was gone, she was spending time with Kara, or checking herself in for care, but she could just as easily have been crashing on someone's couch, trying to make it through the day."

Rye shook her head. "You never have been one to sugarcoat things."

"I won't lie to you. If I did, you might not believe me when I tell you, Pru, your mother loved you. She loved us. She did the best she could."

Rye wiped her eyes. Her mother had called her Prudence, sometimes Priddy. Her father had always called her Pru until she asked him to stop. It had been so long since she'd heard him say it.

"Would you be upset if I asked Reuben about getting in touch with Kara?" Rye asked. "Maybe she knows what happened to Mom."

Hardy reached over and pushed a strand of auburn hair out of her eyes and tucked it behind her ear, as he had done when she was young. "Ask Reuben where Kara is because you want to know more about your sister. If I were you, I'd save conversations about your mom until you get to know both of them better." He sighed. "Even though it feels like we got the short end of the stick, you had a lot more of your mom's time and love than Kara ever did."

Rye hadn't thought about it that way, but her father was right. "Point taken. I'll go slow. Either way, it might be nice to learn more about our family, right?"

Hardy stood slowly, shaking off the cold and stiffness before pulling Rye to her feet. He tucked her under his chin, into the same spot she'd fit into since she'd reached her full height in the seventh grade. "You're the only family I've needed for a long time, but yes. It might be time to open our little circle wider. If you're ready?"

She squeezed her father tight. "You know what? I think I am."

AUTHORS' ACKNOWLEDGMENTS

OUR DEEPEST GRATITUDE GOES TO BEN MILLER-Callihan for his ongoing encouragement, promotion, and cheerleading of this wonderful cast of characters. We are grateful to Courtney Miller-Callihan and the Handspun Literary Agency community of writers, where we feel at home, as well as the resourcing and friendships that have come from "Sisters in Crime."

Our ever-growing fictional world is always bettered by our beta readers, and "Death in Disguise" was no exception. Jeff Deck, Nadine Donnell, Nancy Hardy, Dea-Sue Pelletier, and Don Tirabassi were wonderful. A big shout out to Diane Wendorf, who shared her King Cake secrets with Hardy Rye, and to Heidi Blair, whose relationship with her grown sons has fostered many a moment between Wanda, Rye, and Lance. Last, but certainly not least, we thank the incredible Brain Mill Press team for their curiosity, editorial expertise, and gentle nudges that have pushed us to refine these stories into a joyful escape.

To our readers, you are the carrot (well, croissant and coffee!) we chase during the sticky writing sessions, and the long days spent checking to be sure that half the book isn't taking place in a single day. Thank you for your outpouring of love for these characters, and for us, the lowly cat herders!

To Donald, to Matt and Julia, to David and the boys—you are the best! Thank you for your steadfast support of our coziest dreams. We couldn't walk this path without you.

ABOUT
THE AUTHORS

After teaching and working in early education for a decade, Maria Mankin has published six books with Pilgrim Press and has contributed essays to several anthologies. She is also a co-author of *Circ*, a mystery set in Skegness England, published by Pigeon Park Press, and *Pitching Our Tents: Poetry of Hospitality*. She is a regular contributor to Living Psalms, a collection in which the Psalms are reinterpreted in poetry and art as a reflection of God's work of justice and compassion. In 2024, Maria received an Impact on Education Award for her work with elementary grade students and staff.

Maren C. Tirabassi's forty-four years' experience in mainline ministry shaped Wanda Duff's professional life (but not her personality). Tirabassi is a former Poet Laureate of the city of Portsmouth, New Hampshire, and the recipient of the 2023 Lifetime Achievement Award from the New Hampshire Humanities Council. She has published twenty-two nonfiction titles and poetry and short stories in fifteen anthologies but enjoys most of all writing cozies.

9 781948 559867